NUMBERED

A Novel by Crissi Langwell

Cover Art & Design: MoorBooks Design
Inside art: Franzi, exile_artist, Santitep Mongkolsin
Editor: Sarah Villanueva

ISBN: 978-0-9967717-7-1

This book is also available as an ebook.
Please visit the author's website to find out where to purchase this book.

www.crissilangwell.com

"No one looks back and regrets leaving this world.
What's regretted is how real we thought it was." ~ Rumi

Table of Contents

Arrival

Noelle

100 days left

Underneath the sun's rays streaming through the windows, the walls are blinding, the exact shade of snow on a sunny day. The woman taking me on a tour of the facility is explaining the daily schedule and showing me around room to room, floor to floor, but I barely hear her as my eyes struggle to adjust to the brightness. Just the light alone makes this place different from my darkened loft apartment. Correction, formerly mine. Now I live at River's End, a facility for the dying. The name is painfully cheesy, but I chose this place because it was only a short drive from everything I knew. Now that I'm enclosed in these stark white walls, my access to the outside world completely shut off, I see it wouldn't have mattered if I'd stayed in California, or moved to Egypt. I've heard Egypt actually has a nice facility for those in their final days, located inside a real pyramid.

"Noelle."

She's looking at me expectantly, and I realize I haven't heard anything she's said.

"Sorry, what?"

"I said, this is where you'll be staying." She waves a badge over a panel near my head. The wall folds open and a twin-sized cot moves forward, a small table and lamp next to it. The furniture is metal, and the bedding is white—just like the walls. "This cubby is assigned to you and it will open with your ID."

I glance down at my wrist, the slim bracelet's digital display flashing between my name, my ID number, and the number of days I have left. One hundred. The number matches the one at the back of my neck, a gift every human receives at birth.

"You can set your belongings here, if you'd like," the aide continues, nodding at the bag slung over my shoulder. It's so light, I'd forgotten I was carrying it. All that's in the bag are my headphones and my digital pad, which is loaded up with my favorite music, books, and a few photos of my family. The clothes I'd packed are gone, confiscated by the admissions nurse. In exchange, she'd handed me a neatly folded bundle of light green clothing made of soft cotton material and embroidered with white leaves and flowers at the hems of the shirt and pants. Even my underwear and socks were traded for ones owned by the facility. Once dressed, I'd handed her the rest of my clothing, giving up the last of my individuality.

"I still don't understand why I can't just wear my old clothes," I say, and the aide offers me a sympathetic smile.

"It's just easier this way. I know it's hard to understand, but it's one of the ways we take the stress out of your final days. Now you don't have to worry about deciding what you're going to wear, and every day you have a freshly laundered outfit to put on."

"What if I want to swim?" She'd shown me a pool in a dome covered courtyard, located behind the main level. It was surrounded by lounge chairs, a café, and a gym. "Or if I want to work out?"

"There are bathing suits and gym clothes on the ground level," she says. She waves the badge over the panel again, and the wall closes around the retreating bed. "Now, about your floor. You may have noticed you're one of the youngest people here." I hadn't. I look around, realizing for the first time that I'm sharing the room with dozens of old people, most of them sitting in wheelchairs while staring at nothing. The room smells more sterile than the first floor, a mixture of antiseptic and peppermint covering a faint chlorine odor. An older man sits at a table while an aide spoons soup into his mouth, and two old women clank their walkers with each step as they walk at a turtle's pace toward the Dixie cups lined up at the nurse's station. A sleeping man lies on the bed next to me, his toothless mouth wide open. Other than the jangling of metal walkers on linoleum, the snores escaping from my neighbor's mouth, and the murmur of voices at the nursing station, the room is quiet. And ancient. Apparently I live in a nursing home.

"I guess it's not normal for someone to die in their thirties," I say, though this doesn't make sense. My neighbor left for a facility last month, and she was only a few years older than me. And my brother... Well, I can only assume he's gone; his expiration date was two years ago.

"It's actually the opposite," the aide says. "Each floor is dedicated to a certain age range. This floor is generally just for people sixty and older, but your floor is completely booked. This room has more cubbies because, well..." She trailed off, her eyes sweeping the room, and I understand. *Because more of them have expired.* That's when she looks at my hair, and I know what she's going to say before she even opens her mouth.

"I know, at least our hair looks the same." I touch my silver hair self-consciously. I'd found my first gray strand in my teens, and dyed my hair every six weeks to hide the evidence. It became a losing battle in my twenties, and I finally gave in and let my hair go natural. What was the point in making that much effort? There was no one I cared to impress.

"Actually, I've been wanting to tell you how beautiful your hair is. I hope my hair looks like this when I'm older."

"You said I'm one of the youngest," I say, brushing aside her age comment with a change of subject. "Who are the other people that still don't get a senior's discount?"

"Just one other person." She nods, indicating just beyond me. I turn to see a man around my age lying on a cot, his eyes closed. I study him for a moment, taking in his dark hair and shadow of a beard, the outline of his muscles under the green fabric of his scrubs, his bare foot hanging off the side of the cot as if he's ready to stand and run at a moment's notice. I have a feeling he's still awake, probably listening to everything we're saying. "That's Ryder. Today is his first day, too." She gives me a knowing smile. "Maybe you two will become friends."

"Maybe." *I doubt it.* It's not like I had many friends in my former life. The closest friendships I had were with the people I worked with, and "friendship" is a generous way to put it. On my last day at work, my boss threw me the obligatory lunch on the company dime, offering my coworkers one last chance to say goodbye. Some shed a few tears, and I appreciated the sentiment, but I believe it was more out of their own fear of mortality than about saying goodbye. Mostly, they were curious about what I was going to do before my number was up.

I'd given myself two extra weeks in between work and my transition to the facility. I pretended it was so I could cross off the many things left on my bucket list, which is what most people would have done. But really, I spent those two weeks alone. Of the little I knew about River's

End, the one thing I did know was that I would never be alone again. I imagined hundreds of people living in one large building, and for the most part, I wasn't wrong.

The bucket list idea felt dumb. I'd crafted one in my teens, a time when I was much less cynical than I am now. Most of the items on that list remained unfulfilled goals. Hike the Pacific Crest Trail. Take a Mediterranean cruise. Spend a month living in a hut in Bali. That sort of thing. If I saw something interesting in one of the books I was reading, I added it to the list. Back then, thirty-two seemed so far away. But as I got older, I realized how short my time really was. The goals I hoped to fulfill one day suddenly felt too big to accomplish in such a short amount of time. And then they felt unimportant. I kept the list pinned to my wall as a reminder of things I wanted to accomplish. It served more as a reminder that my life would soon be forgotten. Eventually I folded up the Bucket List and put it away. I stopped caring about the things I hadn't done yet. Once I was gone, I was gone. It wouldn't matter if I took a trip around the world or not, or even went skydiving.

For the record, I did go skydiving—but mostly because I wanted to cross at least one thing off my list.

The aide—*Hannah*, I finally remember—finishes the tour with a look at the other resident floors. The third level, the one I'm *supposed* to be on, is home to people aged twenty to fifty-nine, though most of them seem my age or younger. They all appear fresh, beautiful, and much cooler than I am despite wearing the exact same plant outfit.

The top floor, bathed in bright yellow walls, is the children's level. It's the only floor that has any kind of color. An aide sits in a chair, surrounded by kids sitting cross-legged on vibrant rugs as they sing a repeat-after-me song about a hippopotamus. To the side of them is a section for art, with easels and tables covered in painted papers. Another section of the room has toys in colored bins. The room is very much like any classroom you'd see in an elementary school, making it easy to forget that all of these children will be dead in a few short months. When Hannah turns to leave, I reluctantly follow her back to the elevators. There's something comforting about this level.

Following the tour, I sit at the edge of my cot, unsure what to do first. I consider beginning that book I downloaded before I got here, but I'm not really in a reading mood. I glance hopefully at Ryder, wrinkling my nose at his closed eyes. Twisting in my cot, I position myself so I can see him better. I'd barely looked at him before, just long enough to notice he was a good looking guy. Now that I'm facing him four cots away, I realize *good looking* is an understatement. I have a thing for thick eyebrows, and if I weren't so far away, I'd have a hard time not running a finger over them. They match the darkness of his slightly mussed hair, swept up from his forehead as if he spent his life in the wind. His skin is smooth, though I note the dark shadows under his closed eyes and the sharp edge to his cheeks. He stirs slightly and I drop my eyes, peeking back when I think it's safe. My line of vision travels the carved path of his jaw and rough unshaven face to the Roman slope of his nose, resting on the soft hills of his mouth, which part when he licks his upper lip. I jump when I realize he's watching me. The indigo blue of his eyes hold mine, just like the breath caught in my lungs. I avert my eyes, pretending I wasn't just studying him like a stalker. When I look back, his eyes are closed again. I let out the air I was holding, unraveling my hands from the blanket I didn't even know I was clutching.

There's still fifteen minutes until lunchtime. Even though I'm not hungry, I figure it's a good way to pass the time and stop acting weird around handsome men. Hannah had advised me to eat in the third floor cafeteria, warning me of the bland pureed food they served the seniors. I get up to leave, but pause as I look one last time back at Ryder. Maybe I don't have to go alone.

"Hey," I whisper once I reach him. I touch his shoulder, but he remains still. I stare at him, willing him to open his eyes. His chest rises and falls, his breathing even as if he really is sleeping. "If you're awake, I'm grabbing lunch upstairs. And, uh…" *What was I doing?* We didn't even know each other. And I was still acting weird. "Seeing that we're the only ones here that still have their real teeth…" His mouth twitches, and I know I have him. But I don't. He keeps his eyes closed. "All right, then," I say, now feeling more awkward than ever.

Lunch is pizza, which feels rather cliché surrounded by a bunch of people who look like they've just graduated college. I long for a beer to wash down the admittedly delicious meal, but alcohol isn't allowed on the premises. Instead I have a root beer. I haven't had soda since I was a child, or pizza. I haven't even had sugar since then, so afraid of the health ramifications.

When I was twelve, the doctor ran tests and told my parents I would die of a heart attack on my expiration date. When my mom finally let me know, I swore off sugar. I stopped eating fried foods. I began running, trying to win the race against the end of my life, hoping to see the number increase so I could live to see thirty-five, forty, sixty, ninety-nine. I thought I could change my fate if I was healthy enough.

Obviously, I couldn't.

I snag another slice of pizza, going for the sun-dried tomato and feta slice this time, then refill my soda. Just because I can, I also grab a bowl of ice cream. My stomach is bursting, but I don't care. I've been disciplined all my life. I could eat myself sick, and it no longer matters.

"Is anyone sitting here?" I look up from my plate, my mouth full of pizza, to see Ryder standing above me. I'm suddenly aware of my tray, and the sauce dribbling from the corner of my mouth. I quickly swipe it with the back of my hand, then wave my hands at the five empty seats. He sits two seats away. I feel even more like a pig when I glance at his tray—a salad and water. He proceeds to pick at his salad, as if it's more than he can handle. He catches me looking at his plate, and then looks at mine, wrinkling his nose.

"You don't approve?" The words come out harsher than I intended, a likely side effect of the blush heating across my cheeks. I'm more than full, but wash the pizza down with a spoonful of ice cream, trying to hide my embarrassment.

"It's all good," he says. I can tell he's trying not to look at my plate. He spears a leaf of lettuce, then chews it slowly as if it were a piece of steak. His silence eats at me, and my explanation finally bubbles over.

"I've spent my whole life being healthy. I run every day. I only drink on occasion. Vegetables are my staple. But we're here. What's the point? We might as well eat what we want while we still can."

"Oh, so you're one of those."

"One of what?"

His eyes crinkle at the corners, his mouth slightly turns up. "A Bucket Lister."

"Excuse me?"

"You know what I'm talking about. You're one of those people who have a list of things to do before you die, except your list includes foods you never got to eat on the other side."

"I'll have you know that I have no such list," I say, denying my teenage goals. He thinks he's got me pegged, but he doesn't even know me. "I ate, slept, and worked every day on repeat until they came to take me away."

"I bet you went skydiving."

I stand up, almost knocking over my half full glass of soda. I know I'm overreacting, but I can't help it. I'm mortified because all my reactions around him are wrong, and I'm flustered because I don't know what to make of him. I desperately want to start over. Instead I say, "You don't even know my name, and you're pretending like you know everything about me. You don't know anything."

He looks at me for a moment, and I'm frozen under his gaze. He still appears tired, but his face relaxes with amusement.

"I know your name is Noelle, and my name is Ryder," he says, putting his hand out. I fight the urge to reach for his hand, knowing I'll give myself away if I do. To curb my impulses, I pick up my tray, making my hands unavailable. This isn't lost on him, and I can see the laugh deepen in his expression. "I know you have 100 days from today, according to the number on the back of your neck, just like me. I know you sleep a few cots away from me and are one of the only people on our floor without a walker. I know your eyes are blue because they're unmistakable, even from across the room. I know you're much too young to have hair that silver, but it's stunning on you. I know you're scared to be here because it means it's over. And I know you chew the inside of your cheek when you're nervous, or someone gets too close, or you find someone attractive, or all three."

I unclench my teeth, letting my cheek go as he grins over his nearly untouched salad.

"It's nice to meet you, Noelle," he continues.

My heart pounds inside my chest, from anger and anxiousness over everything he said. "You don't know me," I finally say, his laugh following me as I walk away. I don't look back as I discard my food, knowing he's still watching.

It's going to be a long one hundred days.

Home

Noelle

97 days left

I had a goldfish up until a few days ago. It was the biggest commitment I'd ever made to a living creature, which felt like a huge risk when I broke down and bought the damn thing. With my pending expiration date, I promised myself I'd never take on any responsibility that would last longer than my life. This was why, at age twenty-two, I'd opted to get my tubes tied. I knew I couldn't have children. How fair would that be? I'd die before they were old enough to care for themselves. I'm still bitter that my parents chose to have Skye and me, and I was twenty-seven when they died.

But the goldfish felt like a safe choice. I didn't name it, calling it "Fish" if I felt the need to call it anything. It was an impulse decision at the time. I'd stayed too long near the pen of adoptable dogs, refusing to pet them so I wouldn't grow attached. Still, I could feel my heartstrings vibrating, my childhood longing for a dog resurrected by a few floppy ears and wagging tails. So, I tore myself away and bought a fish instead. It was kind of like choosing to eat a bag of chips to keep from inhaling a bowl of ice cream. This fish was my Band-Aid to the loneliness I felt. I knew I'd fall in love with a dog. But a fish? If it looked like it would live longer than me, I'd just flush it.

That fish grew to twice its size in the year I had it, probably nourished by all the stories I told it. He knew my deepest longings, my regrets, and my struggle with time. During my final week, I kept promising to flush it tomorrow. Every day, tomorrow. On night 101, I picked up Fish's bowl and set it outside my neighbor's door with a note: "Please take care of me. I'm a really good listener." The next morning, as the aides led me from my apartment for the very last time, the fishbowl was gone.

I miss Fish.

It's now been three days since I came to River's End, and each day feels longer than the last. I have no one to talk with. That never bothered me before, but then again, I always had someplace familiar to come home to. Here, I have nothing and no one. Not even Ryder. He's been sleeping this whole time, though he sometimes gets up to eat. We haven't even talked since the first day. At first I brushed it off, figuring he was just taking advantage of the hours upon hours of free time we now had. But by the second day, it began to get old; I can't help feeling slighted. It's not like I expected us to be best friends or anything, but I at least hoped we could connect on some level. It doesn't help that I still find him wildly attractive, which only adds to my frustration. That, and I don't even know how to approach him. Sometimes I catch him looking at me during meals. When our eyes meet, he'll give me a lopsided smile as if there's a joke he knows and I don't. But it's always from across the room. He no longer sits with me in the cafeteria; he doesn't sit with anyone. He just keeps to himself, eating his sad salad, presumably counting down the days until he's dead.

It infuriates me. It's just like me. It's nothing like me.

I'm the first one awake, which isn't a surprise. Here in the old folks' home, the seniors tend to sleep more hours than they're awake. But the dim light coming in through the windows tells me I'm up earlier than usual; the sun hasn't yet risen. I sit up, swinging my legs over the side of the bed so I can lace my tennis shoes. I glance in Ryder's direction, just as I do every morning I get up for a run. For the first time, he's not there, which surprises me. His cubby is folded back into the wall, leaving a hole in the row of sleeping bodies.

What if he's dead? The sadness that follows this thought surprises me, and I push it back where it came from.

I take the stairs to the first level, skipping down the steps as I shake the sleep from my legs. It could be argued that it's pointless to workout at all, except there's not much else to do. Besides, exercise is when I feel the most alive—when my heart is racing, my skin sticky with sweat, my breath labored, every nerve on fire. It's when I feel powerful, like I can run straight through the wall that surrounds this so-called oasis and forget all about this whole dying business.

Before I head to the treadmill, I take a few rounds at the punching bags, warming up my muscles and letting out some unreleased tension. I've been kickboxing since I was a child, starting when my dad decided Skye and I needed to learn how to defend ourselves. Mostly, though, I think this was my dad's way of bonding with us. Years before we were born, he was a Navy Seal, and this history shaped much of who he was and how he parented. It wasn't that he was strict with us, but that he expected us to hold our own in every situation. By the time I could ride a bike, I could also hold a perfect fighting stance, sidestep a direct attack, and throw a mean punch. Dad had made sure Skye and I knew everything that he learned in the Navy, to the point that reacting to an unexpected attack was as natural as breathing. The one time Skye tested me, our coffee table ended up in pieces, my brother sprawled out on top of it as I stood over him. He never did that again.

Once I'm limber, I slip on my headphones and head to the treadmill. I'd bought these things as a joke, drawn to them because they were so retro, like something from the year 2000. But the joke was on me—I liked them so much more than the usual mind projection everyone else used.

Even my mom had asked why I'd prefer headphones over the convenience of internal sound waves. My obsession with the early 2000s amused her because she'd lived them. Maybe that was why I listened to her old music and collected things from her era—because it was familiar through osmosis.

But these headphones also represented a simpler time. Back then, the sky had been blue, which I wouldn't have believed had I not seen her childhood photos. It was nothing like the gray smog that now covers the sun and hides the stars and moon. I'd never seen a constellation or shooting star, even though we'd learned about them in astronomy in college. But my mom told me stories of camping in her backyard with her sisters—in the open air!—watching the Perseid meteor showers every August. She even told me about the year her grandfather had roasted a pig over a spit, a thought that both horrified and amazed me since pigs were now an endangered species, and the thought of killing any kind of animal felt caveman-ish. Apparently they didn't stop at pigs, but also ate cows, chickens, sheep, seafood, and something called sushi made of raw saltwater fish—all now endangered and protected under global law due to overpopulation and the heavy toll on the meat industry.

This was one part of the early 2000s I was not obsessed with. I'd take cultured meat created in a lab over a slaughtered animal any day. I'd never even seen a pig or a cow in my life, and the thought of eating any kind of raw meat made me want to puke. It also seemed strange to eat anything that came out of the ocean. My mom told me stories of eating crab fresh off the boat after her uncles caught them in the deep part of the ocean. Now fishing is outlawed since the lack of oxygen in the water creates dead spots that span hundreds of thousands of miles.

But despite the weird eating habits from the old days, I still love everything I know about this historic time, going way beyond the headphones. Before moving to River's End, I'd spend hours watching old movies my mom called "cult classics" from her childhood; including a series called *Twilight,* about sparkly vampires and hot werewolves; a dystopian series called *The Hunger Games,* about kids who were forced to kill each other; and this one movie called *Mean Girls,* which mostly amused me because my mom knew every line. I aced my U.S. History class that covered 1970-2020, and wore my mother's old yoga pants and sweatshirt when I did my oral report to look like a 2010 teen. I even paid close attention in Environmental Studies. It was a mandatory class everyone else hated, but I found it fascinating. I thought it was particularly interesting how our country didn't take global warming seriously when my mom was a kid, even though all the signs were there—the dramatic change in weather, the catastrophic earthquakes and tropical storms, the declining air quality…. I'd listen to my mom's stories of having a garbage man take away their garbage instead of using it for energy, or how they used gasoline for a car instead of driving water-powered vehicles. They had actual grass in the yard and mowed it every weekend, and bought food from a grocery store and threw away edible lettuce just because it was slightly wilted. This all seemed so wasteful, but it was the norm of her time. They didn't know our oceans would heat up, lose oxygen, and kill fish and whales in large quantities, or that we'd be forced to wear masks for extended periods outside. They had no idea we'd run out of room for farms and now had to rely on vegetables from vertical sky farms that towered over the city like skyscrapers. When the people my mom's age threw things away for the landfills of the past, they didn't know we'd eventually run out of places to dump it.

And when they were young, they had no idea they'd one day know the date of their death and how they would die. I'd give anything to live in a time before our earth was covered in smog and large portions of the ocean were dead. Maybe I could have made a difference back then. But more than that, I'd give anything to live in a time when I didn't know my expiration. My date of death has always weighed me down like a backpack full of bricks.

I set my running pace on the treadmill, then look out the window as I begin a slow jog to warm up. I watch a lone swimmer arc one arm over the other in powerful strokes through the pool. He touches one side, then gracefully slips under, reappearing a few feet out on his way back to the other side. It's like a dance, the way he carves through the water, the way the ripples slip over his skin, the way the glow of the outside lights glistens off his back and sculpted arms. I feel breathless, and I've hardly started running. I increase my speed, keeping my eyes on my heart rate. But soon I drift back to the swimmer. He's resting now at the end of the pool, and I realize with a start who it is. *Ryder.* He's facing my direction, and I quickly look away. I doubt he sees me; his view is probably obscured by the reflection of the dawn, the pink clouds hovering high above the glass dome that protects our air. I'm tempted to hop off the treadmill and be gone before he notices I'm here. But then I realize I'm being a coward.

"You were in here first," I remind myself, admiring his physique as he towels himself dry. He enters and looks around the room before glancing at me. I see all this out of the corner of my eye, refusing to acknowledge him. My heart rate increases on the monitor as I sense him coming closer. Then he's right next to me. He doesn't even change into dry clothes or put on shoes. He just powers up the treadmill and starts running. I'm both bothered and turned on by this, which pisses me off even more. *He's ignored you for days,* I keep reminding myself, irritated by the droplets of pool water that are flying off him as he runs, cooling my heated skin and causing ripples in places that haven't rippled in a while. The guy has slept since we got here, appearing weak and barely eating. Now he's running as if marathons are his pastime.

I punch the speed rate and start running faster, pulling energy from the music in my ears. He does the same, landing on a speed faster than mine. I wait about thirty seconds and then accelerate more. I can hear his bare feet slapping against the belt as he runs, the sound louder than my music. I think about turning my music up to drown him out. But I don't. As angry as he's making me, I want to hear him. We keep outrunning each other—me, and then him, and then me again. I'm sprinting now, running faster and longer than I've ever run in my life. My legs are burning, my lungs complaining, sweat soaking my pastel tank top to a forest green. I realize I'm going to have to let this go, but before I can slow the machine, he does first. I keep running a few seconds longer, pretending I still have more in me, and then I reduce my speed to a walking pace, matching his exactly. I can't help but look at him, blushing when he grins. We're both breathing hard, and his chiseled chest glistens from sweat instead of pool water. We slow to a stop, and I get down. My legs feel shaky, like they aren't even part of my body, and I know once I sit I'm not getting back up. I head for the showers, but he stops me by grabbing my hand.

"Let's start over," he says as I turn back to him. He lets go of my hand, then holds his toward me. "I'm Ryder."

I look at his hand before placing mine in it. His grip is warm, sweaty, strong. But he holds my hand gently without shaking it.

"I'm Noelle."

"It's nice to meet you."

There's an awkward silence between us. I pull my hand back. Are we friends now? Or just strangers on friendly terms?

"Uh, I should probably shower," I say at the same time he says, "Coffee?" I can't help laughing—the polite kind of laughter when I don't know what else to say. It's my nervous habit. Laugh, and maybe the discomfort will disappear…or at least hide under the feigned humor. Ryder motions for me to go first. "I'll shower, and then, yes, let's get coffee," I say.

I don't linger, suddenly glad for all the automatic perks of the facility. A robotic sweeper captures my sweaty clothes from the ground. Thanks to the preferences programmed into my ID, the shower water is the perfect temperature. I don't even have to towel off, as the warm air from the vents blows every drop of water from my body. When I leave the shower, a tray ejects from the wall, holding a set of clothing in my exact size.

I check my appearance in the mirror before leaving the changing room. My hair is still wet and I'm not wearing any makeup. I fight the urge to put on some mascara. I don't want to give Ryder the impression that I think this is more than it is. I regret the decision as soon as I reach the coffee shop. He's freshly showered, and somehow his still damp hair looks a million times better than mine. His eyes light up when he sees me, his smile revealing perfect teeth and a dimple, and I wonder just how translucent my eyelashes must look without any color at all.

"You clean up nice," he says, pulling my chair out for me—a surprising move. While I'd never had a serious relationship, I'd dated a few guys in my time. Not one of them ever pulled my chair out for me. In fact, they hardly noticed me at all. My generation began the same year technology advanced enough to predict dates of death, and knowledge of our expiration date kind of ruined us. We were known as the Genesis Generation—Gen-Gen for short—and were known for our "Me First" attitudes. Everyone around my age and younger was into experiences, trying to fit as many in before their time was up. The smaller the number, the more frantic these goals became. This priority caused a decrease in volunteerism, monetary donations, and common courtesy—including pulling chairs out for your date.

"I'd order for you, but I don't know your preference," Ryder says, holding up his wrist. "I'm still not used to these bracelets. Everything is too easy here."

"It's not much different than a Smart Watch," I say. I'm confused when he shakes his head. "You didn't have one?"

"Nope," he says. "And before you ask, I also didn't have a Smart Phone, Smart House, Smart Car, or Smart Refrigerator. Nothing I had was smart."

My eyes widen. "How did you get your food?" I thought of my refrigerator at home that was programmed to automatically order my staple foods when I ran out.

"The old-fashioned way," he says. "I called Zon and re-ordered by phone. But when I was growing up, it was even more rustic than that. We grew our vegetables and cultivated our own meat."

"You were farmers," I say. He shakes his head.

"No, we were just poor."

"But you had land to grow vegetables?"

"No," he says. "We used the side paneling and roof of our house."

I'm not sure what to say, so I order instead. I wave my ID over the panel on the table, and a screen appears on the glass surface. I mull over the choices, then go with a latte, heavy foam. When my coffee arrives, I consider leaving with it so I can see what's for breakfast.

"I'm sorry," Ryder says. The apology catches me off guard. This is new, too. "I'm not really a mean guy," he continues.

"You haven't exactly been mean," I say, recalling a few times when I was short with him. I should be the one apologizing.

"No, but I've been reclusive."

"Oh?"

"Yes, *oh*," he says, and he shoots me a smile before his face turns serious. "It's hard to explain. I guess I'm just angry. I shouldn't be here. None of us should. If we're really going to die in three months like they say we are, we should be able to stay in the outside world. It's not fair that they have to take us away from everyone we love and everything we know just so they can make our lives comfortable. It doesn't even make sense."

"It does to me."

"How?"

I pause for a moment, thinking back to just this past week. Every day I'd dealt with this differently. One day I was closing out all my accounts and cleaning my apartment as I prepared for the end. The next, I was leaving my mess everywhere in the house because it no longer mattered—I soon wouldn't be there to see it. But one thing was consistent—besides Fish, I had no one left to say goodbye to.

"I think it's nice," I tell him. "Everything about life is hard. You grow up, get a job, work, try to make ends meet. But when you reach this final stage, everything is suddenly paid for."

"Or rather, we already paid for it."

"I didn't," I say.

"You paid taxes."

I don't have anything to say to this. It still seems like a small price to pay for three months of carefree living.

"And what if this whole thing is a ruse? Like population control or something?" he continues. I roll my eyes.

"Now you sound like my brother. He was just as paranoid as you are."

"Was?"

"He expired," I say, trying to sound like I'm sure of it. "Just like we will in…" I look at my ID bracelet. "Ninety-seven days." The number makes my stomach plummet. It does every time I pay attention to my limited time. "I can't believe it's ending." I look at him. "And don't say that it isn't, or that it's planned, or we can stop it. That's just false hope. I've finally come to terms that my life is over, even if I still have moments when it all seems surreal. To think otherwise means I go backward, and I don't want to. I want to spend my final days with everything taken care of, in total comfort, staying in this white and green resort called River's End."

He sits back in his chair and takes a sip of his coffee. I do the same. I realize this is all a mistake. Just because we're around the same age and dying on the same day doesn't mean we have to be friends. It doesn't mean we have to be anything.

"Look, I have reasons to believe this whole thing is a sham," he says. "I'm sorry if that sounds a little too conspiracy theory to you, but I have actual proof."

"And that is…"

"I can't tell you."

I fume at his words, more than I should. At this moment, it's not Ryder I see in front of me, but Skye, just as I remembered him on the last day I ever saw him. It was our parents' farewell party, and I was already having a hard time accepting that I'd never see them again. He, on the other hand, was more concerned about a secret government plot than the fact that we were about to be orphans.

"I'm not heartless," Skye had said. "They're my parents, too. I love them, but I don't agree that they have to die."

"Not this again."

"I'm serious, Noelle. This whole game is just that—a game. No one or thing can predict the exact date of their death, not even a computer." His own number gave him less than two years to live, a time that's come and gone.

I know it's Skye's words affecting me, but I can't hear them anymore, even if they're coming out of Ryder's mouth. We're here, and this is the end. I can't bring myself to have hope in anything else. I push my chair back as I get ready to leave.

"Wait," he says, and I do, feeling like a pushover. "I just...never mind."

"Right. Okay." I grab my coffee and turn around. He doesn't stop me this time, and while I'm disappointed, I'm not surprised. I feel like an idiot that we even got this far into pretending like there's any kind of connection. Our only similarity is our expiration date.

I take a shortcut across the courtyard, zig-zagging around sunbathers on my way to the sliding doors. Ryder will probably eat on the third floor with the other Gen-Gens, so I opt to stay on the second floor and enjoy gummy porridge for breakfast. I eat next to an old woman, trying not to notice she's in bad need of a shave, or that most of her meal is landing back in the bowl from her shaky hands. When I've finished my cereal, my guilty conscience taps at me until I finally turn and take her spoon, feeding her the last half of her breakfast and wiping her chin in between bites.

"Thank you, love," she croaks, offering a wide, toothless smile. Despite my frustration, something lightens inside me.

"The pleasure is mine," I say, patting her hand.

I start to clear our dishes, but an aide waves me away. With nothing to do, I retreat to the couch by the window and watch the swimmers in the pool. I pretend I'm not looking for Ryder as I scan the grounds. I feel bad about how I left things.

I'd thought everything would be easy once I got here, sure I'd finally escape my ghosts. I constantly felt like I was struggling in the outside world. I was the last one left in my family. I refused to be close to anyone, choosing to walk through life alone. I thought I'd find a sense of peace once I reached my hundredth day. Instead, all my ghosts followed me here and are louder than ever. To make it worse, I realize that I don't want to be alone anymore. With Ryder, I feel like I found someone who understands, even though I'm making a mess of everything. I'm angry, just like him. I'm not so sure about his conspiracy theories, but I can't fault him for finding something to blame. I'm also tied up in knots over being so close to dying. I hadn't ever admitted that before, not even to myself. Plus, it's only been three days, and I'm going stir crazy. If I don't find something more to do in the short time I have left, I'm going to go insane.

I need a purpose.

3

Orphan

Noelle

97 days left

I take the elevator upstairs, greeted by the sunshine walls of the top floor. The kids are all playing in separate areas of the large room, gathered in groups around Legos, puzzles, board games, and other activities. All, except one boy. I notice him sitting in the corner, picking at something imaginary on the ground in front of him while everyone else seems to have a friend. He never looks up, though he flinches when a ball from one group hits the wall next to him.

An older boy runs up to retrieve the ball. "Sorry, kid," he tosses over his shoulder as he heads back. The younger boy says nothing.

I look around and notice Hannah, the woman who showed me around, leading a group of girls in a beading project.

"Can I help?" I ask. She looks up, surprised, then smiles.

"I had a feeling I'd see you here," she says.

"You did?" I didn't even know I'd be here. "How?"

"You seemed most interested when I brought you to this floor. You must love kids."

Not exactly.

"I was never around kids much in my…in my former life. I just have nothing to do, and taking a yoga or meditation class doesn't sound fun."

"So, you want to help?" she asks. I nod. "We're going to do an art lesson in a few minutes if you want to start setting up for that." She tells me where to find the paint and poster board, and I get to work. Soon, everyone in the class is wearing an apron and standing in front of an easel. One easel remains empty, however, saved for the boy who remains in the corner of the room.

"What's his story?" I ask Hannah once everyone is painting.

"That's Devon," she says. "He's been here for a week and hasn't spoken since. According to his foster parents, they've never heard him speak."

"He was a foster," I muse. "What happened to his birth parents?" Devon looks up momentarily from his station across the room, though he's too far away to hear that we're talking about him. The pupils of his eyes are as dark as his skin, and they reveal an unmistakable emotion—fear.

"It's a sad story," Hannah answers. "He was four when they died. It was a car crash. He survived, but they didn't. It was many years before they were supposed to expire, though there's a rumor they'd tampered with their numbers, making it appear they had longer to live. Maybe they believed it would give them more years." She shakes her head. "If they did believe this, then they're selfish people."

"Why?"

"They didn't change Devon's number."

The boy stays where he is for the entire art lesson, turning his body when Hannah tries to coax him to join in. "It will be fun," she promises, but now he faces the wall, unwilling to budge. I'm distracted by his refusal as the other kids enjoy creating their interpretation of a summer's day. A young girl raises her hand, and I join her since Hannah is still with Devon. On her poster board are a painting of a yellow sun, a blue stripe for a sky, a large tree, and a girl in a dress with a smile as big as her face.

"Will there be trees in Infinity?" the young painter asks me. Her question catches me off guard. It's a valid question—after all, it's supposed to be something to look forward to when this life ends. My own parents had told me these stories when I was younger, starting with the moment I began asking questions about our expiration dates.

"Only your body dies," my mother said, smoothing my hair from my face as I lay my head in her lap. "But your soul never does. You'll finally be able to go to Infinity."

"What's Infinity?" I asked, and she peered into my face with a look of surprise.

"It's the most beautiful place you could ever imagine," she said. "It's full of everything you love, and things you didn't even know you loved."

"Are there puppies?" I asked. I'd been asking my parents for a dog for as long as I could remember, but they still hadn't caved.

"There are puppies," she said with a laugh. "And kittens, and hillsides covered in trees, oceans with crashing waves, sandcastles that reach up to the sky, and playgrounds that stretch as far as you can see."

"And fairies?" I asked.

"And fairies," she agreed. "Mermaids, too. And unicorns. Everything will be there."

"Will you?"

She gave me a sad smile, and then looked away. I thought I saw moisture forming in her eyes. It was gone when she looked back at me.

"I'll be there, Daddy will be there, even your brother Skye will be there. We'll all be there, waiting for you to join us, where we can be a family forever."

"Until we die."

"No, honey. Forever. Infinity is forever."

Years later, I realize Infinity is a fairytale parents tell their kids to help them accept the natural cycle of life and death. In truth, nothing happens when you die. You just cease to exist. You're forgotten. And if you're like me, the last of your family, there will never be another soul that will speak your name again.

"Yes," I tell the girl looking up at me. "There are trees in Infinity. There's everything you've ever dreamed of, everything you've ever loved, and things you don't even know you love."

She beams at my answer, and goes back to adding blue to her sky.

After art is music. A few teens from the other side of the room help clean up the paint mess, while another group helps gather everyone in a circle. Hannah has since given up on Devon, and I, with nothing better to do, decide to try my luck with him. The worst that will happen is rejection, and I've gotten pretty used to that feeling. But the fact that I expect his rejection makes it better.

"Hey." I settle in next to him against the wall. He scoots about a half-foot away from me, and I don't try to close the space. "I'm going to sit here if that's okay. You don't have to talk or anything. I just don't know anyone here, and I'm feeling a little shy. Is it okay if I'm here?"

He doesn't answer, and I pretend that means yes.

"Great. Let me know if they play your favorite song." I'm making light of it, hoping it will help reveal a crack I can push my way through. But in all reality, I get it.

Devon remains silent as the music starts. He doesn't tap his foot, or hum, or even sway his body when one of the teens takes over the guitar and starts strumming a song I recognize as completely inappropriate for kids. I look up in alarm, then laugh when I realize he's changed all the lyrics to more kid-friendly ones. The other teens are laughing too, then join him with the chorus. Soon, the whole room is full of singers, drummers, dancers, and tumblers. I stay with Devon, helping him hold up the wall, but I clap with the energy of the room. For a moment, it's easy to forget the end. This is what living is supposed to look like.

I leave at lunchtime, my heart full but my stomach empty. My breakfast mush is forgotten, and I long for a heartier meal. Something Hannah forgot to tell me in our tour is that this is a truly vegetarian facility—no cultured meat at all—and I'm craving a Spamburger something fierce. I skip the second-floor smorgasbord of purees and head for the Gen-Gen section, hoping for something that at least pretends to be meat. I'm graced with soy-sauce soaked carrot dogs, which don't taste so bad with enough ketchup and mustard but do nothing to fill me up. It's not even that I used to eat a lot of lab meat before I came here, it's the fact that it's been taken away.

"The chili almost tastes like beef," Ryder whispers in my ear from behind. I turn, noticing his full bowl, just part of a packed tray.

"You've had beef?" I ask. He wrinkles his nose, then shakes his head.

"Nah. But if I had, it would probably taste better than this chili."

I look at his tray. "No salad?"

"Are you judging my food?" he asks, but there's a smile in his eyes.

I roll my eyes and turn back to my carrot dog.

"Come on, Noelle, stop pretending we're not friends. Sit with us."

"Us?"

Ryder points his tray toward a table of guys in the center of the room. They wave in our direction. "You've made friends?" I ask, feeling a tightening in my chest. I'm embarrassed by my jealousy, and I relax my expression, hoping he doesn't notice.

"Hey, if we're all dying anyway, we may as well meet others just like us. After all, we're in this together."

No, we're not, I want to tell him. We die alone, no one in it with us at all. But I don't say this. Instead, I follow him to the table, putting on my best smile, even though I'd rather sit against a wall, refusing to talk with anyone.

"Guys, this is Noelle. She's the only other person I know who prefers the smell of denture tabs and diaper cream, which is why we're roomies in the senior ward."

"You're the hottest grandma I've ever met," one of the guys says, holding his fist out. I play along, bumping fists while sticking my tongue out at him.

"Pay no attention to him," Ryder says. "Colby is just mad he has to die a virgin."

"Hey, I got more tail than you wish you had, old man," Colby said, tossing a chili bean at him. Ryder ducks and the bean lands somewhere on the ground behind us.

"So, that's Colby," he continues. "And Eric, Keith, and Shane. At the other table over there are the girls, Danika, Jules, Jeanette, and Spring."

"You've been busy," I say. He's slept for days, and now he has eight new friends?

"I had to find people who don't hate me." Again, he's smiling, but this joke feels a little true.

"Oh, we hate you. But we also feel sorry for you," Colby quips.

"I don't hate you," I hiss. "I just got irritated. Besides, I was only gone for three hours." Ryder takes my hand and pulls me from the table. I'm not expecting it, but I don't fight him.

"I'm teasing you. Relax. I just thought it might be better if we're not alone. It's not like we're overflowing with friends on our floor. Besides, they approached me."

"But why?"

"Colby overheard our conversation this morning. He was interested in what I had to say. A lot of them are feeling the same way about the whole expiration thing."

"Not this again. So, now you're making me be friends with a bunch of other crazy people."

He squeezes my hand. "I'm not making you do anything," he promises. "But don't discount them. They're a bit younger than us, but they're smart. And fun."

This time I do pull my hand away. "Why are you even including me? We're obviously so different."

"I think we have a lot more in common than you think," he says. "We even have the same expiration date. That's something, right?"

I think back to my parents and the identical numbers on the back of their necks.

"It's just a number," I lie.

"Wrong," he says. "It's destiny."

I don't know how to feel when Ryder leads me back to the table. I'd been the one who initiated a friendship with him, but now he's acting like this friendship is his idea, and even including other people in the mix. It's not that I'm against meeting other people. Admittedly, I'm intrigued by the idea. Still, I feel like a fifth wheel—or tenth wheel, in this case. Even worse, it sounds like they're all as crazy as Skye was.

Worst of all? I'm afraid to believe them. If I do, it will mean my whole life is a lie, that my parents didn't have to die, that this facility taking care of us is really unsafe. To believe them is riskier than anything.

At the table, I chew my carrot dog while the guys take over the conversation. There's not really much for me to say. Ryder seems to have forgotten his tendency for day-long naps and is now one of the boys. It's not like I knew him, I keep reminding myself. And yet, he feels more like a stranger than before. A couple of times, he looks over at me and shoots me a smile, almost like he's checking in. But he doesn't say anything. His hand stays near mine resting on the bench, but he doesn't touch it. I wish I'd just sat alone. I glance over at the table nearby, the one with the girls whose names I can no longer recall, and consider joining them. When they all break into laughter, I think differently. Why poison their fun with my awkwardness?

"The worst was saying goodbye to my dog," Eric says. Or was it Evan? No, it was Eric.

"No, the worst was saying goodbye to your girlfriend," another guy says. I don't remember his name, but he has olive-colored skin and striking green eyes.

"You had a girlfriend?" Ryder asks, then laughs with disbelief. "I can't believe you'd do that to yourself. It's not like you didn't know your expiration date. Do you like punishing yourself?"

"You wouldn't understand," the guy says. "She was special."

"They're all special, Shane." Ryder laughs, then looks at me as if I'm going to join in. I don't. I mean, I also think Shane is stupid for getting into a relationship when he knew he was going to die. But Ryder doesn't have to know I agree with him.

"For me, the worst is saying goodbye to your parents," Keith says. His expression is more serious than the other guys'. "I've known most of my life I was going before them, and it still didn't make it easier."

"At least you had parents to say goodbye to," Ryder says. "My parents died when I was 15. They didn't even have a real plan for me. I was left to my aunt, and she couldn't have cared less whether I was there or not. I left and took care of myself. When it was my time to go, I had no one to wish me goodbye."

His parents died on the same day as each other, too. Apparently, this is an epidemic. The realization that we have more in common washes over me, appearing initially as surprise, but then merging into a heated rage that starts as a seed in my belly, growing into a raging wildfire that consumes my breath. I'm fully aware that this doesn't make sense. But what sticks to me is his lament that he didn't get to say goodbye to his parents. Lots of people lost their parents too early. *Like me.*

I look away while the guys continue talking, forgotten as I sit next to Ryder. I've never felt more alone in my life, including all the times my coworkers grabbed drinks together while I stayed home with Fish. The last few days stab at me and all my insecurities. I came here determined to keep to myself, but meeting Ryder changed everything—and I don't know what to make of it. The guy slept for the first few days and ignored me when he was awake. Then today comes and he's swimming laps and making friends, and I'm...*jealous.*

I grab my tray and leave the table. No one stops me. I spend the afternoon at the pool, half-reading the book I brought with me. It feels good to be in the sun, especially since the glass dome keeps out the polluted air so I don't have to wear a mask. I let the warmth wash away my bad mood. I've resigned myself to spend the rest of my days alone, save for the time I spend on the children's floor. This decision feels good, as I know it will be the best use of my time. But when Ryder sits down at the foot of my lounge chair, my irritation returns with a vengeance.

"What do you want?" I ask him, glaring over the top of my book.

"I could ask the same thing of you. Ever since I met you, you've been nothing but angry with me."

"Me?" I put the book down and sit with a steel spine. "You're the one who's been terrible! You've slept for days, ignored me, and have acted like you're so much better than me. You barely said two words to me at lunch. Then you act as if you've got the cornerstone on pain as if you're the only one who is hurting by being here. Newsflash, buddy, none of us want to be here, because being here means we're taken from everything we know. Out there, I had a life! I had my own space. I had a purpose. But here? I have nothing and no one! I can't even lift a finger without someone doing it for me. So for you to act like you're the only one who's lost something is completely selfish and unfair."

"I never said I did."

"But you did!" I insist. "At the table. When that one guy was talking about saying goodbye to his parents, and you told him you had it worse."

"We were all doing that, Noelle."

"I wasn't."

"No, you weren't. In fact, you never said anything because you think you're better than all of us."

"Excuse me?"

"You heard me," he says. "You say I'm acting like I have the cornerstone on pain? Speak for yourself. You sit there and act as if everything is okay, but it's not. If it were okay, you'd understand that I need time to process, that we all need time to process. *You* need time to process. I'm doing the best I can here, and I don't need you to tell me how I should be acting and all the things I'm doing wrong. I don't want to be here. I don't have a choice, but it doesn't mean I have to accept it right away. I need time, and you're not even giving me that. You tell me I don't know *you*? You don't know *me*!"

His words hit me like a bullet, and my chest tightens. He's right. I can't let him know he's right, but he is. He stands up and walks away, and everything inside me wants to call him back, to apologize, to start over. But my eyes are filling with tears, and I don't want him to see how his words affected me. He's gone, and I dissolve into tears right next to the pool, alone in a crowd of people living on borrowed time.

4

Dying

Ryder
97 days left

I was already dying before I came here. Lung cancer, Aunt Bryn had told me before I ran away for the last time—a surprise since I had no symptoms at all. I swam every day and ran cross country for the track team. My lungs felt like they were made of steel, and yet, supposedly they were failing me. Aunt Bryn had known for years that this was how I was going to die. My parents had too, but I didn't learn about it until a few years after their death. Aunt Bryn mentioned it as if she were telling me we were out of milk, appearing shocked that I didn't already know. She took me to her physician, Dr. Caste, a friendly man who stood out like a comforting cup of cocoa in the cold days of my life. Even when I ran away, I continued to see him, hoping he'd find some way to reverse the damage

I still couldn't feel. We both knew that was impossible—the numbers on the back of my neck told the truth. Still, I felt that if anyone could extend my life, it would be him.

Nothing agreed with me. Dr. Caste put me on a cocktail of medication, changing pills periodically as I complained of side effects. I constantly felt short of breath, my lips taking on a bluish tint as I fought for oxygen. I stayed indoors as much as possible to avoid the toxic air outside. Most days, I could hardly lift my head. At this point, I was working as a busser at a restaurant and in danger of losing my job because of all the days I needed to call out. I wasn't sure how I was going to make rent. My food had dwindled to a jar of beans and a stack of corn tortillas, which I lived on for every meal. Sometimes I'd wake up and realize I'd missed a whole day. I'd show up for more tests, reading the answer on Dr. Caste's face before he even told me the results. I began to wonder if I'd even make it to thirty, as my digital number promised. I wasn't even sure I'd make it to eighteen.

I was taken by surprise when a new doctor sat where Dr. Caste once did as I came in for my appointment. It hadn't occurred to me to pay attention to anyone else's number, so engrossed with my own mortality. Dr. Caste expired, Dr. Singh told me, and then looked over my charts while I digested this information. My new doctor asked me about each pill and supplement I was taking, his brow furrowing deeper as he pored over the list.

"We're going to try an experimental drug." Dr. Singh made a few notes on my charts. I didn't ask questions as he took my chart and folded it in half, placing it in the inner pocket of his jacket. He typed quickly into the computer, and then printed two new sheets, handing me one of them. On it was the name of one medication—Kreptophan—instead of the fifteen different medicines I was taking before.

"Shouldn't I taper off?" I asked. I knew I wasn't the medical professional in the room, but I had researched the drugs I'd been on. A few of them were highly addictive, with warnings that included how to stop using them.

"Normally I'd say yes," Dr. Singh said. "But this new drug is supposed to support your system as you heal. It will absorb your withdrawal symptoms, and repair any damage to your organs."

"Damage? You mean from the cancer?" He'd nodded, but the look on his face said something different. He instructed me to discard any leftover medication and to see him the following week for testing.

It took three days to notice the difference. The heaviness in my head was gone. I felt like running instead of the weighted steps I usually took. My appetite grew, an unfortunate effect since I still had no food. I was no longer sick. At least, I no longer felt it. Most importantly, I could breathe! I practiced long inhales often, amazed every time my chest expanded without pain. When I visited Dr. Singh, he seemed pleased with my progress. A year later, he told me I could stop taking the medication altogether and live a happy life until my expiration date.

"There's nothing we can do about your number," he said, and the same troubled look I'd seen on our first day together flashed over his face. I should have known something was wrong back then.

A decade passed, and I lived a normal enough life. At each checkup, Dr. Singh would tell me I was in perfect health and send me on my way. But last year, another doctor took his place. Dr. Griffin revealed she had just completed her residency when she took over Dr. Singh's patients. She didn't know what had happened to him, just that he was no longer working at the hospital. This time I'd been aware of his expiration date—he still had about forty years left.

"Did he move his practice?" I asked, deciding I'd figure out a way to move with him. But Dr. Griffin didn't know.

"Are you still using Kreptophan?" she asked, thumbing through my charts. I shook my head.

"No, that was the last medication Dr. Singh had me on," I said. "I went off that about eleven years ago, and haven't had to take any medication since. I've been just fine without it." I was in the best shape of my life, starting each day with a five-mile run, and ending with weightlifting and calisthenics in the expansive living room of my loft apartment. My life was everything I thought it would never be. I'd managed to get my degree in computer science, land a programming job, and live a comfortable life near downtown San Francisco with a view of the city. The only thing missing was someone to share it with, but that was out of the question as long as my number remained low.

"I see." She continued to look over the papers and then went into my file on her computer. "Since your expiration date is coming up, we're going to need to run some tests," she said, typing a few things in. She scheduled a few labs that could be conducted the same day.

Three hours later, I was back in Dr. Griffin's office, staring at the results of the tests. "This can't be right." *Cancer.* It was back.

"We'll get started on these medications immediately," she assured me, handing me a list with names I couldn't pronounce.

"What about the Kreptophan?" I asked her. She shook her head, concern painted over her forehead.

"I'm afraid Dr. Singh did you quite a disservice by putting you on that drug and then taking you off all medications. Kreptophan was found to be inefficient for cancer patients more than two decades ago."

"But I feel better," I insisted.

"It may have been the placebo effect," she said.

"A placebo when I wasn't taking any medication for years?"

"We could have tackled this earlier had you been taking these medications." By the way she kept fiddling with my file, I could tell she was flustered. I didn't care; I was pissed.

"And yet, here I am at twenty-nine years old, healthy as an ox."

"An ox with cancer," she said. She set the papers down and looked me in the eye. "Look, Mr. Jamison—"

"Ryder," I interrupted.

"Ryder, the fact of the matter is that you have a terminal disease, and it will get worse if it's untreated. I have updated your records to indicate the new medications you will be taking."

"But I only have a year left," I said.

"You'll have less if we don't start treating this immediately."

"And if I don't?"

Any kindness the doctor possessed immediately left the room as she gave me an icy stare.

"Mr. Jamison," she said coolly. "If you refuse treatment, I will consider this a suicide attempt. Any unsuccessful attempts at suicide are punishable by law. You could spend your final year in prison. You wouldn't want that, Mr. Jamison, would you?"

I realized she had me by the balls. I signed the paperwork she placed in front of me, agreeing to begin taking the medicines she prescribed and to attend weekly doctor's visits for regular lab tests. I was assured that some of these tests would reveal whether or not I was faithful in taking my medicines.

"See you next week!" she said cheerfully.

 ❀ ❀ ❀

That was nine months ago. Every week I went back to Dr. Griffin, who ignored any complaint over how I was feeling as she sung praises about my progress. It seemed gray skin and blue lips, shortness of breath, weight loss, lack of energy, and constant nausea was a sign of improvement. When I wasn't curled around a toilet or relying on a CPAP machine for air, I was on my computer, trying to crack the code to the hospital's system so I could regain control over my life. The security was ironclad, but I was determined to figure out a way to hack the system and change my records so I could get off these damn medications. I was sure they were responsible for how I was feeling. I wasn't even convinced I had cancer.

I received a message a week before I came to the facility, delivered by bike messenger and written in familiar handwriting. *Dr. Singh.* He confirmed my suspicions about the medicine, that they were, in fact, killing me to coincide with my expiration date. He gave me a password to get into their computer system, and then shared how to delete my charts so they couldn't be accessed. I had to wait until day 101, after I'd been discharged from the hospital's outpatient care and put in the care of the facility. No one would know about the medications I was ordered to take.

"Destroy this note immediately," were Dr. Singh's final instructions. I committed his words to memory and then burned the paper in the kitchen sink. On my last night, I got into the system, deleting my files one by one. I flushed my medication, stripping the labels from the canisters and disposing of them in trash bins down the street. I used up all my energy to hide any evidence that I'd been under a physician's care. My charts now read "unknown cause" under cause of death, and medication "none."

My first few days at the facility, I could hardly eat or do anything other than sleep. I stopped cold turkey, with no medication to absorb the terrible side effects as the drugs left my system. But just like last time, it took three days to heal. This morning, I woke up feeling like I could run a marathon. I also felt like a caged tiger, with more energy than I'd had in almost a year and nowhere to release it.

So when Noelle came at me with her "cornerstone of pain" speech, I wanted to put her in her place. When she accused me of being rude by sleeping or ignoring her, I wanted to educate her on what it's like to come off heavy drugs. When she told me I was crazy for believing conspiracy theories, I wanted to let her know how it feels to be killed slowly by your doctor and to face prison if you don't comply.

Instead, I walked away. I didn't want to say something I'd regret—and anything I had to say at that moment, I'd regret. The first time I saw her, I saw something different in her. For so long, I've been avoiding relationships. When I left Aunt Bryn's house, I promised to never get attached to another human being again. They only let you down, and I didn't have enough time for that kind of disappointment. But knowing what I do now, I realize I'm ready for a real connection, the kind where someone knows my thoughts and feelings before I express them, and likes me anyway. Maybe even loves me. I'd take "like", though. And when Noelle sat on my bed, trying to coax me into joining her for lunch, I knew she was the one I'd been hoping for. It was in her voice, the way she moved, the words she chose. I was so afraid of throwing up on her, the drugs running their final course through my body, I pretended to be asleep. But I peeked when she wasn't looking, taking in the way her striking silver hair framed her pale face in shimmering waves, the sprinkle of freckles that floated over her nose and cheeks, the icy blue of her eyes under thick dark lashes, the rose petal color of her lips which she held open slightly, revealing perfect pearls for teeth. I saw her delicate hands which she rested gently in her lap, dressed in the same green scrubs the facility made us wear. I saw all this in a matter of three seconds, memorizing her features, and then seeing the outline of her shape behind my closed eyelids as she continued to coax me to join her for lunch. When she walked away, I wanted to call her back, to tell her what was going on, to confess the pain I was experiencing and the secrets running through me. But I didn't know if I could trust her. I didn't know who I could trust. I put my faith in Dr. Caste so many years ago, finding comfort in his grandfatherly face, and he'd been the one to start me on the regiment meant to end my life.

What if Noelle's pretty face and petite figure were just a mask to something hurtful? I now know she's who she says she is, just a patient like me. She wears her emotions too loosely to be hiding anything. But when I first came here, it was when I finally had my life in my own hands. I wasn't about to lose that independence on blind trust.

Still, old habits die hard. I'd spent so many years keeping people at a safe distance, I keep doing this with Noelle. I'd turned a corner this morning only to offend her without even trying. Then at lunch, I lost my ability to say anything to her at all. I knew she was uncomfortable, sitting around a bunch of guys who were saying the same things I was trying to tell her about the establishment. Don't get me wrong, I felt just as awkward around them as she apparently did. It wasn't like me to be one of the guys. But when Colby introduced himself, admitting his own doubts about the numbers after overhearing Noelle and I talking, I changed my mind about being a loner. It was a relief to meet others who felt the same way. I tried to include Noelle on this, wanting her to learn what I already knew— that this whole numbers thing was bullshit. Unfortunately it backfired. During lunch, I could feel her anger growing as she stiffened next to me. Every time I smiled at her, she never returned it. And when she got up to leave, I'd already been expecting it.

And it pisses me off.

The truth is all around her, and she's refusing to listen, insisting on living in her bubble until the day her number is up. She isn't even trying to fight for more time, viewing River's End as a blessing rather than the place that does the government's dirty work for them. All the perks and resort-like amenities? It's just a ruse for what will happen on our final day.

From inside the Welcome Center, I watch her as she remains by the pool. She wipes her eyes, and I feel bad that I'm the one who made her cry. She leans back on her chair, staring at the people in the water. Everyone is laughing and playing as if they're on vacation. It's surreal, really, and I'm not sure I'll ever get used to it. Even knowing our time isn't predicted as perfectly as those in charge would have us believe, I still live with a limited lifespan mindset. If I can't figure out a way to escape my number, my time really will be up in ninety-seven days. You won't find me horsing around in the pool.

I look back at Noelle's lounge chair, alarmed to see it empty. I scan the grounds and see her walking toward the first-floor entrance. I don't want her to see me, to even think I've been here watching her. Does it matter? Probably not. Still, to explain myself will make her see I care more than I wish to reveal. I take the stairs, knowing she'll be on the elevator. By the time she waves her wrist over her cubby panel, I'm lying on my bed, masking my shortness of breath through slow inhales and exhales.

"Sleeping again, what a surprise," I hear her mutter, even though she's four cots away. She probably wants me to hear. If she knew the half of it, she'd regret her words. I feel guilty; it's my fault she doesn't know.

She places her book inside her cubby and then closes it again. I know all this by sound, predicting her next moves as I hear the cubby close again and her sneakers walking away. I'm up, leaving my bed open as I run to the elevator, watching the numbers reach three, and then four before stopping. The children's floor. I'd skipped the tour on my first day here, telling the aide I just wanted to sleep, so I never did see what was up there. But by the signs at each level, I know what every floor holds. The children's level is the only one I haven't been on. There was no reason. Now, there is.

Rather than wait for the elevator, I take the stairs again, two at a time. It feels good to move my body like this again. I reach the top floor and cautiously open the door. I'm greeted by yellow walls, paintings of bright flowers, and laughter. I peek around the corner and see Noelle with a group of girls. She's braiding one girl's hair while the others wait their turn, all the while talking and smiling in a way I haven't seen from her. She's happy. She looks up before I can duck around the corner again. I see her roll her eyes, but then she nods her head in a gesture that beckons me to her. Embarrassed, I join her with the kids, standing awkwardly nearby while she finishes banding the girl's tight braid.

"Give me a few minutes, okay?" she says. The girls groan loudly but don't try to stop her from leaving. I follow her to the empty nursery and she closes the door behind us.

"I'm sorry," she says, looking down at her feet. I lift her chin with my finger until she's looking at me again.

"Don't be sorry. Otherwise, I have to be sorry, too." She smiles at this, breaking the wall between us. "This is hard on all of us. There's been a lot of change. It's hard not to take it out on other people. I'm afraid I've been guilty of that, so really, I'm sorry, too. You don't deserve anything but kindness."

"Neither do you," she says. "And I didn't realize how much this whole thing has been affecting me until what you said near the pool. I thought I was fine. There was no one left to say goodbye to when I came here, so I figured all my days here would be just like all my days on the other side. I've tried really hard not to get attached to anything so that this transition would be easier. Obviously, I failed."

"You too?" I ask. "I've spent years without any close friendships just because I didn't want to miss anyone when I came here. This morning, I woke up thinking of my mailman, of all people. I thought about the dog that lived next door that barked every time his owners left him behind. I thought about clam chowder at the Wharf and the sounds of seagulls at the pier. I thought about what it felt like to wake up and go to work, even on days I didn't want to, and how I'd give anything to have those days back. And I thought of a big juicy lab steak, instead of the rabbit food and tofu they're trying to kill us with here."

"Oh my God, me too! I'd die for a burger."

"Or anything barbecued. Or even shepherd's pie."

"I think we're having tofu pot pie for dinner," she says, hiding a grin behind her hand. I nudge her side with my arm, and she pulls away, laughing.

"Thing is, I miss everything, and most of it is stuff I didn't even know I'd miss."

"Same," she says. "I'm realizing I wasted time being alone because I'm so homesick, it hurts." Her face falls as she says it, and before I think about it, my arm is around her shoulder. For a second, we linger that way. She even leans into me. But it's as if reality hits us both at the same time. She pulls away as I'm taking my arm back. She crinkles her nose when our eyes meet. I can read her without her having to say a word. We're too used to putting up walls.

She walks a few steps away, and then peers at me over her shoulder.

"Want to meet the kids?"

Human

Ryder
97 days left

"Really?" I ask. She grins and takes my hand, leading me to the elevator. Once inside, she lets go, as if remembering our distance. My hand remains warm, my fingers remembering her touch.

Once the doors open, I follow her into the play area. I feel overwhelmed by shyness, which quickly dissipates. A young girl tugs at my shirt and I look down. She's crying, holding up an imaginary owie on her finger. I pick her up and kiss it, only to be accosted by more little people holding their fingers out toward me. I don't know whether to laugh or cry, as I realize they just miss their parents. All my years of pushing people aside are forgotten as I kiss owie after owie, give bear hugs, teach how to tie knots, and learn how to braid hair. I win a game of chess against a teenager who believes he can beat anyone, and "lose" to a shy six-year-old who rewards me with a gap-toothed smile.

All the while, my eyes continuously drift to a young boy sitting by himself on the other side of the room. I feel his eyes on me when I'm not looking at him. When I do, he averts his gaze quickly. I respect the distance he's keeping for a while, letting him continue as if he doesn't care. I know better, though. I've played this game for years.

"That's Devon. He's an orphan," Noelle whispers to me when she catches me looking at him.

"Like us," I murmur. She nods.

"Except he was four when it happened. It was a car accident, and he was the only survivor."

I take a sharp inhale, then shake my head. "That's rough." Because of these facilities for the dying, most of us have never seen a dead or dying body in our life. This little boy not only saw corpses, but they were his own parents.

"He hasn't spoken since, I've been told," Noelle continues. She grimaces. "I don't know what's going on in his precious head. He won't let anyone in. I can only imagine the hurt he's hiding."

My attention remains on Devon, even as the other kids clamor to keep me focused on them. I fake it, filling their need for something kind of like a father. I feel like a fraud as I play the part. As soon as I can break away, I do.

I head for Devon and sit down next to him. I recognize the fear in his dark eyes, and how it trades places with indifference just as quickly.

"Don't worry," I say to him. "I'm just trying to get some alone time. Is it okay if I take it with you?" I don't expect him to answer. He even shifts a little away from me. "Oh, I know that move," I say. I still don't look at him, but keep watch out the corner of my eye. "Don't worry, I don't want to sit too close to anyone, either. So just stay on your side, okay?" This time I do peek at him, and I catch the twitch at the corner of his mouth. We sit silently for a few minutes, both watching the kids playing on the other side of the room. "You know the hardest part about being here?" I say, breaking the momentary silence. I don't wait for an answer. "It's all these kids that miss their parents. I feel bad because they think I'm like a dad or something. But I'm not. I never was, and I never will be. I don't even know what it's like to be a dad." I shift my body so that I'm facing him. He's picking at something on the ground, refusing to look in my direction. But he doesn't move away. "My dad died when I was fifteen." Devon still doesn't look up, but his fidgeting slows, and I know he's listening. "But before that, I hardly saw him. It's like he and my mom were too busy with work and each other to worry about me. Now that I'm older, I wonder if it's because he didn't want to get close to me because he was afraid." I'm no longer trying to win Devon over. Instead, I'm spilling my secrets to an eight-year-old stranger who refuses to speak. And as much as I'm fighting it, I'm tearing up. "I know this because I did the same thing. *Do*. I do the same thing. I try not to get close to anyone because I'm just going to have to say goodbye. It worked for a while, but you know what? It's stopped working. I miss my home. I miss the people I worked with. I miss the guy who made me a coffee at the corner café." I wipe my eyes with the back of my hand, laughing lightly at the stupidity of crying over my former barista. It seems my life can be summed up in a series of lists, all naming the stuff I'd miss most and will probably never see again, like my mailman and the coffee guy. "It doesn't matter how hard you try to protect yourself from loving," I tell Devon. "The heart will always win in the end."

Devon stops picking and stares at his hands. The aide rings a bell in the center of the room, and all the kids line up in front of her.

"Dinner," Noelle calls to me over the sound of chattering children. "Do you want to eat with them?"

I nod because I do. I get up and note that Devon gets up, too. He hesitates for a moment, and I wonder if he's waiting to see what I do. He must have caught himself because he then walks ahead of me to the line. I join Noelle, and we walk together behind the kids. I have this unfamiliar urge to take her hand, despite the argument we were in just hours ago. I fight the urge and keep my hands to myself. I know this feeling has everything to do with the kids. There's a sense of light inside me I've never experienced before. It feels like I'm finally living.

The kids' menu is way more fun than the food on the other floors, which totally seems unfair. They have cheese and faux pepperoni pizza, corn tofu dogs, zucchini fries, even veggie burgers that don't taste half bad. For dessert is build-your-own sundaes, which I notice the kids add to their dinner-filled trays. Root beer floats and natural sodas make up the drink choices.

"We're eating here from now on," I whisper to Noelle, which makes her laugh.

"Noelle, sit with us!" a girl calls from a group of twelve-year-olds. She looks at me, raising her eyebrows in a question.

"Go," I say. "I have my own lunch buddy." I nod over at Devon, and she looks past my shoulder.

"Good luck," she says, then joins the girls, all their hair fashioned into elaborate braids.

I head for Devon, who keeps his eyes on his plate of food as he eats but is also obviously aware of my arrival. This time I don't speak. The moment has passed, and to be honest, I'm a little embarrassed that I said so much to him. He's a kid, and I treated him like a therapist.

And so we eat in silence. I reach for the ketchup at the same time he does, our hands brushing together before he shrinks back, almost like he's been burned.

"Go ahead," I say, pushing the ketchup toward him. He doesn't move right away, but I resolve not to touch it again until he's had some. He caves and takes the ketchup, pouring some on the side of his zucchini fries. He puts the ketchup back on the table, and then a few seconds later he pushes it in my direction. Progress. "Thank you," I say, acting as if it's no big deal. Inside, I'm crowing. I add ketchup to my own fries. Then, I create a ketchup smiley face on the table. This time, Devon smiles before he can cover his mouth.

As slow as I try to eat, I still finish way too fast. The bland carrot dogs at lunch were awful, even with tons of ketchup and mustard. I'm still starving.

"I'm going to get more," I say, acting as if Devon will miss me when I'm gone. "Do you want anything while I'm up?" This time, I pause in hopes for an answer. He remains silent. "Would you like an ice cream sundae?" That's when I see it—the slightest nod. "Good man," I say, turning before he can see my Cheshire Cat grin. I grab another veggie burger and then build two ice cream sundaes. I add several cherries to Devon's. When I get back, he looks at me for the first time. He doesn't say anything, but it's another step in the right direction.

I wonder what it's like in his shoes. At his age, I never thought about the whole numbers thing. I knew about it; every kid did. But I didn't understand what it was, exactly. I didn't know that dead meant DEAD, as in, gone and never heard from again. I knew my parents had numbers much lower than mine, but the reality didn't occur to me until a year or so before my parents died. Even then, it didn't mean anything until I realized I'd have no one left to take care of me. I freaked out when those questions arose. But this kid found out the answers at four years old—too young to have to know what death really means.

❀ ❀ ❀

Death was all I could think about after my parents left. I was older than Devon, but still not prepared. "This is your room," Aunt Bryn had said, opening the door to a walk-in closet at the end of the hall. There were still a few hangers, and the room smelled like mothballs, but all I could think of were my parents' bodies lying side by side, motionless in a sterile room of their new home at a facility. A mattress pad lay in the back of the closet, and there was room at the foot of my bed for my things. I hadn't brought much, most of it left behind for the estate sale that would happen at the end of the week. I kept recalling things I'd miss, but I missed my parents most of all.

I was aware that a closet was not a bedroom, and I knew Aunt Bryn was aware, too. Her room was rather large, with an oversized bed and enough space to do her morning aerobics, which I soon learned was a daily routine despite her prominent thighs and protruding belly, plus her nightly habit of ice cream and a glass of sherry. I didn't think Aunt Bryn was completely heartless in my room choice, though. Her apartment only had one bedroom, and I suppose she thought the closet would be a good spot for a teenage boy. I would have preferred the couch, though. The mothballs made my eyes water.

I hadn't been awake when my parents left that morning. It wasn't even their 100th day, so I hadn't expected it. My aunt later revealed that they'd decided to take a camping trip in their final days and would be picked up there. They didn't tell me because they didn't want me to get upset on their final day, Aunt Bryn said. I knew better. It was because they didn't want to *see* me upset, and they didn't want to say goodbye. So they stripped me of everything final—last hug, last look, last goodnight—leaving me with moments I never knew were my last. Upset? I wasn't upset. Upset felt like too kind of a word. I hated them, but silently. Outwardly, I stared out my window while Aunt Bryn cooked us dinner. I spoke only when spoken to. I never argued. I longed for the day when I could be on my own, in charge of my own life, and free of people who disappointed me.

But that would be later. For now, I was stuck with Aunt Bryn, who never wanted to be a parent. She never told me that, but it was obvious in the way she looked at me with her chin jutted forward, how she redid every one of my chores, and how she lamented her lack of storage space now that I was living in her closet. She kept revealing all my parents' secrets—the pregnancy they terminated a few years back, my father's affair when I was younger, and the many vacations they didn't go on because I was a kid and would just get in their way. She always ended these omissions with "I wasn't supposed to tell you that" or "you didn't hear that from me"—as if I had anyone to tell. These secrets chipped away at me. Every one of them took a chunk from my innocence, making me see my parents in a different light. These secrets transformed my parents from demigods to mere humans, then eventually into monsters.

The kisses goodnight, the light left on in the hall, the soft smiles on long car rides, the family hikes in the hills behind our house…they faded under the dark shadow of infidelity and unwanted children, and were smothered by the ultimate act of abandonment. The final blow was my "diagnosis" of cancer, but I'd been preparing to leave months before that.

⚪ ⚪ ⚪

I want to forget, but know I never will. It's part of my core, like tar that's filled in every crack of what I thought was a perfect life.

I mentally shake myself free from the memory as Devon scrapes the last of his ice cream from the fountain glass, using the long spoon to reach the chocolate that's settled at the bottom. When he's done, he gives a satisfied sigh and sits back in his chair. I get the impression he hasn't enjoyed much in the days since his parents died, but this might be one of the lighter moments.

"You don't ever have to speak," I say to him, stacking his dishes with mine on my tray. "Never, if you don't want to. And don't let anyone tell you otherwise. You've been through enough."

He mumbles something. I'm not even sure if it's words, it's so soft.

"What?" I ask.

"I saw them die," he whispers, fat tears falling on his hands gripping the table.

"Oh, bud." I scoot closer so I can wrap my arm around him. He leans against me, and my heart breaks and swells at the same time. Then I listen as he tells me everything—the deer that jumped in front of them...the tree that sunk into their engine and through the glass...his mother's screams into the night...his father's empty stare...the rain...the rain...the rain...his mother's broken breathing...her final words...I love you...be a good boy...Infinity isn't far away...I see your father...silence...silence...please   Momma...wake up...don't leave me...DON'T LEAVE ME!...don't leave me...come back...come back...come back...

...please...

...please...

...please...

...please...

Miracle

Noelle

93 days left

One week down, thirteen more to go. My life has been reduced to weeks, days, minutes…and this place will never feel like home. Every day there's a new schedule of activities. This morning was paddle boarding in the pool, chanting and meditation in the garden, or a baking class in the second-floor kitchen. This afternoon was ceramics or painting, a poetry workshop, or aerobics in the gym. Tonight there will be s'mores at the various fire pits with a music jam on one side of the courtyard, and on the other side, a movie projected onto the outer wall of the building. It should all feel perfect, like going away on a cruise ship. Except, this cruise ship has been docked for a week, won't move for at least ninety-three more days, and we're not allowed to disembark.

I'm restless. My legs feel jumpy despite my daily runs. The days are blending into each other, marked only by meals and activities. I regret coming here, even though I had no choice. I no longer see the point. To make our lives easier? No, it's to make us wish the end would just get here. If I feel this way at a week, I can only imagine how I'll feel as more time passes.

The sole highlight of my days is the time I spend with the kids. Ryder joins me every time I go, though I know he's only there for Devon. When I first saw them talking together, I felt jealous all over again. I was sure I'd be the one to crack the kid and get him to start speaking. I knew it would take time, but I was determined to work with him until he opened up. For Ryder to get him to start talking on the first day they met felt completely unfair. But when I watch him with all the kids, it makes sense. He has this dad-like appeal to many of them, especially the boys. I think that's what Devon needs most—someone who's like a father. My jealousy is short-lived as I watch the way Ryder dedicates his entire attention to him, and how hungry Devon is for someone to focus this intently on him. The boy went from being mute to never running out of words. Whenever we visit, Devon is Ryder's shadow. He eats the same foods Ryder eats, copies Ryder's mannerisms, even uses the bathroom at the same time. I thought Ryder would become annoyed at this, but he seems to look forward to their time together, just as much.

One of the teens is reading the kids a story before their nap time, sharing an alternative Peter Pan adventure about Tiger Lily to the group, a chapter each day. We all listen as Peter Pan fashions tiny boats out of leaves, floating them toward Tiger Lily until they transform into butterflies that float over her head. Ryder is sitting next to me, Devon curled up in his lap. Most eight-year-olds normally wouldn't feel the need to cuddle, but Devon isn't an ordinary kid. Last night before we went to bed, I'd asked Ryder how he felt about Devon's clinging affection. Ryder admitted he'd worried about the appropriateness of it all, as well. But he also figured Devon's emotional age was stuck somewhere around four years old, the day his whole world came crashing down.

This makes sense, and I peek at the boy's face as he listens to the story. One finger is in his mouth, his eyes half-lidded as he listens with his head resting against Ryder's chest, content.

The story ends, and the kids obediently retreat to the edges of the room, opening their cubbies and climbing on their beds. I help a few of the younger girls, kissing them on the cheeks before pulling the covers up to their chins. The aides never do this. They're great at making sure everything happens in a timely fashion, and their moods are always upbeat, but they aren't very nurturing. I wonder if it's a staff rule to never hug or comfort a child, which, if true, only adds to my growing distaste of this facility. To make up for it, I try to mother the kids as best I can, especially the younger ones.

I wait at the perimeter for Ryder to finish tucking Devon in, but am distracted by a soft mewing noise. As far as I know, animals aren't allowed here, so the sound seems very out of place. I tiptoe toward the sound, my ears perked. The door to the nursery is slightly ajar. When I nudge it open with my foot, I see Hannah with her back to me, rocking from one foot to the other. I open the door more, and her head whips around, a look of panic on her face. She relaxes when she sees me, though she still looks nervous. My eyes widen when I realize what she's holding.

"A baby?" The sight of the pink bundled infant crying in her arms strikes me as strange, almost foreign. It's then that I realize I've only seen school-age children here—no toddlers or babies, even though this nursery exists. "Is she yours?" I ask, even though I know the answer. I wince when she shakes her head no. The child is so young and yet barely alive. "How much longer does she have?"

"Twenty-eight days," Hannah says, grimacing as she looks down at the baby. "I don't even know why I brought her here. I shouldn't have."

"Where else would she go?"

Hannah gives me a look of confusion, then of understanding. "You don't know, do you?"

"Know what?"

"What happens to the younger kids?" She sits in the rocking chair, making shushing noises as the baby continues to cry. "Most facilities don't even take kids younger than five. We do, but only under certain circumstances, like when a family member's expiration is close enough that they must be here, too."

"So if they don't come here, where do they go?" I ask.

"Generally, they'll stay with their parents until the day before their expiration, especially babies. But when an infant is born with a low number, some parents opt to euthanize their child immediately."

"That's terrible!" I say. Hannah appears shocked at my outburst. "You don't think so?"

"No, actually. I think it's kind. The parent is choosing to end that child's suffering, and making the most peaceful choice for the whole family. Can you imagine how hard it might be for older siblings to bond with their baby sister or brother only to have to say goodbye a few weeks later? Now, that's cruel." She shushes at the baby again, whose little cries are getting louder. "Hand me that bottle, will you? I've tried everything else, I may as well try this again." I retrieve the bottle from the table and place it in Hannah's outstretched hand. She tries to coax the nipple into the baby's mouth, but the infant turns her head away with a vibrating howl. "I don't know what else could be wrong," Hannah says, standing again and rocking the baby. She holds her toward me. "Do you want to try?"

"Me?" Hannah is already placing the baby in my arms, showing me how to support her neck. I'm afraid to make any sudden movements, sure that if I do, I'll drop her. The baby's fists are up in the air, her little body rigid as she continues to cry. With her mouth wide open, I can see her tiny pink tongue is covered in white spots. "Is that milk, or something else?"

Hannah peers into the baby's mouth, then gives a sigh of realization. "Thrush," she says, moving to the other side of the room and opening a cabinet. "My cousin's son had it last year. She gave him these antibiotic drops in a yellow bottle...here they are." She pulls something off the shelf and comes back. She holds the dropper in the baby's open mouth and releases the medicine. The baby pauses in surprise, then continues to cry. Her cries weaken, though, eventually quieting into passive hiccups. "Here, chase it down with this," Hannah says, handing me the bottle. This time the baby takes it, her dark eyes looking into mine as she drinks. With her head full of dark hair and caramel skin, she looks Spanish. Eventually, she drifts off to sleep with the bottle still in her mouth.

"What's her name?" I ask.

"Jane Doe," Hannah replies. I shake my head.

"That's not a name."

"I know, but she doesn't have one. At least, her mother didn't tell me her name. I don't think she gave her one."

I place the sleeping baby carefully in the crib, holding my breath as I remove my arms. She remains asleep. We tiptoe out of the room, and I close the door behind us.

"Why is she here?" I ask.

Hannah gives me a sheepish look. "I don't know. A moment of weakness, I suppose. I'd seen the mother a few times when she was pregnant, at the supermarket near my house. I think she knew I worked here because I often shop in my work clothes. Today she handed the baby to me. She doesn't speak English, so I don't know what she said to me, but I could see the baby's low number for myself. I knew she wanted me to care for her. I figured she didn't realize what happens to babies who are handed over, and I didn't have the heart to tell her otherwise. It took some persuading, but I managed to talk my supervisor into letting the baby stay here, but with conditions—I can't get attached, and it can't take away from my normal duties." She grimaces. "I can already tell it's not going to work, though. I've been with her for two hours, and haven't gotten anything else done." She shakes her head sadly. "I'll probably end up giving her to my supervisor, but I just had to try."

"I'll take care of her." I utter the words before I even have time to think about what I'm volunteering for. The realization washes over me as Hannah's face lights up. I push aside all my doubts, trying to hide my uncertainty as she throws her arms around me.

"Thank you so much!" she says, then begins going over all the details, including the baby's new sleeping arrangements beside me on the senior floor. I'm only half-listening, even though I know I should be paying better attention. What did I do? This is the first baby I've ever held, and now, all of a sudden, I'm in charge of keeping her alive? This is so much more than just keeping her from expiring before her time, it's about not breaking her. I'm not even sure I'm capable of that kind of responsibility, or even why I've volunteered. For four weeks, I'll be the one to hold, feed, bathe, and soothe her. I'll be like her mother. I'll probably fall in love with her. And then, I'll have to say goodbye to her.

But on the other hand, I'll be the one to hold, feed, bathe, and soothe her, be her mother, fall in love with her...

Underneath my fears of keeping this fragile creature alive is a sense of devotion. I want to give her the best life possible in her four short weeks, and give her the kind of love her mother would have given her. I want her to feel safe and comfortable. And when she leaves this world, I want her to fall into her forever sleep having only known soft words, sweet caresses, and warm embraces. I want her to know she's loved. I want her life to matter.

But first, she needs a name.

❀ ❀ ❀

"How about Betty?" Ryder asks, leaning back on the couch. We'd just finished dinner and are digesting on the senior floor as the staff set up for the evening's activities. I loved his reaction when I told him about the baby. "She's a lucky girl," he'd said, never once questioning what I was thinking. I'd done more than enough questioning for the two of us, anyway, but a negative reaction from him would have wounded me.

"Betty? That sounds like a grandmother's name." I look down at her tiny face. I'd fashioned a sling out of a stretchy blanket Hannah gave me, allowing the baby to remain close to me. She's sleeping, having taken another bottle with no issue. I lift the edge of the blanket so I can peer at her face, studying the way her heart-shaped lips push out as she dreams. I've only known her a few hours, and I can't stop looking at her. My fear is fading by the minute, getting lost in the sweet scent at the top of her head, the downy softness of her newborn skin, and the impossible smallness of her toes that curl whenever I touch them.

"Betty *was* my grandmother's name," he says. "Yeah, I guess she needs something a little younger. How about Anna?"

I wrinkle my nose. "It feels too plain."

"Griselda?"

"Too... I don't even know. Too much of a mouthful." How did parents name their children, anyway? It seems like such a huge deal—you're adding a title to a baby before you really know who they are, and that's what they will be called for the rest of their life. What if you name a baby Sarah, and then realize she's more of a Christina?

"It might take me a day or two to figure this out," I say to Ryder. He peers over my shoulder to look at her. Warmth spreads over me and I realize just how perfect everything feels right at this moment. I can feel the baby's soft breathing against my belly, and Ryder's heartbeat against my shoulder. I feel pulled in two directions—one to remain this way for as long as possible, and the other to turn my head so I can meet his mouth.

"So, s'mores or movie?" I ask Ryder, fighting my attraction by acting casual.

"Movie," he says. "It's the latest Marvel superhero movie, and I promised Devon I'd take him to see it."

"So much for bedtimes, right?"

"The aides are looking the other way while I break him out of there," he teases, standing up and stretching. "What about you? It looks like little Betty is out for the night."

"Push that name all you want, I'm still not calling her Betty." I peek at her again. "Hannah says I have to feed her every four hours, so I might as well kick back and watch the movie with you and Devon, and then feed her again when it's over."

While Ryder leaves to execute his escape plan on the children's floor, I head outside. The smoggy sky is tinted orange by the sunset, and the color is mirrored in a dozen or so fire pits burning around the perimeter of the courtyard, surrounded by people with marshmallows on sticks. The facility band, which is just a few of the aides with instruments, begins playing in the corner of the facility's courtyard. I find a spot against a tree that seems perfect for viewing the movie, sitting cross-legged so I can rest the bundled baby against my knee. I peek at her again, searching her face for any sign of a name. It's funny, in my teens I'd dreamed up names of my imaginary future child, before I'd decided I'd never have children, and came up with dozens at least. Ainsley. Rose. Anastasia. Rebecca. Looking at this child's tiny face, none of them are right. Still, I can't keep calling her "the baby," and I'm definitely never calling her "Jane Doe."

"Noelle!" I look up and see Spring waving to me. I don't know her well, having only noticed her a few times since learning her name a few days ago. She's with the same three friends at one of the fire pits, and the memory of the bronzed teens comes back to me. These girls are everything I'd wished I'd been in my twenties—thin, tan, tall, and blonde. Instead, I was short with brown hair, pale skin, and a tendency to gain weight any time I loosened my food rules. My feelings of inadequacy never faded in my thirties, and I still feel awkward around these girls. They're young and fun, with no evidence of their pending expiration. I'm awkward and old, with the silver hair to prove it. I want to shrink as Spring breaks away from the group and jogs over to me.

"It's true," she exclaims, crouching beside me in an attempt to peer at the bundle in my lap. I push the side of the blanket aside, and she gasps, looking closer. "She's like a little doll! I don't think I've ever seen anything so tiny! What's her name?"

"I haven't figured it out yet."

"Well, I'm sure whatever you decide, it will be perfect." She waves at the other girls, and suddenly I'm surrounded, these perfect blonde creatures fawning over the baby as I smile like a proud parent. It feels real and fake all at the same time. I'm in a game of pretend, playing house, acting the part of this baby's mother even though she'll be taken away in four short weeks.

"This is Danika, Jules, and Jeannette," Spring says. I nod, pretending I didn't already know their names since we were never introduced.

"How long is she...I mean, how long do you get to keep her?" Jules asks.

"Twenty-eight days," I say. I try to sound nonchalant, as if it doesn't matter, but Jules sighs at the number.

"It's so soon," she murmurs. The baby stirs and then opens her eyes, and the girls fuss over her as they crowd in closer.

"And a few weeks later, I'll be gone, too," I remind her. Danika wrinkles her nose.

"I hate thinking about it," she says. "I try not to, but it feels like it's all I can think about. I can't escape it here."

"Same," I whisper, relieved to admit it aloud.

"It's like, everything is provided for us here, we don't have to worry about anything. Our life is supposed to be easy, but there's nothing to distract us from the end," Spring says.

"That is, if you're not so bored, you wish for the end," I say.

"I don't think you're going to be bored anymore," Jules coos, touching the baby's cheek with a finger. "Can I hold her?" I loosen the wrap and carefully lift her, coaching Jules on how to hold a newborn despite not knowing how just hours earlier. She sits back on her knees, rocking the baby side to side making shushing noises. A small cry erupts from her arms, and Jules shoots me a sheepish look. "I guess she doesn't like me."

"She's probably hungry," I say. I touch a few buttons on my ID bracelet. In moments, an aide brings me a warm bottle of formula. "Did you want to feed her?" I ask Jules. Her face lights up as she takes the bottle. The baby's cries stop as she eagerly drinks.

"I should have known you'd be surrounded by mother hens." I look up as Ryder and Devon join us. Devon kneels next to Jules, watching the baby drink. "Isn't she a cutie?" Ryder asks as he sits next to me.

"She's a damn miracle," I say, my heart swelling at all the attention she's getting. It's going to be hard not getting attached to this little girl.

Devon whispers something, then looks at me quick. He's still not big on talking in large crowds, and generally only speaks to Ryder.

"What'd you say, buddy?" Ryder asks. The boy gets up and hides next to Ryder, leaning up to whisper in his ear. "Milagro?" Ryder asks. The word has a nice ring to it, and I feel something pull inside me. Devon whispers again. Ryder smiles, then looks at me. "Milagro is Spanish for miracle," he says. He turns back to Devon. "How'd you know that?" It appears that Devon's mother was fluent in Spanish and had tried teaching him before she died. It's a sweet story, but I'm buzzing over the word...the name.

"Mila," I say. "Her name is Milagro, but Mila for short."

Ryder takes my hand and squeezes it. "It's perfect," he says.

Parenthood

Noelle

90 days left

"Looks like she still has all her fingers and toes," Dr. Patrick says, winking at me as he checks Mila's reflexes in her foot. There are no shots to worry about or future appointments to make. Even this visit is out of the ordinary, but I insisted she be looked over, especially after her recent bout of thrush. The milky whiteness is now gone, and the doctor seems pleased with her progress. "She just as healthy as any baby her age."

"Then why is she dying in less than four weeks?" The question slips out of my mouth before I can censor myself. I'm glad, though. My life is now in two different segments—before Mila and after. My flippant attitude about our short life spans no longer exists, especially when it comes to hers. I still question the theories my brother swore by and Ryder hinted at, but I'm starting to wonder if they're so crazy after all. I'm beginning to hope the conspiracies are true.

"These things happen," he says. He takes his stethoscope out of his ears and rests it around his neck. He pauses, appearing to find the right words as he fiddles with a lion-shaped insignia embroidered on his collar. "Her chart says SIDS, but that could mean a number of things" he finally says. "An infection or virus, a breathing problem, or some other issue that hasn't yet revealed itself. The important thing is, Mila will be given a happy life before she goes to Infinity, and you're a saint for giving it to her."

I roll my eyes, but a part of me aches. I now have a reason to wish Infinity was a real place. Dr. Patrick wishes us well and I gather Mila into my blanket wrap, pulling it tight around me before grabbing my bag. She's naturally his youngest patient, but especially on this floor. A line of elderly people wait a few feet away, headed by Ms. Richards, a woman who must be pushing 150.

"How's the sweet blossom today?" she croaks to me, flashing me a crooked smile. She's probably the only person over the age of ninety who still has all her own teeth, even if they're like corn kernels under a maze of red lipstick. She motions toward me and I pull the blanket aside. Mila peeks through, her dark eyes shining under long lashes. "She's sure a pretty little thing, isn't she?" Ms. Richards purrs, her bony finger stroking Mila's tiny one.

"She sure is," I say, swelling as if I'm responsible for her looks. I leave the doctor's corner and head for the couch. I'll have to share the TV with Elmo and Leo, but neither one of them will care if I turn it on. Leo spends his day staring at one spot, which always depends on the way his head is tilted. Elmo, on the other hand, is more alert but doesn't speak at all. He prefers to watch everyone, and he settles on staring at me as I sink into the couch.

"Hello boys," I say, then do my best to ignore the weight of Elmo's eyes. I touch the button on my ID bracelet and an aide shows up with a bottle. "Thanks, Steph," I say, and she gives me an obvious shake of her head. "What?"

"You know you won't be able to keep Mila forever, right?" she says. She nods toward the nurse's station. "Nurse Sherry has been talking."

I look in the direction she's indicating, and turn away quickly when I see the robust woman watching me.

"What's she saying?"

"That Hannah should have never brought that child in here, and that you're a resident, not one of the aides. You're not supposed to be working, you're supposed to be relaxing."

"But letting everyone do everything for me is boring," I say.

"Really? Because I'd give anything to be able to sit down and have an aide be my beck and call," Steph snaps.

"It's not that I don't appreciate it, it's just that I have nothing to do, no purpose. But with Mila, I do. Besides, I want to take care of her. If I want to do something, shouldn't I be allowed to?"

"Not necessarily. There are rules."

"Is there a rule against caring for a child?" I ask. Steph pushes her mouth to one side, brow furrowed.

"I don't know," she finally says. "But if there is, Nurse Sherry will find it. I'm just warning you, this whole mommy dearest thing might end soon." She leaves, but her words wear at me like acid. To her, they're probably just that—words. But to me, it's like ripping my heart out, cutting it open, and then only giving back half. I've slipped into caring for Mila like slipping into a well-worn pair of jeans. I've even weathered the late night feedings, understanding that each moment I have with her is precious and few. I've memorized every one of her features, her tiny sighs, and the way she curls her toes and stretches her arms. I feel like I might even be able to understand the different meanings of each cry, hearing the language within her wordless tones.

This isn't a game like Steph insinuated. I may not be Mila's real mother, but it doesn't matter. That girl has stolen my heart, and by the way she looks into my eyes, I can feel our connection. There is no nurse, no rule, no anything that will take Mila away from me, I swear it.

She drifts off while she drinks, and I move the bottle away and cover her so the light won't disturb her. I can feel her tiny chest rise and fall against my belly, the rhythm flowing through me and pulling at my eyelids. I look up at the television, watching as a woman weaves a blanket with yarn cords as big as her arm. In, over, and through. It's either this channel or a movie, and Mila is too cozy for me to reach for the remote. That, and I'm not about to call an aide over to help me—it might end up being Steph. And so, arm knitting it is. I watch until my eyes grow heavy, sure that I can knit a blanket for Mila, floating away from the couch, the room, the facility, the earth. The air ripples around me, sending rings of light every place I touch. The stars are singing and I smell vanilla. I turn my head and I'm back home, my mother standing in front of the oven holding a pan of cookies.

"Would you like one?" she asks and hands me a cookie. I bite into it, and the sweetness bursts in my mouth like sunshine, the warm chocolate coating my tongue, the chewy center offering me satisfaction as I chew.

"Am I dreaming?" I ask her, and she nods before going back to baking. I have questions for her, but I can't think of them. Instead, I just watch her bake, lulled into absolute comfort that starts in my belly and radiates out the top of my head. I recall an afternoon like this years ago, but there was a reason behind the cookies. What was the reason? Oh yeah, it was for a party. *Her* party. And my father's. Their end-of-life party. The comfortable feeling evaporates and I sit up straight, staring at my mother's back. Something's different. Something's missing. *The numbers.* The back of her neck is bare. I reach to the back of my neck and feel skin.

"Where are our numbers?" I demand, hopping off my stool and looking around to see if I've dropped it. Skye walks in, holding something in his hand. He gives me a sideways grin, then heads for the sink. His hand is bleeding. No, what's in his hand is bleeding. I take my own hand from my neck, shocked to see the blood covering my fingers.

"The numbers aren't real," he says, his blue eyes piercing mine as he drops the devices into the sink. I rush forward, but not before he turns on the garbage disposal, mincing our numbers as I'm pulled from the room, through space, back to the couch with a lurch.

※ ※ ※

"Sorry, I didn't mean to wake you." My eyes feel heavy, and I blink a few times before I come back to reality. I look up and see Ryder standing beside me.

"You didn't," I mumble, sitting up and stretching as best as I can without disturbing Mila. "I was dreaming."

"I hope it was good."

"There were cookies involved." I feel shaken by the dream, but it's also awakened my sweet tooth. I'm craving cookies as if they're cocaine. I crane my neck to see the clock near the nurse's station, disappointed that it's so far away from dinnertime. Nurse Sherry is handing out meds at the station, but I feel like she's keeping one eye on me.

She probably isn't, but it doesn't matter. Steph's words weigh heavy like a stone in my gut, and my odd dream adds to the weight.

"Let's get out of here," I say to Ryder, carefully prying myself from the couch. He's got the diaper bag and lets me lead the way.

"This doesn't have anything to do with cookies, does it?" he asks.

"This has everything to do with cookies." In the hall, I press the button to the elevator and wait for it to arrive.

"So much for my run this morning." There's a smile on his face, though, and he doesn't seem to mind the sugar quest.

"Think of it as fuel," I say. "Besides, I haven't had a run since Mila arrived. Count yourself lucky."

"You know, you could always put her in a carrier when you go on the treadmill," Ryder points out. "Or let me care for her while you take a break. You're going to burn yourself out." The elevator arrives and we get in. He pushes the floor button that leads to the cookies and the door closes.

"I don't want to miss a moment." And now, I'm afraid my moments are even fewer.

We each order cookies and a coffee at the café. For someone who's worried about food choices, Ryder inhales his cookie before I even take a bite. I raise an amused eyebrow at him, and he shrugs in response before ordering another with the digital waiter.

"They may not let me keep her," I finally tell him, unable to keep it inside any longer. He wraps an arm around my shoulder and squeezes.

"I'm sorry," he says. "How do you know?"

"That one aide with the purple hair, Steph, told me. She said Nurse Sherry is against the whole thing. They believe it's creating too much work for me when I'm not supposed to be working at all, but it's total crap. For the first time in my life everything makes sense, and now they want to take it all away. They want to take *Mila* away."

"Are you sure? Did anyone else say anything to you?"

"No," I admit. "But I saw the way Nurse Sherry was looking at me. It wasn't friendly."

"That woman wouldn't know how to be friendly if it was part of her job description," Ryder says. "I think she was born with a frown."

Mila stirs, and I quickly order her a bottle. Before she even starts to cry, I have the nipple in her mouth. I'm determined to ensure she doesn't bother anyone in hopes that this might extend my time with her. With my hands full, Ryder feeds me bites of cookie. It's nothing like the ones my mother used to make, but it's a worthy substitute. They're even warm, though I believe each cookie is toasted before it's served. The effect is satisfying—melted chocolate chips coat my tongue, fed directly from Ryder's fingers. I laugh just as he's giving me another bite, and chocolate brushes against my cheek.

"You're not very good at this," he jokes, taking a finger and wiping away the chocolate. He licks his finger clean.

"Actually, eating is the one thing I'm good at. I think you're the one who's not very good at helping someone eat."

"I haven't had a lot of practice," he says. "Here, let me try again." This time he purposely misses my mouth and cookie smears on my cheek and down my shirt.

"Hey!" I squeal. Mila protests against me, and I duck my head as I try to stop laughing. "Shhh," I hush at her, and her wide eyes watch me carefully. "That's not fair," I say to Ryder. "I'm completely defenseless."

"I don't know what you're talking about. I'm just trying to help."

"Right," I say, freeing one of my hands and grabbing the cookie before he can offer any more help.

"Speaking of helping out, why don't you let me take over so you can take a break? I can give her a bottle just as well as you can."

"If it's anything like your cookie feeding skills, I think I'll pass."

"Seriously," he insists. "Go do something for yourself. Workout, take a nap, go on that skydiving trip you never took. I don't care. Just go do something without a baby attached to you."

"I'm fine, really," I say, but he's already untying the blanket that's wrapped around me. "You don't take no for an answer, do you?"

"I do," he says. "But not this time. You don't even know you need a break. You couldn't even stay awake after lunch."

"That's not—"

"Noelle, stop arguing. I'll take good care of her. You can have her back at dinner; that's only a few hours away. Stop wasting time."

"Fine," I say. I shrug off the blanket and instruct him on how to tie it around his back and shoulder. I secretly love that he's not only taking her but willing to wear her as if he's a mother kangaroo. Once she's burped, I place her inside the fold of the blanket.

"You have to make sure she's positioned just right, and the knot needs to be secure," I tell him. He gives me a sideways smile, almost laughing at me, but he listens, just the same. "By the way, I *have* gone skydiving," I say, and then turn and leave before I change my mind.

"I knew you were a bucket lister!" he calls after me, and my grin takes over my face.

I have no idea what to do with myself. It's only been a few days, but I feel lost without Mila. I decide to take Ryder's advice and head for the gym.

My legs feel jumpy in anticipation, and I jog toward the dressing room to change. Once on the treadmill, my body remembers what it's supposed to do. I start slow, but soon I'm running my regular pace, my chest expanding as I run toward nowhere fast. My heart is pounding, and it's never felt better. My ponytail is wet at the end from where it's brushing against my neck. My tank top clings to my skin and my breath is short with each inhale and exhale. Every muscle in my body thanks me. I feel it all. I hadn't realized how much I missed this.

I run for thirty minutes, and then consider ending with a few rounds at the punching bag, but I just don't have it in me. The last couple of nights have caught up with me. I'd tried to hide my exhaustion, but Ryder hadn't been fooled. I guess it's a little hard to keep it secret when you're falling asleep to a show on arm knitting. I do a quick circuit on the machines instead, mostly just stretching my muscles, before I finally head to the showers. How do mothers even get time to shower? Standing under the spraying water feels like a novelty. Just a few days ago this had been an everyday activity. Now, it's the best thing in the world. I stand there for at least twenty minutes before I even start to soap up, drinking in the quiet, the solitude, the feel of the water pelting my skin, and the equal parts hot steam and cool air swirling around me.

My mind wanders back to another time when I tried to find comfort under the hot spray, my tears washing down the drain as I sobbed into the water. I was only seventeen, but it felt like my life was already ending. My mother's words echoed through my head, owning me, defining me, consuming me...

In the end, my heart would fail.

❀ ❀ ❀

I'd never thought to ask how I was going to die. I didn't even know that was an option. I knew I would die at thirty-two, but I didn't realize how fast the years would pass. With my eighteenth birthday in a few weeks, I was more than halfway there. I had fifteen years to do everything I ever wanted. I began doing the math. If I went to college for four years, I'd have only ten years in a career. A masters was out of the question. What about a dog? My friend's dog was twelve and wasn't slowing down. I couldn't chance it.

A slow realization melted over me. I couldn't have kids; they'd be too young when my expiration came. My devastation started as a piece of sand in my belly, growing to the size of a pebble, then a stone, then a boulder that crushed my soul and stole my whole being. I always figured I'd have kids. It was never a question. It wasn't like I professed that to be my identity or lifelong dream, but it was on the expected path of my life. Now that life was dead, just like I'd be in too little years.

❀ ❀ ❀

Now in the gym shower, the water continues its comforting spray on my back. I realize I'm crying, though the tears mingle with shower water. In the short time I've been at this facility, I've relaxed the rules I've placed on myself. The day my mother told me I'd die of a heart attack, I swore I'd never form bonds with anyone. No relationships, no close friendships, nothing. There was too much to risk. Here, I've let Ryder in, though I'm not sure that even counts because we're both scheduled to go at the same time. But Mila? She counts.

What am I even doing? I'm not her mother. And in less than four weeks, I'll be forced to let her go. Will I survive the inevitable heartbreak? When my parents left, I stayed in my room for three days, unable to face anyone. I couldn't eat, could barely breathe, and I felt utterly alone. Skye had taken off, and I was left to face my sudden status as an orphan all by myself. Even now, I can hardly think of my parents without also acknowledging the huge empty place inside from their loss. How will it feel to say goodbye to Mila? Why am I even putting myself through this?

Because I love her, and because this is the closest I'll ever be to being a mother. That dream was stolen from me with my expiration date, and when I made that decision permanent with one simple trip to the doctor. Now, I get a chance to experience something I never knew I could— being a child's mother...being Mila's mother. With her dark complexion and midnight eyes, she looks nothing like me, and yet, that little girl is every part of me, knit into every cell and fiber of my body as if we're one. I've known her three days, and yet, I can no longer separate my life from hers, or hers from mine.

I have hours until dinnertime, and I can't stand it. My body feels tired, but my soul is alive. I'm tired of being away from her. I turn off the water and bypass the air dryers, slipping on the clean clothes waiting for me while my skin is still dripping wet. I don't care. I run across the courtyard, past bodies soaking up their final days of the sun, through the first-floor lobby, beyond brand new residents in awe of a facility that does everything for them, and up the stairs because the elevator is too slow. I throw open the doors to the second level and scan the floor, searching until I see Ryder holding Mila. I smile and start for them. But then I realize the problem.

"No! Stop!" I scream as Nurse Sherry, flanked by two guards, takes Mila from his arms.

8

Gone

Ryder

90 days left

Noelle runs toward me, her wild and wet hair clinging to her panicked face as I feel Mila lifted from my arms. I never should have told her to go. I'd promised her we'd be fine, and I lied. I hadn't taken her seriously when she told me her fears. I should have known better. Of course it wasn't fine. Nothing here is fine. Why would this be any different?

"Give her back!" Noelle screams, rushing at Nurse Sherry. If it weren't for the security guards, she would have ripped Mila from the nurse's arms, maybe even have done some damage. The guards grab Noelle, holding both of her arms as she struggles to get free. "That's my baby!" She pulls as Nurse Sherry begins to walk away, but the guards have a firm grip on her. "Let me go! Ryder, bring her back!"

I rush after the nurse but know it won't do any good. I've already argued with the woman, and she wouldn't budge.

❀ ❀ ❀

"Babies are to remain in the nursery if their legal guardian isn't in the facility with them," Nurse Sherry said, pointing to a line in the packet of papers in front of her. Noelle had only been gone an hour when she approached me, and I had a suspicion the nurse planned it that way. "It says so right here. Ms. Edison is not the child's legal guardian, and therefore cannot care for the child the way she has been for the past few days."

"But what will it hurt?" I demanded. "We're all dying. In less than a month, Mila will be gone. Can't she know what it feels like to have a mother in her last days?"

"Ms. Edison is not her mother."

"Why does this matter?"

Nurse Sherry set the packet down and took off her reading glasses, then met me with her cold gaze. "It matters because the safety of these children depends on us. What's stopping any person in this facility from taking a child and hurting them as they claim they are only caring for them like a parent?"

"Noelle would never hurt Mila."

"I'm not saying she would," Nurse Sherry said. "But if I allow her to take this child as if she's her own, I'm opening the door for any person in here to take a child for the wrong reasons. The risk is greater than the benefit."

I did my best to plead my case. When the nurse wouldn't back down, I stood up and prepared to leave, Mila still secure in the blanket wrapped around the two of us. That was when she got the guards involved. One of them tapped the electric stick at his side, insinuating what would happen if I didn't comply. Though I'd never seen the guards use their sticks in the facility, I was well aware of what those sticks could do. The scars on my back no longer hurt, but the decade-old memory still did. I knew they'd use them, even if I was still holding an infant. I had no choice but to hand her over.

◈ ◈ ◈

"You can at least give her an explanation," I say to Nurse Sherry as she reaches the elevator. "She deserves that."

"Mr. Jamison, we're through here. I'll kindly ask you to stop following me. If you can't comply, I will have no choice but to bar you from the children's floor altogether, you and Ms. Edison." She stops and turns, Mila cradled in her arms. "I'm sure you understand what's at stake."

I understand all right. I turn and see Noelle, still held by the guards. When she sees I've given up, her face crumples.

"No!" she screams, breaking free from the guards. Sticks drawn, the guards give chase.

"Noelle, stop!" I yell, but it's too late. One of them taps her on the back, and she crumples to the ground, writhing in pain. He zaps her again and she screams.

"She's down, dammit!" The officer points it at me, and I stop, hands up.

"Don't think I won't use this on you, too, buddy," he threatens. He turns to leave with the other officer, and I fall to the ground beside Noelle. She's twisted in agony, her face contorted as tears cover her cheeks. An aide kneels beside me and injects her with something. Her purple hair falls against her eye, and she brushes it aside. This must be Steph, the nurse's aide Noelle was telling me about.

"What did you give her?" I ask.

"It's just a sedative. It takes away the pain, and she'll sleep it off. By morning, she'll just feel bruised." Steph shakes her head. "I warned her. It could have been worse." I bristle at her casual attitude.

"How could it have been worse?"

The aide sheaths the needle and stands up.

"This baby could reach expiration early."

Steph's insinuation is clear: they could have killed Mila right there. They still have that power, though Nurse Sherry's nursery comment gives me hope that she'll remain alive. It's all I have to cling to.

A few aides rush forward to tend to Noelle, but I wave them off. She remains still, her hair covering her face, her body in a fetal position. I lift her into my arms, and her head falls against me. She's awake, and I can tell it takes all her effort to look at me.

"She's okay, Noelle. Just trust me." I know that's a tall order. She trusted me to care for Mila, and now the baby is gone.

I wave Noelle's arm over the panel near her cubby, and her bed rolls out. Once she's on the bed, I take her shoes off and pull the blanket over her. It's not even cold, and yet I tuck her in. I start to leave, but she whimpers. When I look down at her, the questions are in her eyes. I sit back down, rest my hand on her shoulder, and tell her everything that happened.

"I'm so sorry," I say. She fights off sleep for a minute longer before the drugs pull her under. I watch the soft rise and fall of her shoulders as she breathes, the way her silver hair frames her face, the dark circles under her long lashes. Her freckles. Her lips. The way she seems centuries old and so very young. I wish we had met under different circumstances. If I'd known her, I would have gone through with the whole bucket list thing, only because I was doing it with her. Last dip in the ocean. Last barbecue with friends. Last beer in a bar or Sunday morning in bed. On their own, I don't care about them. But if I'd had them with her, I would have insisted we experience every last thing we could. Instead, our shared "last" is being stuck in this facility until we die. No ocean. No freedom. No safety, unless we play by the rules.

And yet, I still have her. If we weren't being lied to, it would be enough. But with her, I'm determined to break free. Ten days off the medication, and I feel the best I have in a long time. I am more convinced than ever that Dr. Singh saved my life. Even more, I'm convinced that none of us are really dying. Okay, maybe a few of the seniors are on their last legs. But the majority of us? We're supposed to live long lives. I'm sure there's a deeper reason for the death countdown, and it's not because some computer can figure out the exact date and cause of our death.

The room empties as everyone leaves for dinner. I stay behind, not really hungry, and not wanting to leave Noelle alone. I feel protective of her. Partially it's because I feel like I owe her, but I also don't trust what will happen to her if I leave. So I sit awkwardly on her bed, her body curled around the place I'm sitting, my hand still on her shoulder. Eventually, she turns, and I see the place where the guard zapped her with the stick. There are two small holes in the back of her shirt, almost like cigarette burns. I lift the fabric and wince at her wounds. The raised black burns are surrounded by angry red skin. I cautiously touch the redness and it feels hot. When I summon an aide with a jar of salve, I'm glad it's another girl and not Steph.

"I can apply it," she says, but I shake my head. I don't want anyone to touch her. If she were awake, this would probably sting. But since she's in deep sleep, I apply the salve liberally. Her shirt sticks to the medicine when I lower it, but it's better than letting the wounds fester like mine had years ago.

I eventually lower myself to the floor and lean against the bed. From here, I can't see the room, only the inside of her cubby. I can almost pretend I'm not here at all, that the two of us are someplace else where our moves aren't watched. I feel like we're living in a fishbowl. This is the closest I'll ever come to being unseen.

I had a space like this at my aunt's house—not the closet bedroom I slept in, but a hidden spot on her roof where I could look out on the pastures that surrounded her home. Before I was bold enough to leave, this was my escape. When she was in another part of the house, I'd slip outside and out the back, scale the fence, and climb the drainpipe until I reached the roof. From there, I'd maneuver around our rooftop vegetable garden until I reached a fake window that led to nowhere. The roof was flat and empty in this spot, and if I backed all the way up to the window, I was cased in on three sides. For some reason, this made me feel safe. It was artificial, just like the windows, but something about being hidden this way made me feel more secure than I had in a long time. Once, Aunt Bryn had gone outside at sunset, calling my name as she scanned our neighborhood street. I scooted deeper into my hiding spot, mostly concealed by plants and shadows, but still somewhat visible. All she had to do was look up and she'd see me. But she never did. I was invisible.

I'm invisible now. The lights dim as they do every night at bedtime—dark enough to fall asleep, but light enough to make it to the bathroom, if necessary. There are no bed checks, as there's no rule we have to actually be in bed, so the fact that my bed is still secure in its cubby is of no concern. No one even checks on Noelle, which is both relieving and bothersome. I guess it doesn't matter since we're supposed to be dying, anyway.

I make a bed on the floor next to her, trying to find the comfiest spot on the hard linoleum. My hip aches and I turn several times before I finally reach the point past caring. I'm almost asleep when I hear her moaning. In an instant, I'm back at her side. She's still asleep, but her eyes are squeezed tight. I touch her arm, hoping to rouse her from her dream, but she remains stuck in sleep. Cautiously, I lower myself behind her, fitting my body against the back of hers. I keep my hands to myself, not wanting to overstep my bounds. She sighs and scoots into me, and my body reacts. I close my eyes, willing myself to calm back down. Baseball. Grandma. My dog that died when I was eight. The smell of her hair. Dammit, this is going to be harder than I thought. She uses the same shampoo I do, the same we all do, and yet it smells different on her. Like pine forest and salty ocean air. On me, it just smells like soap.

I brush her hair aside and, in the dim light, look at the number on her neck. Ninety. Just like mine. Ninety days to wake up, eat meals, breathe air, see the same things, do the same things. No variety. No adventure. Just here. But with *her*. I slip my hand behind her back and touch the device. I wish I could remove it, I wish I could remove both of ours, but tampering with it is punishable by law. There was a rumor about some guy who did this, and he died instantly. I don't understand why, but I'm not about to test the theory.

I must have fallen asleep because the next time I open my eyes, the soft morning light reaches our side of the room, reflecting in Noelle's open eyes as she watches me. My arm circles her waist, hers are folded in front of her, and our faces are a half foot apart. I smile, but I keep my mouth closed, not wanting to blast her with morning breath. Her eyes are puffy. A piece of hair has drifted over her forehead, and I brush it aside.

"Good morning," I whisper. She doesn't speak, but the recognition is there. "Do you feel okay?" I lightly touch her back. She winces and I pull away instantly.

"I'm fine," she whispers. I touch her cheek, and she takes my hand and guides it away from her face. I realize I'm being too familiar with her. When I look closer, I realize she's been crying. I draw her close to me, and she leans her head against my neck, her hands pressed lightly against my chest. But then she stiffens, pushing against me. I pull back, trying to read where she's at, what she's feeling, and recognize the fury in her expression.

"Hey, it's all going to be okay," I say. "After breakfast, we'll go upstairs to check on Mila and see what our options are."

"No," she says. The tone of her voice is firm.

"It's okay. I mean, it's not okay what happened, but you are still allowed to see her. Nurse Sherry said—"

"No, Ryder. No. *We* will not go check on Mila."

"Oh." I sit up, realizing what's going on. "I'm, uh, I just thought we could go together, but if you want to be alone, I can—"

"What I want is for you leave," she says.

"But—"

"Leave!" she shouts, disregarding the sleeping bodies that surround us. My skin flushes. I don't even know what to say. She rolls over and faces the inside of her cubby, cutting off the conversation. I stare at her back, seeing the shaky way it moves up and down with each breath, seeing the two small holes burnt into her shirt, seeing her number peeking out from behind her silver hair. Eighty-nine. One less day.

As hurt as I am over her rejection, I'm even more upset with myself. I did this. I messed up. And the longer I sit here, the more I'm making a fool of myself. Our lives could be over in three months, and I'm wasting it by chasing someone who isn't mine, and making a huge mess of it while I do. As strong as my urge is to comfort her while she tries to hide her tears, it's apparent she wants nothing from me.

I leave her, retreating to my own bed and lying down. I'm only there for a few minutes before I leave the room altogether and head for the pool. As far as Noelle's concerned, I'm the reason Mila was taken away. She has no reason to forgive me. Life is too short for that.

Pain

Noelle
89 days left

I watch him as he sleeps. I'm alarmed to find him in my bed and comforted at the same time. Every muscle feels like lead inside my skin, and the area where the guard hit me is on fire. But Ryder's arm resting across my waist feels nice. I don't want to like it. I want to hate him, to push him off the bed, to hurt him exactly the way I'm hurting. He'd been the last one to hold her before Nurse Sherry stepped in. He didn't fight hard enough to keep her in the room.

But how hard did he need to fight? Until they hit him with the sticks? Until they killed him? Even in my grief, I know he isn't to blame. I know that if I were the one holding her, the outcome would have been the same. They still would have taken her and there's nothing I could have done to stop them.

This safe place suddenly isn't safe anymore.

What am I even doing? Whether I lose her now or later, it's going to hurt just like this. I can feel the hole growing inside me, a burn that hurts worse than the ones at my back. I opened myself up to this, even after I swore I never would. And now, I want to crawl into the earth and die. I want to fast-forward to the day I leave this world. I want to disappear, to be forgotten, to be free of everyone and everything. Nothing means anything. *Nothing.* If losing my damn fish broke my heart, what was I expecting by caring for a baby? I regret ever stepping foot on the children's floor and meeting her. I should have minded my own business when I heard her crying. I should have said no when Hannah placed her in my arms. After all, I was never meant to be anyone's mother.

❀ ❀ ❀

"You're so young, though," the receptionist said, looking down at the clipboard and then back at me. I regretted placing my "ailment" on the sheet. I should have just said routine appointment, not hysterectomy. "I'm sorry, it's none of my business."

"It's not," I agreed with her, and her eyes widened before she looked away. Instantly I felt bad for being so direct. "I'm twenty-two, old enough. Plus, I'm dying in ten years," I explained, and I tried to ignore the inevitable sadness in her eyes when she looked back at me. "I just don't want any accidents to happen."

"Sign here, and here," she said, handing me a clipboard with several lines highlighted. I scribbled my signature, then found a seat.

"Ms. Edison?" A friendly woman with long blonde hair stood in the doorway. She led me to a back room where I could change. "Is there anyone here with you that can take your things?" she asked. I shook my head, suddenly aware of just how alone I was. My parents didn't even know I was here. I didn't want them to know what I was doing, even though it made all the sense in the world. I played the numbers game in my head, calculating the milestones in my imaginary child's life. If my child was born on this day, she would be three when her grandparents died and eight when her Uncle Skye died. She'd be a ten-year-old orphan when I died, with no one left to care for her. I couldn't do that to her.

"It's just me," I said. The nurse smiled reassuringly.

"I'll be your person," she said. I knew she only meant that she'd hold on to my things, but her words still affected me. I turned to undress in the room before she could see my watery eyes.

She and another nurse wheeled me to the operating room on a bed, weighted down by warm, heavy blankets. My heart was pounding, regret coursing through my veins. The doctor and his staff leaned over me, and another nurse injected something into the IV next to my head.

"Noelle, I want you to count backward from one hundred," he said. I did, my eyes fighting to stay open. The last number I remembered was ninety-seven.

I was in a curtained room by myself when I opened my eyes. I could hear the voices of the nurses beyond the room, a steady stream of beeps, and the sound of rolling wheels in the hallway. I shivered under my blankets, wishing I'd told someone what I was doing. I desperately needed my mother. The shivering went to my head, the dizziness causing both nausea and panic.

"Nurse," I moaned, and the curtain moved aside.

"Whoops," the nurse said as I vomited across the bed, and she moved quickly to place a spit tray under my chin to catch the rest. There was a dull ache in my lower abdomen, but I couldn't feel my legs, indicating that I was still under the effects of the drugs.

"Sorry," I whispered when I was done.

"Think nothing of it," the nurse said. "I see this all the time. The anesthesia is wearing off, and sometimes it can make you feel dizzy." She removed my blanket and gown, giving me new ones as another nurse injected something into my IV.

"For the nausea," the nurse explained, and I felt a cool calmness come over me. I leaned back in my bed as she checked my vitals. "Will someone be here to pick you up today?" she asked. She must have seen the look of alarm on my face. "I take that as a no. This is normally an outpatient procedure, but we'll keep you here overnight for observation. You should be fine to leave on your own tomorrow."

I didn't want to be there by myself, and I didn't want to leave by myself the next day. I wanted to call my mom, tell her everything, have her come here so she could be my person, hold my hand, and let me cry before bringing me home. At the same time, I was facing some hard goodbyes in just a few short years. My parents were going to die soon, so was my brother. Once they were gone, I'd have no one left. I figured I might as well get used to being on my own.

Still, I desperately needed someone…anyone.

"Wait," I said as the nurse began to leave the room. "There was a nurse here with blonde hair, a woman. She has my things."

"Your things are right there on the table next to you," the nurse said, pointing near my head. I turned and saw my clothes in a folded file and my purse.

"Is she still here?" I asked. The nurse nodded and left to find her. In a few minutes, the first nurse, the one with the blonde hair, opened the curtain.

"What can I help you with, sweetie?" she asked. I couldn't even get the words out before I start crying. She rushed to my side, taking my hand as I mourned my future, my invisible children, the impending deaths of my family, and how utterly alone I felt in this moment, and would for the rest of my life.

I don't even know her name. It seems strange that I didn't learn the name of someone who held my hand in such a pivotal moment of my life. It was also the last moment I ever let someone in like that…at least before I came to River's End. I've spent ten years keeping people out. So why have I softened my stance here? Losing Mila is the worst blow I've felt in a long time.

The tears won't stop, and it makes me angry. I'm pissed that they took her from me, but I'm even angrier that I let myself get close to her.

"I'm done," I whisper. Even if I can see her again, I won't. She'll forget me. In a few weeks, she'll be gone, and she won't even know the difference. Neither will I. Maybe I'll forget her, too. Maybe I won't remember how her soft hair feels tucked underneath my chin, how her tiny chest feels rising and falling against mine, or how all her fingers curl perfectly around one of mine. Maybe I won't remember her milky breath or her obsidian eyes, or how she'd watch me as if she loved me while I held her bottle to her mouth. Maybe I'll forget the sound of her sighs when she's content, the wail of her cries when she's not, or the way her little lips smacked in between feedings. I hope I forget.

I know I never will.

Ryder begins to stir, and I swipe at my tears. I consider pretending to still be asleep, but he opens his eyes before I can close mine. It takes him a few seconds, but then he smiles. My heart aches with longing before I harden it. I'm done, even with him. From here on out, I'm on my own. He reaches over and brushes a piece of my hair from my forehead.

"Good morning," he murmurs. I don't respond. I can't. I might betray myself. "Do you feel okay?" He touches my back, and the pain shoots through me.

"I'm fine," I mutter. His fingers brush against my cheek, and I take his hand and move it away before I do something I regret, like smile. He gives me a sympathetic look, and all of a sudden I'm in his arms. I inhale the musky smell of his body as he holds me against his solid chest. His closeness fills a deep space inside me. I feel like my missing piece has been found, and at the same time, I feel like I need so much more.

I'm done.

I push against him as every part of my body screams for him. My body is betraying me.

"Hey, it's all going to be okay," he says. "After breakfast, we'll go upstairs to check on Mila and see what our options are."

I'm done.

"No."

"It's okay. I mean, it's not okay what happened, but you are still allowed to see her. Nurse Sherry said—"

"No, Ryder. No. *We* will not go check on Mila."

The look on his face cuts straight through me. I want to turn away, but I stand my ground and look him firmly in the eye so that we never need to have this conversation again.

"Oh," he says. I guard my heart as his face falls. He sits up, running his hands through his hair. "I'm, uh, I just thought we could go together, but if you want to be alone, I can—"

"What I want is for you to leave."

"But—"

"Leave!" I turn on my side before my tears begin falling. I measure my breaths, keeping them slow so that he doesn't know I'm crying. It seems like forever before he leaves. When he does, I count to ten and then let out the sob that's been bursting in my throat, hiding it in my pillow. I stay there, trying not to move in case it looks like an invitation. I'm making a huge mess of everything. Why does this hurt so damn much?

I wish all this was over. Eighty-nine more days of this hell.

Breathe

Ryder
88 days left

Swimming has always been my escape. There was a pool at my childhood home, and my dad taught me to swim as soon as I knew how to walk. Over the summer, my parents enrolled me in every swim camp there was. While other boys my age played football or baseball, I was swimming laps at the community center or in my backyard. My parents didn't always get things right with me, but this was one of the things they did. I loved swimming. I loved the way it felt to glide through the water, moving at a fast, easy pace with each arm stroke. I felt powerful, as if I were flying. I didn't do it for the competitiveness, though I'd earned my fair share of medals. I did it for the solitude, the peacefulness, the chance to escape my fear of growing up.... It was a moment when I could hide below the surface, lose myself to the rhythm of each arm slicing through the water, pretend like I was the only person left on earth.

My aunt's home did not have a pool. I still had the school's pool for when I had team practices or competitions, but I no longer had a place of my own to go to—not legally, that is. At night, I'd slip out of my aunt's house and ride my bike to my former home across town. I'd sneak past the "For Sale" sign on the lawn and jimmy the latch to the backyard. Silently, I'd roll back the pool covering and ease into the water. Then I'd spend the next hour swimming back and forth in the long pool, the moon my only source of light. At first, it felt strange to be there. It still felt like my home, but in many ways, it didn't. When I peeked in the windows, the house held furniture that wasn't ours. The backyard lawn was gone, replaced with small rocks and various potted plants. Our old rusty table and chairs were traded in for wooden chairs and a small bistro table with a pot of flowers. But the pool, that never changed. I was soon able to look past the foreign items, feeling at home as soon as my body hit the water. I kept a careful watch on the sale sign, waiting for it to disappear. Even when it did, I continued taking chances, counting on its vacancy to prolong my nighttime escape from reality. As long as the driveway was clear, so was I. I'd lost every other part of my life; this was the only place I could be me.

🌀 🌀 🌀

In the early part of this morning, the facility's pool offers me the same kind of solitude my childhood pool did back then. During the day, it's near impossible to find quiet. People treat this place like a resort, not a place for the dying. In the heat of the afternoons, grown adults jump in the pool like kids or float on inflatable rafts. But in the early hours, the pool is empty. I can almost pretend I'm back home, gliding through the water as if every piece of my life is in place.

I curl one arm over my head after the other, trying to keep my focus on even breathing and strong strokes. Distraction eats at me in the shape of Noelle's face, the curve of her waist, the smell of her hair, the hurt in her eyes. I fall back and forth between drowning in my guilt and burning in my vindication. I did everything I could. Didn't I? I should have done more. What more can I do? I want to save her. I want her to open her eyes. I want to break out of this place and just live my life.

Stroke. Glide. Stroke. Glide. Breathe.

The fiery red sun hovers just above the fence line, casting a pink hue across the grey sky. I pull myself from the water and sit on the pool's edge. For a moment, I remember what it was like to feel the breeze against my wet skin after a swim. Here, the air is always the same— funneled through the filtration system. Yes, it's cleaner. There's no need for a mask when we go "outside" in the domed courtyard. But just once more, I'd like to feel the wildness of the wind instead of the managed air in a controlled environment.

I remove my goggles and shake the water from my hair, letting my feet dangle below me. Through the wall of windows, I can see our floor, though the reflection of cloudy sunlight bars me from seeing inside. I wonder if Noelle is looking outside. When I'm inside looking out, I sometimes peer past the facility's property to see the rest of the world, pretending I'm not here but someplace else in the world, and this is just an ordinary day. I long for ordinary days. At least I was in control of the mundane. Here, I'm not in control of anything. I might not be sick anymore, but what good is that going to do me? As far as I can tell, there's no way out of here. This place may look like a hotel, but it's as secure as a prison, and all I can do is sit here and wait for my execution.

As a few early risers walk from the facility toward the pool, I towel off and head for the showers. The water is a perfect 105 degrees, as always. I try to turn the water down once I step inside, but the system overrides the knobs. This was the preference I chose, so this is what I get—no variations allowed. When I turn off the water, I'm greeted by a blast of hot air—no need for a towel.

"Maybe you'll dress me, too?" I mutter as I exit the shower and grab my shirt. A robot rolls forward and attempts to take my shirt. "Get out of here," I tell it, and it obeys my command. I finish dressing, then head toward the cafeteria by way of the stairs. I have no desire for warm mush, so I climb to the Gen-Gen level. When I open the doors I'm met by the smell of bacon. Vegan bacon, sure, but it sure smells real. I'm also met by Noelle's lowered head, bent over a book while she bites a piece of her bacon. I'm not fooled; she knows I'm here.

"Ryder! Over here!" Colby is waving from a table in the center, sitting with some guy I've never seen before. I glance back at Noelle just in time to see her avert her eyes back to her book. I'm torn. I know she's only pretending to read. I want to wrap my arms around her and soothe her hurt. Instead, I let her be.

"Hey," I say, taking the seat next to Colby.

"Hey man, this is Thom. Thom, meet Ryder." Colby says, and Thom points his knuckles at me. I bump them, trying to figure out what's off about him. His dark hair is pulled back in a ponytail at the base of his neck and he's wearing the same green scrubs we all are, but his shows off his bulging muscles while mine is draped a little looser. I'm no slouch, but Thom makes me feel like a string bean in his presence. But it isn't the herculean way he drapes himself over the table that has me on alert, it's the familiar way Colby is treating him. I recall the natural walls that were in place when I first met Colby. He'd welcomed me in, but there was no back-patting or knowing looks like there is with this guy.

"What's going on?" I finally ask. The conversation stops. I ignore Thom's icy stare as I give Colby my attention. "How is it that you guys know each other so well?"

Thom and Colby glance at each other, then back at me. "Support group," they say at the same time. It seems rehearsed.

"I call bullshit."

"Nah, man. We were part of the same weekly group, trying to cope with this end-of-life shit." Colby nods over at Thom. "This guy was kind of the chairman of our group, but it's not really a permanent role, if you know what I mean."

I eye both of them as my breakfast arrives, trying to see who will reveal the truth. A look. A word. Anything that will feed the suspicion in the pit of my belly. I chew on my bacon, waiting for someone to confirm that there's more to this story than a support group. Thom meets my gaze with narrowed eyes.

"Look, dude, if you want trouble, you can go elsewhere."

"Ryder's cool," Colby says to Thom, and it makes me feel even more alone...and jealous. I'm not in this group, I'm on the outside—allowed to hang out, but not to know their secrets. I'm not convinced of this whole support group story, and they don't trust me enough to tell the real story. I bite back my disbelief, meeting Colby's hopeful smile with a shrug. "Sorry man, I guess this place is just messing with my head."

"It's all good," Colby says. "Kick back and enjoy the ride. There's no reason to stress. That reminds me—Thom, have you tried ordering from your ID band yet? Watch this." He punches in a few buttons and a robot wheels to him.

"This way to your massage, sir," the machine says in a woman's voice. Thom shakes his head, a smirk on his face.

"Maybe later," Colby says, touching the cancel button on his band so that the robot retreats. "I've had a massage almost every day I've been here."

"By a robot?" I ask.

"Nah, a real masseuse," he says.

"Probably the only action you're getting, too," Thom says, then ducks as Colby cuffs his head.

"You just wait. One massage and you'll be addicted. Speaking of action…" Colby nods in Noelle's direction. "What's up with you two?"

"Nothing," I say a little too quickly.

"I heard about the baby. That's rough."

I glance at Noelle over my shoulder, watching as she picks up her book and leaves the table without even looking my way. "I think she blames me. I told her we could check on Mila today, but she brushed me off. It was more than that, though. She acted like she didn't even *want* to see her."

"That's weird. She was practically her mother for the past few days."

"It's complicated," I say. I eat the last bite of my pancakes and stand just as a robot comes to clear my space. "I better go."

"What, you already lined up another date?" Colby teases.

"Nah, a massage," I say. Even Thom laughs as I leave. I don't want to get into the whole Noelle thing with them. It's beginning to make more sense, what's going on. She's shutting down. She's a loner, like me; so when she took care of Mila, she'd opened herself up to feelings she probably had never experienced before—and to the deep hurt she likely felt when the baby was taken away. It scared her, I'm sure of it, which is why she's pushing me away and acting as if she'll never see Mila again.

🌀 🌀 🌀

I find Noelle curled up on a couch in the corner. The TV is on, but she isn't watching. Instead, she's staring out the window. Her face reveals nothing. There are no tears, no anger, no emotion at all to let me know where she's at. Maybe she's at peace, and anything I say will stir up emotions that aren't there. Jules walks up to her, and I take a step back toward the wall in an effort to be invisible. She places a hand on Noelle's shoulder, who jumps at her touch, and then shrinks in an effort to get out from under her friend's hand. It's slight, and I see Noelle recover instantly, flashing Jules a grin as if everything is okay. I know better though. Their conversation is brief. Jules gives her a hug, and Noelle leaves the couch for her cot. I follow, putting my hand over hers when she waves it over her panel. She whips around as her bed rolls out, sighing when she sees it's me.

"Leave me alone." She looks away from me, but I tilt her chin back in my direction, then stroke the side of her face as the tears finally spill over.

"Don't push me away," I whisper. She closes her eyes, her mouth trembling. "Look at me." She does, and her whole face crumples. I pull her against me as she fights back her sobs and loses, holding her carefully so I don't hurt the wounds on her back. She shudders in my arms, and I lift her so she doesn't collapse. I lie with her on the bed, and she curls into me, her face against my chest as I keep her close. Her tears move into shaky breathing, and then into deep inhales. I keep hold of her as she sleeps, smoothing her silver hair now and then. I stay awake; I'm not tired. I'm only partially conscious of the room that surrounds us. My focus is on her as I face the inside of her cubby, blocking the rest of the world out.

"Why did I have to meet you here?" I whisper into her hair. I wonder how different we'd be if we'd met on the outside. Would we have even known each other? Would we have found something to connect on? Would the walls we placed around ourselves have come down for each other? Maybe it's better that we hadn't met. I just regret that I only have a few months left with her—if she'll have me.

She sleeps for almost two hours. I stay in the same position the whole time, even as my arm cramps and eventually goes numb under her head. Nothing could make me move. Not fire, not that evil Nurse Sherry—nothing and no one. I would stay here for days if need be. Luckily, that's not the case. She stirs, stretching her body against me before opening her eyes. I hold my breath as her blue eyes search mine. Then I take a chance and lower my lips to hers, my heart racing, time slowing, my fear of rejection gripping me. She meets me halfway, her lips touch mine and break through every single brick of the walls we keep trying to rebuild. My hands are in her hair, on her back, at her hip, against her face. She clutches my shirt and I become her air. I practice as much restraint as I can muster, aware that we're in an open room with prying eyes. But if we weren't, I'm not sure I'd be able to stop.

She's the first to break away. She lowers her head and puts her hand against my chest, pressing lightly. I kiss her forehead, and she wraps her arms around me.

"I want to see Mila," she whispers.

"Right now?"

"Right now."

I brush her hair from her face and caress the side of her cheek. "You have so much love in you, I hope you never feel the need to bottle it up again."

"It's hard," she says. "But I keep thinking of her all by herself in that nursery. I know it's going to hurt, but I have to give her as much love as I can until her final day."

"You know that Nurse Sherry is enforcing time limits on visits, right?"

Her mouth sets in a fine line, her eyes narrowing with the same fire I'd seen in our earliest days together. But then she shakes her head.

"Well, then we use every single second we're allowed. It's not perfect, but it's something, I guess."

We take the elevator to the third floor. It's free time, but the kids stop what they're doing when they see us enter.

"Noelle!" one of the girls squeals, and she's soon surrounded by a crowd of girls wondering if she can braid their hair, tie their shoes, teach them to crochet, and use crayon as lipstick on them.

I feel a pair of arms wrap around my waist and look down to see Devon's curly-haired head pressed against my abdomen. It's been almost a full day since I've seen him, and I instantly feel bad. I wrap my arm around his shoulders and squeeze.

"Hey, buddy."

"I've been watching out for Milagro," he says, lifting his head. "No one was picking her up when she was crying, so I did. I changed her diaper, just like Noelle does, and I gave her a bottle, too. Is that okay?"

I look over his head toward Noelle, watching as she gives an apologetic wave to the girls before disappearing into the nursery.

"That's perfect," I tell him, drinking in the pride on his face. "Noelle will be so happy to hear you've been taking great care of Mila for her."

"No one else is doing it," he whispers. "I saw one aide come in and feed her, but no one else. They close the door so we can't hear her crying, but I hear. I snuck in when no one was looking. I'll keep doing it if you want."

I feel bad. An eight-year-old shouldn't be in charge of an infant; he should be playing with friends and enjoying his final days. But I can tell this is important to him.

"I don't want to take you away from your fun," I say.

"I want to take care of her," he insists. He hops from one foot to the other while he waits for an answer. Thing is, I'm not the one to give it.

"You'll have to talk with Noelle," I say. Through the window, I see her rocking Mila on her shoulder. My heart swells and breaks at the same time as she presses her mouth to the baby's dark hair, then looks down at her. Her mouth is moving, and I know she's singing. I wish I could hear her, but I want to give her this time. "Let's ask her in a little bit, though, okay?"

I help Devon build a village of Lego houses, and then help him destroy each structure as if we're Godzilla, stomping on anything in our path. One of the teens rings the bell, signaling lunchtime, and I help Devon clean up. He gets in line, and checks behind him to make sure I'm still there. I glance at Noelle, but she's not budging. I join Devon and we move single file to the cafeteria where they have veggie corn dogs, cheese pizza, and milkshakes. I still miss lab meat, but I'm starting to get used to the vegetarian options. I hardly mind the tofu as I crunch into the corn dog. I order a second lunch for Noelle before we head back. Once we're in the bright yellow kids' room, Devon makes a beeline for the nursery. He's already pleading his case when I get there.

"I'll move my cot near the nursery so I'll hear her every time," he promises. She looks at me over his head, shooting me a perplexed look.

"He's already been doing it since she was brought here last night," I say. She grows tense as I relay what Devon told me.

"I should be here," she mutters. Devon looks to me, and I pat his shoulder.

"Hey bud, give us a few minutes, okay?" I'm relieved when he leaves without asking questions. "He'll be your extra pair of hands," I tell Noelle. She shakes her head.

"It's not that I don't think he's capable. I know he is. But it isn't fair. They took her from me, and then stick her in this room as if she's a piece of furniture."

"But she's alive," I say cautiously. Her eyes flash as she turns to me, but then she softens.

"I know," she says, then she sighs. "I don't get it. This place was supposed to be so magical, our last months made comfortable and wonderful so that we leave this world on a high note. Instead, it feels like we're being punished. We don't even get a choice about being here, only which facility we get to die at. Other than that, we have no freedom whatsoever. We're here so that the rest of the world doesn't have to deal with the messiness of death. This isn't to make our lives better, it's to shield the outside world from reality." She looks down at Mila, smoothing the hair on her forehead and kissing her on the top of her head. "And then there's Mila and every other baby that has a shortened life span. Why is she even in here? She should be with her mother."

"But her mother gave her up," I point out.

"Because she didn't know any better," Noelle says. "She was probably afraid. No one on the outside knows how to deal with death because of facilities like this. They're afraid to see death. They don't talk about it. There's so much focus on bucket lists and living a full life, and ending it at a facility where every single thing is taken care of for you. But when it comes to death itself? No one knows what to do. Think about it. Who talked to you about what it would be like to lose your parents?"

"No one," I admit. "But my family was fractured like that. My parents didn't talk about a lot of negative things with me. And my aunt? She hardly talked to me at all."

"I think most families were like that," Noelle says. "I love my parents, but they never once talked to me about what it would be like after they died. I spent my whole life pushing people away, avoiding any kind of attachment because I was so afraid of getting hurt. And I'm not alone. Parents are giving their babies up to facilities to avoid the pain of loving them and then letting them go. Look out there." She gestures to the kids in the room. "These kids should be with their families, not locked up here like they're orphans. And Mila? She shouldn't be left in a room to cry. She should be in the arms of someone who loves her."

"Like you," I say.

"Like her real mother."

11

Skye

Noelle
88 days left

It's hard to say goodbye to Mila. When the aide informs me that my time is up, I want to fight her on it. But I don't want to lose my chance to see her tomorrow, or the next day, or every day until she expires.

Devon reassures me he'll take good care of her. It bothers me that I'm depending on an eight-year-old to care for a newborn. Ryder believes he can do it, and I'm fairly certain he's right. I just don't think it's fair. I should be able to trust that a facility of caregivers would ensure Mila is loved and cared for until her last breath. The fact that I can't lights a fire inside me.

Ryder and I are escorted away from the third floor, even though we insist it's unnecessary. "It's so nice of you two to make sure we get to our floor safely," I say to the guards as we ride the elevator. One of them is the officer that struck me last night. He gives me a side glance and places his hand on his stick. "You don't scare me," I say, my nervousness buried under my anger at the whole situation. Ryder takes my hand and squeezes it. I'm not sure if it's in support or to quiet me, but I decide I've said enough anyway. Tomorrow is a new day, and I won't let anything get in my way.

"Come with me," Ryder says when we reach our floor. We leave the guards behind as he leads me to the stairwell.

"Are we going back?"

"No," he says. "We're going to the second floor."

I follow him up the stairs, racing to keep up with him once he bursts through the doors and stalks across the floor. He makes a beeline for Colby, who's sitting at a table in the corner, talking with the same guy I saw him eating breakfast with this morning. Ryder pulls a chair out for me and then takes one directly across from Colby.

"Whatever you two know, I want to know, too."

"I don't know what you're talking about, man," Colby says, sitting back with a bored look on his face.

"Yes, you do. You know something, and so do I."

Colby isn't the only one whose interest is piqued. I peer into Ryder's face, wondering what he's talking about.

"You first," the other guy says.

"Hold on," I say. "What the heck is going on? And who's this guy?"

"This is Thom," Ryder tells me. "These two apparently go way back. They say it's from some support group, but they're about to tell us the real story."

Colby and the new guy glance at each other. Thom finally leans forward, resting his elbows on the table. "After you tell us yours."

Ryder's jaw tenses and I see a flash of anger cross his face. He glances at me and then nods. "When I came here, I was detoxing from the medicine my doctor was giving me," he says. "They were trying to kill me, to get me to believe I was actually dying of cancer. I was dying all right, but not because of some disease." As he continues his story, I feel my body grow cold. I recall how he'd ignored me in those first few days, but also how pale and weak he appeared. Days later, he swam laps in the pool and then ran on the treadmill as if he had all the energy in the world. I don't think he'd lie to me. But if all this is true, what else don't I know?

"How did you know to quit the medicine?" Colby asks.

"A doctor clued me in. He had taken over my care years ago and took me off the meds I had been on. The same thing was happening back then, but I was too young to know what he was saving me from. Eventually they caught on, or he just disappeared." Ryder tells us of his new doctor, the treatment plan she placed him on, and how he got worse instead of better. "Just before I came here, my former doctor sent me a letter letting me know that the medications were killing me." He pauses, looks Thom and

Colby square in the face. "If any of this comes back to bite me in the ass, I'll know that you two ratted."

"Anything you say stays here," Thom says.

"He also gave me his former colleague's login information. I was able to alter my information so that it didn't show I was dying of cancer. I changed my cause of death to 'unknown'. No one here knows what my life was like before I walked through these doors. Now, I'm miraculously cured, and yet my number is still the same. I believe this is all a sham, that none of us are actually dying on a specific date without help and these numbers on the back of our necks are just props."

"No, they're real all right," Colby says. Ryder touches his neck and squints at Colby.

"How so?"

"When that timer reaches zero, your life will end—but not because of some divine reason. There's a needle filled with some sort of poison, set to inject you once you reach your expiration date. That is if the authorities want you to die."

"And if I remove it?" Ryder asks.

"Then it kills you early," Thom says.

"Unless you have the right tool," Colby says, a sly look on his face.

"What's that supposed to—"

"Shit." Thom is looking at the television in the center of the room. On the screen, a news reporter stands in front of several police cars. The camera pans out, and I lean closer, studying a man with platinum hair flanked by two officers. A chill runs through me. It can't be. His head hugs his chest, hiding his face, but I know it's him. I touch my own hair, my eyes glued to the screen as the officers carry him by the arms, his feet dragging on the ground with his hands cuffed behind his back.

"How do you know all this?" Ryder probes them.

"Because that's one of our guys," Colby says in a low voice. "Noelle, I believe you know who I'm talking about." My eyes don't leave the screen to acknowledge Colby, even though his words are just as shocking as what's unfolding in front of me. On the TV, Skye lifts his head and looks directly at the camera—at me—his icy blue eyes a perfect match to my mother's, to my own. My hand covers my mouth, tears spring to my eyes. He has bruises on his cheek and a cut above his eyebrow, and a few new lines add to the character of his face. But it's him.

"We're live in Guerneville, California, where authorities have arrested Skye Edison. Reports confirm Edison, a fugitive, has been captured in Armstrong Redwoods, a forest on federal land in Guerneville that was shut down ten years ago due to budget cuts," a female voice says over the video. "Edison was alone at the time of his arrest but is believed to have worked with an underground network being investigated by the FBI. He was found with a cache of weapons, stolen property, and is accused of crimes against the government."

"Crimes against the government," Colby spits out. "They mean tampering with his number. But they can't say that because the world would know their secret."

"Shhh," I demand, my eyes never leaving the screen.

"It's all a lie," Skye suddenly yells. "The numbers are a lie. They're killing you, all of you."

An aide runs to the television and turns it off before he says anything else.

"Pretend like you didn't see anything," Colby hisses. "Look at me." I do, and the normal laid-back expression he's usually wearing is traded for one that's much more serious. "The staff knows who you are. They know you're Skye's sister. They've been watching you. Now that he's been arrested, they're going to wonder what you know." I look at Ryder, but he's deep in conversation with Thom.

"But I don't know anything," I say, turning back to Colby.

"And that's how it needs to stay."

"Attention all residents. Please return to your assigned floor immediately," a voice sounds over the loudspeaker.

"How do you know all this?" I ask. Ryder has my hand, trying to lead me to the stairs, but I plant myself. We're the only ones in this room who don't belong here, and the hair on the back of my neck prickles as I realize we're the center of attention; all of the aides are facing us, waiting for us to leave.

"The less you know, the better." Colby leaves the table with Thom, never looking back.

"Face forward, Noelle. Let's go." Ryder's voice is quiet, but his tone is unmistakably forceful. I obey, holding his hand tightly as we head to the stairwell. I start to ask questions but he cuts me off. "Not now," he whispers.

I'm in the dark. Something is going on, and I don't know what.

"Just act natural," he says as he pushes the door open at our floor. As soon as we cross the threshold, I can feel Nurse Sherry's eyes on me. I smile up at Ryder as if he's just said something humorous. He grins back at me and squeezes my hand. He leans down and gives me a kiss on the mouth for good measure. I wish I weren't so terrified inside. My thoughts are spiraling. Skye. Mila. Our limited number of days. The lies I've been told. My parents. Oh God, my parents. Did they die for no reason? What are the authorities going to do to my brother?

How the hell are we going to get out of this alive?

Nurse Sherry dictates new rules for our floor. Of all of them, there's only one I hear—we're prohibited from visiting other floors. The courtyard is the only place we're all allowed to be together, and only after we've signed out with the charge nurse. I can hear the words that aren't being said—we'll never see the kids again. I can't see them bringing Mila or Devon to the courtyard. My insides burn, my hands are clenched as tight as the rock forming in my chest. There's grumbling among some of the residents, but I'm sure no one is angrier than me. I open my mouth to protest, but Ryder pulls on my hand. I turn to glare at him

but stop when I see the tears brimming his eyes. I know
he's thinking about Devon. I realize the full gravity of all
this. Not only are we barred from spending time with
Devon and Mila, but they're essentially unprotected.
Devon is my only hope to keep Mila safe, and I can't really
expect him to save her if something happens overnight.

*Something could happen overnight, and there's nothing I can do
to stop it.*

* * *

The rest of the day feels like three. I can't figure out what
to do with myself, or even how to feel. One minute I'm
pacing the floors, wanting to tear Nurse Sherry's eyes out.
The next, I'm sobbing on my bed, wishing the whole
facility would just crumble to the ground and take all of us
with it. Ryder tries to comfort me, and his hand on my
shoulder burns all the way to my bones.

"Go away!" I scream, feeling like a monster as I do.
When he doesn't leave, I turn my back to him, curling
myself into the smallest ball possible as I clutch my pillow.
I know he's hurting, too. I'm not even angry at him. I want
him to go. I want him to stay. I'm ready to lash out at him
if he even tries to touch me, but when he curls his body
behind mine, I break down. He wraps his arms around me
and I scoot closer, letting him be my strength as my heart
breaks wide open. He lets me cry, his arms pulling me in
tight as if I might plummet through the floor, the earth, all
the way to the molten core of this planet. I feel as if I might,

as if there's nothing to hold me here. Why does this even hurt so bad? None of this matters. Whether real or fake, we're all going to die. We've been tricked into signing our own prison sentence. We're all on death row.

I don't move when dinner begins. Neither does Ryder. My tears continue filling my eyes whenever I brush them away, and I wipe my nose on my shirt.

"Wait here," he whispers. When he gets up, he leaves a cold, vacant feeling against me. He's only gone for a moment, though, coming back with some tissue. I blow my nose, feeling truly disgusting as I do. I shoot him an embarrassed smile as I drop the dirty tissues to the floor, not wanting him to see. He blows his own nose, his reddened eyes are watery. Then he leans over me and adds his tissues to my pile.

"We can let the sloth-bot get it," he says. I forget myself for a moment and laugh at the moniker he dubbed the vacuum cleaner. It really does look like a sloth in a way, crawling over the floor as it suctions up anything that's not supposed to be there. He lies back down, and I use his arm as a pillow, facing him. The heaviness settles back over me. He brushes my hair from my face and presses his lips to my forehead. I close my eyes.

"It's not fair," I whisper.

"I know." His words brush against my skin, and I lean up to catch them and the taste of his mouth. I want him to make me forget, to take away the pain. I want a moment to believe none of this is real, that we're on the other side of the wall, the number of our days unknown. I want him. But even more, I want him to take me away from reality.

"Move with me," he whispers, and we both slide to the floor between the bed and the inside of my cubby. The concrete floors are cold on my back, but his hand cradles my head. From where we are, the nursing staff can't see us. They may even forget we're here while everyone is at lunch. Ryder is staring at me intently, and I can see his desire. I tilt my face toward his, but he pulls back. "I want this, Noelle. More than you know. But do *you*? I don't want to push you. But being that time is a funny thing…" He trails off, and I answer him with a nod. "Are you sure?"

If this had been before day one hundred, I never would have gone this far. After seeing Skye on TV, I'm not even sure our numbered days mean anything. But Ryder? I'm sure. I've never been more sure of anything in my life.

"Yes," I whisper, my eyes never breaking from his. He crushes his mouth down on mine, his hands tangle in my hair. I clutch his shirt, drawing him closer to me. He takes it off, then kisses me again, his tongue circling mine in a way that makes me dizzy. I'm sure he's just as aware as I am of our narrow window of solitude, but I wish this moment could last forever. I want to savor it as I memorize every part of him. My hands run over the raised scars on his back and I pause as I realize their familiarity. Two round scars, the same shape as the end of an officer's stick—identical to the ones hardening on my back.

He slips my shirt over my head, then presses against me so that we're skin to skin. His body feels warm against mine, his tan skin smooth as I continue running trails from his back to his shoulder, over his chest, across his neck. I cradle his unshaven face before rubbing my inner arm over his cheek, the bristles sending shivers through me. He slides his pants off, then tugs at mine. He stops just as the elastic waist reaches the top of my hip.

"What's wrong," I whisper. He runs a hand through his hair, his face appearing tormented.

"This is probably unnecessary," he starts.

"What is?"

"I don't have protection. It doesn't matter, I guess. But what if it does?"

What if we survive?

I pull his hand so that he's on top of me again. The blue-green of his eyes swims oceans around me, darkened by his concern. I can feel the giggle rising up inside me, and I clamp my hand over my mouth.

"What?" His concern is replaced by confusion, but I can't stop laughing, shaking beneath him. It's not really funny. It's more ironic than anything. We could die in 88 days. We could die tonight. We could die when we're old, unable to leave our beds. But one thing that won't happen?

"I can't get pregnant," I finally get out, my laughter dying with the words. It's no longer funny. "I made sure I couldn't years ago. I just...I did the math. Having a kid wasn't in the cards. At least, it wasn't when the numbers thing was real." I turn my head, the moment slipping away as I realized the gravity of my decision. If we survive this, I still can't have kids.

"You okay?" he asks, guiding my face back toward his. "We don't have to do this." I don't answer. Instead, I slip my pants off the rest of the way and raise my hips to his. He hesitates, hovering above me. My eyes take in the full length of him, the way his core muscles point in the direction of his manhood, how beautiful the shape of his chest is above mine. I look into his face, and warm at the way he's watching me. I know he's still unsure if I'm ready, but honestly, what's the point of waiting?

"Please," I whisper.

I gasp when he enters me, burying my face into his chest to keep from making any sound. He nuzzles my head so that I'm looking up at him again, and it all becomes too real. We're here in the facility, my bed the only thing keeping anyone from seeing us, completely naked and tangled up in each other on the concrete floor. He's looking so intently at me, his eyes burn straight into mine. I look away, but he guides my face back.

"Stay with me," he whispers. I nod, unable to speak. He feels so good inside me, his hands exploring my body, his kisses across my cheeks, my neck, my shoulders, my mouth. Ryder touches me like it's worship, his lips blessing every inch of my skin, his hips molded to mine like hands folded in prayer. I'm as scared as I am liberated by his touch. It's everything to me, but my inner voice, the one that holds everyone at arm's length, is tugging at my soul. *What if he lets you down? What if you care more than he does? What if this is just an item on his bucket list?* I clench my jaw, mentally blocking the voice from continuing. I can't go there. I'm tired of going there. Whether we survive or not, I'm done with living a cautious life. I'm ready to free-fall into every moment. I'm ready to live.

He strokes the side of my cheek, and I look back into his eyes.

"Where'd you go?" he asks, his fingers tracing my jawline. I take a deep breath and smile, turning my head to kiss his fingers.

"I'm right here with you," I say. I reach my head up and touch my lips to his, then part my mouth slightly as an invitation. He accepts, pressing into me harder as our kiss intensifies. It doesn't matter that we're in a facility room on a stone cold floor, or that privacy doesn't exist without secrecy. The numbers, the rules, our loss—none of it matters. At this moment, I only see him. And when he finishes, his eyes lock on mine, our bodies remain connected, my fears evaporate, and I finally understand how it feels to be free. There's no other way to explain what just happened.

Lies

Ryder
87 days left

Her body rises and falls with each breath, her face pressed against my chest. We'd started the night in our own beds, but I crept into her bed a few minutes after the lights went out, wrapping myself around her as she fell asleep. Her body feels natural against mine, and I can't stop inhaling the smell of her hair. Her breathing is hypnotic, and I want to lose myself in the rhythm, fall asleep to it as my lullaby. But I can't. Every time my consciousness fades, I'm jerked awake by what Thom told me.

Noelle is in trouble. We all are, but she's the one I'm worried about. There wasn't enough time for Thom to completely fill me in, but from what I do know, it's not good.

First, our country's leadership has been taken over by The Enforcers, a group of extremists within the government who are working to rapidly decrease the human population. This takeover occurred around 2016. It's not general knowledge, but now that I know, it makes a lot of sense. From what I remember from history class, this was the year a strange election happened and many laws were overturned. Two years later, our environment was suffering and the numbers were introduced. Thom told me that the two are connected.

Second, The Enforcers intend to use Noelle to get what they want. Before Skye was found, The Enforcers planned on extracting information from her. The facility, managed by The Enforcers, planted her in the senior's ward with me, banking on a connection between the two of us. When that didn't pan out as fast as they expected, they brought Mila in. It was all by design. If Noelle didn't tell them what they wanted to hear, they'd torture her. If that didn't work, they'd kill me in front of her. If she still didn't talk, they'd kill Mila. As far as I can tell, Noelle really doesn't know anything about Skye or any of the other rebels. But The Enforcers don't know that. As far as they're concerned, Noelle is their key to getting inside the one group that could mess up everything.

But now Skye's been found, and from what Thom said, things are about to get worse. Skye's arrest on live television publicly revealed the lies behind the numbers, and there's bound to be rioting in the streets and protesters trying to get us out. They no longer need Noelle for information. Now, she'll be used as bait.

"I don't think Skye will talk, even if they use her," Thom said, and I'd gritted my teeth at his callousness.

"So you're saying he'll just let her die."

"None of us want her to die," Thom said. "But there's much more at stake here."

"We're sitting ducks," I breathed. He shook his head.

"Just stay alert. There's more of us on the inside. We have a plan, and you two are part of it."

I don't sleep much tonight. Every time I start to drift, panic shocks me awake. I'm afraid they'll take her if I'm not alert, though I know they could take her no matter what. Thom's words didn't offer much to go by. Without knowing his plan, I feel helpless. I don't even know if I can trust him or Colby, though I don't feel I have a choice. Thom says he's here to protect Noelle, but his reasons are different than mine. To him, she's a liability. To me, she's everything.

I slip out of her bed just as the morning light begins filtering through the windows, and I catch an hour of broken sleep. I wake to her sitting on the edge of my bed. She smiles, then holds her hair back as she leans to kiss me.

"Good morning," she says. Despite every way our lives have changed in the past day, her voice radiates light through my chest. I reach for her wrist and pull her back toward me, using her kiss as my personal caffeine.

"Good morning," I say once her lips leave mine. She ducks her head, a shy smile on her face. I catch the wistfulness within it. She's processing, just like me. I know she's wondering about her brother and worried about Mila. I don't think she realizes how much danger she's in, though. With everything that's gone down, I'm not even sure how to tell her. "Did you sleep well?" I ask. Her lips twist into a secret smile as she nods.

"The best sleep I've ever had," she says.

Her hand stays in mine, my fingers circled loosely around her tiny wrist. She moves her hand so that our fingers are entwined, bringing my palm to her lips. The move catches my breath, bringing back the vision of her body beneath mine, her golden skin, the shape of her collarbone, the scent of her natural perfume.

"Did you?" she asks.

"Like a baby." Technically it's not a lie. I was only a few beds away while Noelle rocked Mila through sleepless nights. However, my reference is a poor choice of words. Her face falls, and she turns her head. "I'm sorry, I wasn't thinking."

"It's okay," she murmurs. Her eyes are shining when she faces me again, and she brushes the tears away. "I don't even know what to worry about most, you know? I worry about her, but I don't know how to save her. I'm worried about Skye, what kind of danger he's in now. I'm worried about you, about me, about all of us." She wipes away another tear, her blue eyes a raging storm. "It's all been a lie. I feel so stupid. I changed my whole life because of this." She gives a laugh, but her fury remains. "I never thought I'd be mad that I wasn't dying."

"I know," I say, sitting up and wrapping my arm around her shoulder. I've suspected our numbers were a lie for so long, I'm not shocked after Skye's proclamation on the news. But I know what it's like to feel betrayed. "The doctors who were supposed to be caring for me were killing me instead. Not quickly, but over time. It took one honest doctor to reveal that something wasn't right, even though all the clues were there. I didn't see them, and I felt completely dumb about it. Then there are my parents. They knew when their number was up, but they did nothing to prepare me. We didn't talk about it. I had no idea where I was going. Even worse, they disappeared a few days before they were supposed to enter a facility. I woke up, and they weren't there. No note. No instructions. Nothing. I later found out they took a camping trip without me, one of those dumb bucket list ideas before their final one hundred days. These were the people I trusted the most, and they completely let me down for their own selfish reasons."

"I'm so sorry, Ryder," Noelle whispers. I shake my head, tilting hers so she's looking at me.

"I'm not saying this to compete with you. I'm telling you because I get how angry you are. I'm still angry. I don't know when I won't be angry. None of this is fair, and none of it makes sense."

She's quiet for a moment and then sits up to face me. "But Thom knows something," she says. "He was talking with you. He told you something important, didn't he? What did he say?"

I pull away, sitting cross-legged at the head of my bed. She does the same at the other end, waiting for me to speak. And I do. I tell her everything I know because she deserves to know all of it. I can't protect her from the truth, and she sure as hell can't protect herself if she doesn't know what she's up against. When I get to the part about Mila, she covers her mouth to suppress a sob.

"Hannah knew," she whispers.

"What?"

"Hannah, the aide. She was in the nursery with Mila when I found them and was all too eager to let me take over her care. She fed me some story about a woman handing the baby to her, and then not having the heart to turn the baby in to the officials. She said she'd promised to take care of her, but realized she couldn't. She roped me in, and I believed her. I'm so damn gullible!"

"No, you have a heart. You care. It's one of the best things about you, one of the things I appreciate the most."

"Well, my heart got me in trouble," she says. "I've spent years making sure I don't care too much about anyone, and they got to me with a baby." She shakes her head. "It's so sick. I mean, it's completely revolting. They used this innocent child—and who knows where she really came from—they just used her as a pawn. She's probably…" Another sob escapes her mouth, and her face crinkles as she fights to keep her tears from falling. "She's probably already dead," she says as she loses the battle and buries her face in her hands. I scoot closer to her and envelop her in my arms, holding her as she cries. I don't want to agree with her, but I do. If the only thing keeping us here is a stack of lies and unknown motives, I can't think of a reason why Mila would still be alive. Wrong. I can think of only one reason—her use as bait hasn't run out.

We eat breakfast without talking, partly because no one else is and partly because the weight of observation rests on our backs. We're being watched; we know it, even if we don't see it. So we contribute only to the sounds of clinking spoons in our oatmeal, sips of orange juice, and the occasional clearing of throats. After our meal, we head for the gym—because what else is there to do? I keep a steady pace on the treadmill, as I plan to stay on there for as long as possible. Noelle, on the other hand, starts sprinting after a short warm up. It's reminiscent of our first morning together in the gym, but this time there's a clenched jaw, narrow-eyed determination to her run. Her breathing is short, her hands closed in tight fists as she glares out the window in front of her. I follow her gaze to the people hanging around the pool, mostly Gen-Gens. No one is swimming. Instead, they sit in tight groups, heads low, deep in conversation. I study each person's worried expression, their hand movements, their furtive glances over their shoulders to see if any of the staff is paying attention. Of course the staff is paying attention. Even if they don't look like they are, I know everyone is scrambling.

Noelle slows her pace to a jog, then a walk before stopping. She rests where she is, clutching the side of her treadmill, her eyes still on everyone outside. Then, without a word, she gets off and heads for the door. I stop my treadmill and hop off, jogging to keep up with her as she stalks outside.

"I'm getting answers," she says before I even have to ask. She finds Spring and the rest of the girls and sits. I take a seat on the outskirts of the huddle, but one of the women moves over to make room for me.

"What do you know?" Spring asks, looking at Noelle first, and then at me.

"I know there were a few people missing on our floor," Noelle says.

"Wait, really?" All of my focus has been on Noelle, I didn't notice anything like this.

"Elmo and Leo have disappeared, and so has Ms. Richards. That old man who walks with the tree branch cane is gone, too. Three women who bunk near the doorway are gone. And that one guy in a wheelchair who hums all the time has also gone missing. That's a lot of people with the same expiration date."

"You didn't say anything," I say. Her face hardens for a moment, and she glares—but not at me. When she turns in my direction, she softens her stance and takes my hand.

"I wasn't sure if I was right or not. I noticed they were missing when we left for breakfast and didn't see them in the dining hall."

"What if they were somewhere else?" I ask.

"Where else would they be?" She glances up at the windows of our floor, and I follow her gaze. Nurse Sherry looks down in the courtyard. I can't tell if she's looking at us, but I'm sure she knows we're here. "Everyone on our floor stays in the same room. If someone isn't there, we can only assume they're gone for good." She turns to Spring. "Is there anyone missing on your floor?" Spring shakes her head.

"Not that I can tell," she says. She tilts her head. "Well, there was that one girl, Patrice. But I think her number was up. I feel bad, she kind of isolated in the last week. With everything that went down, no one noticed she was gone."

"Do you think that guy was telling the truth?" one of the girls pipes in. "You know, the one they arrested. He said the numbers were a lie. Do you think that's true?"

"I don't know," Noelle lies, squeezing my hand. She doesn't mention Skye is her brother, and as far as I can tell, none of them know.

"I think he is," Spring says. "The aide turned that TV off really quick when she realized what was happening. They've been acting strange ever since, making us stay off each other's floors, and now you're telling me a bunch of the seniors are missing. I not only think the numbers are a lie, but I definitely think there's more to this story."

Noelle and I glance at each other. When we look back, Spring gives us a curious look.

"You do, too," she says. "Don't you?"

"Yes," Noelle confirms. She opens her mouth to continue, but an explosion causes us both to jump. I look up, seeing the cracked glass of the dome.

"Get down!" I yell, shielding Noelle as another blast explodes the glass. Glass rains down on us. Small shards pepper my skin and I'm overwhelmed by the smell of burnt air. A whistling hiss flies through the air, and something solid lands a few yards away. Before I can register what it is, it explodes.

Noelle and I run for cover behind the lounge chair. The girls we were just talking to are also hiding. One of them lies motionless beside a nearby chair, blood pooling beside her. A few more devices sail over the wall and land in the courtyard, exploding upon contact. Chanting sounds from the other side of the wall.

The numbers are a lie. We're not dying, we're alive.

The numbers are a lie. We're not dying, we're alive.

The numbers are a lie. We're not dying, we're alive.

"Protesters," Noelle says, straightening from our hiding place. I sit up, scanning the courtyard. I catch sight of Colby and Thom on the other side. Colby's eyes meet mine.

"All residents, return to your floors," a voice sounds over the intercom.

"No!" one woman yells, and many more voices join in her defiance. None of us move. I look up, and Nurse Sherry is still looking down in the courtyard. This time, she's saying something in her ID bracelet. The doors to the lobby burst open, and soldiers march forward. They're in formation until they reach the first group, and then fan out, pouncing on the people closest to them. The group doesn't have a chance to fight back. They fall, unmoving to the ground.

"They're killing them!" Noelle shouts above the screams around us. I take her hand and we run alongside everyone else, taking cover behind a tree. It's the same tree we sat against on her first night with Mila, but this time, the safety of its shelter means something different. I watch as a soldier catches a woman by the shoulder. The resident collapses, and the afternoon sun glints off a small metal device in the soldier's hand. I recognize it immediately.

The last night I visited my childhood home, I knew something was off. The For Sale sign had been missing for weeks, and every time I pushed through the gate, I knew I was taking a chance. At some point, I had to give this up and let my home go—but I still hadn't been able to. This was the only place I could pretend things were normal, hold on to my security, and go back to a time when the world made sense.

I'd only been swimming for a few minutes when the floodlights came on. I nearly choked from surprise. I bobbed my head above the water and saw a man at the sliding door—the same sliding door I'd pressed my nose up against in my youth—holding a rifle and staring straight at me. I froze, our eyes locked. When he began to raise the barrel, I hoisted myself out of the pool and ran, leaving behind my clothes and shoes. I reached the gate as I heard the glass door open, my heart pounding as I fumbled with the lock. My fingers shook as I tried to keep the latch open, and then I shouldered it with all my strength. An overweight officer was exiting the passenger side of his cruiser as I burst through the gate. He took one look at me and placed his hand on his stick.

"Stay right where you are, son."

I didn't listen. I was too scared. I hadn't done anything more than swim laps in the pool, but the sight of the owner's gun was enough to set me in a tailspin. I took off down the road, waiting for the cop to shoot me. My feet hurt, every stone digging their way into my water-softened feet. But I didn't let up. When I heard the cop's heavy steps behind me, I dug in harder, running even as my lungs ached in my chest.

"Hands up, get on the ground!" the cop wheezed behind me. How he was keeping up with me, I didn't know. I'd never run this fast in my life. His stick touched my back and I was down, curled in a fetal position as the electrifying pain radiated through me. He launched himself at me, but I fought through the pain to clock him right in the jaw. I scrambled to my feet again but crumpled as I felt something on my shoulder. As I fell, I took in the second cop's bike on the grass, the small metal device in his hand, and the smirk on his face.

"That will keep him," the officer said. I lay unmoving on the ground, my breath coming out slow and labored. It took everything I had to just breathe. Inhale. Exhale. I couldn't move anything else. Even when the first officer zapped me again with the stick, I remained still. He held it there for about ten seconds, the electricity coursing through my body. I screamed in my mind, gurgled in my throat, begged for my life with my eyes. He laughed in response before finally removing the stick. I felt him touch the back of my neck.

"You're lucky, son. Your number was almost up."

Noelle's number stares me in the face as we crouch behind the tree. Eighty-seven, and it means nothing. We could die eighty years from now, or we could die today.

"They're not dead," I whisper. "They're stunned. It's how the officers are getting people to comply without using lethal force."

"What do we do?"

I don't know. Running doesn't feel safe. If they catch us, there's no telling what they'll do. I watch as aides stack the stunned bodies on rolling carts as if they're luggage.

One woman's head hits the concrete as she's hoisted onto the cart. The aide nudges her head back on the cart, then stacks another body on top of her. The lack of care is telling. If we get caught, our bodies will be at their mercy, and there's nothing we can do to protect ourselves.

But if we comply, then what? What's in store for us? With the target on Noelle's back, there's no way we'll walk back inside unnoticed. What if what's inside is worse than what's happening here?

As I'm contemplating, Noelle nudges me.

"Look," she says. She nods her head toward the lobby, and I see Colby walking in a line, his hands on his head just like everyone else as they walk through the open doorway. I glance through the line and see Thom further back. He glances in my direction, then nods.

Tonight, he mouths. I give a slight nod back, then stand.

"What are you doing?" Noelle hisses. "Is this really the smartest thing to do?"

"It's the only thing to do." I hold my hand out to her, and she stares at it. "Trust me," I say. I lean down, my lips against her ear. "Something's happening tonight. Whatever the plan is, it's already in motion." I stand back up, and this time she accepts my waiting hand as I help her to her feet. We place our hands on our head and get in line, passing the bodies of a few stunned residents on the way. The officers hardly pay us any attention, but I feel Nurse Sherry's eyes on us as we slowly make our way single file into the lobby and up the stairs.

When we reach our floor, it's as if nothing happened. Our elderly roommates rest around the room watching TV, playing board games, or staring off in space. One of the nurses sits at her usual table, handing out medication to the seniors waiting in line. Nurse Sherry has left her post by the window and is now inside the glass cage of her office, writing something down at her desk. I hold Noelle's hand in mine, and we walk to the window that overlooks the courtyard, surveying the damage. The last few people shuffle in line, hands on their head as the officers follow behind. But our attention is captured by what's beyond the wall. Buildings burn in the distance, the smoke darkening an already gray sky.

"They're rioting," Noelle says softly. I wrap my arms around her from behind, and she holds on to my forearms as she leans against me. I don't know what's going to happen tonight. I'm sure we're leaving, which scares me to death. We have no idea what we're walking into. But staying scares me even more.

I swallow my fear, staring out at the burning city on the horizon. Whatever happens tonight, I'm ready.

The Pawn

Noelle

86 days left

I awake to two eyes staring into mine. I jerk back, slamming against Ryder behind me. He tightens his grip at my waist in his sleep as the person places a hand over my mouth.

"Shhh," the person whispers. "I'm here to get you out."

My heart is pounding, my adrenaline racing through my veins. In the dim light, I can see her feminine shape inside a tight-fitting bodysuit—a vast difference from the loose-fitting pajama-like clothes we've been wearing for the past two weeks.

I sit up and Ryder stirs. We didn't bother sleeping in separate beds last night, and no one tried to stop us. I can see flashlights over by the door to the stairwell. All around us are sounds of sleeping.

"Ryder, wake up." I rub his arm and he grimaces, stretching before opening his eyes. His reaction isn't as dramatic as mine when he notices the woman standing near us, but he's suddenly wide awake.

"Where's the staff?" he asks, looking toward the nurse's station.

"Sleeping," the woman says, flashing a metal device in her hand—the same one the officers used to knock out defiant residents near the pool. She hands us dark clothing and we change. I'm so grateful to get rid of these green scrubs, I don't even care that I'm dressing out in the open. Once we're changed, she leads us to the three people waiting at the stairwell. We follow them down the stairs silently. When we reach the first-floor landing, one of the guys does a quick check before giving us the all clear.

"We gassed the lobby, but it still doesn't give us a lot of time," the girl explains.

"What about the cameras?" Ryder asks, nodding up at the one pointed directly at us.

"They're on a loop. One of our guys hacked the system. Again, it's not foolproof. It's only good until someone notices, but it buys us some time." She spins her finger in a circle. "Turn around."

We don't question her, we just do. As I feel something touch the number at the back of my neck, I realize we don't know if we can trust them. What if this is just a ruse to get us to give up without a fight? I close my eyes, curl my hands in tight fists, and wait without breathing. There's a slight tug, and my number falls to the ground. Shocked, I bend to pick it up as she works on Ryder's number.

"Careful," she says. "If you touch that needle, you're as good as dead."

I turn the number over and see the needle she's referring to, tucked inside a chamber. The part that was attached to my neck has several small metal disks. I rub my neck where it once was, and it feels raw like an open wound. When I look at my hand I see small spots of blood.

"It will heal in a few weeks," the girl says. She opens her gloved hand toward me and I carefully place the number in her palm. "When the staff comes to, they'll be looking for you." She points to the disks on the back. "This one here is a sensor that can tell whether you're dead or alive. Because it can't feel your heartbeat, it thinks that you're dead. And this one here is a tracking device. This is so they can keep tabs on you wherever you are, or, you know, find your body if you drop dead before your number is up. Speaking of which, I need your ID bracelet. Hold out your wrist."

Both Ryder and I do, and she waves a small black box over each of our wrists, causing the bracelets to fall. She lifts her chin to one of the guys, and he scans our bodies.

"They're clean," he says. She nods, then turns back to us.

"Sometimes they inject people with trackers," she explains. I wish I were surprised by this, but I'm starting to come to terms with how naïve I've been.

They lead us through the lobby. In the dim light, I can see the shape of bodies lying near the wall. The moonlight shines through the glass enclosure separating us from Admissions. I'm alarmed to see embers glowing on the ground, matching the fire in the distance. The whole world is burning, and we've been sheltered from all of it.

The woman waves a device over a panel, and we follow her through the sliding doors, entering a brightly lit hallway. She places a finger on her mouth and motions for us to hide in an alcove while two of the men rush forward. She hands us each a gas mask from her pack, and we quickly put it over our heads, covering our nose and mouths. Then we wait. I hear something drop, and then a hiss. My hands feel sweaty, my heart pounding as the reality of the situation washes over me. We're escaping. We might die.

We might live.

A few minutes pass and the woman motions us forward again. More bodies. I recognize the doctor that looked over Mila—Dr. Patrick—and feel bad. He had been so kind. I crouch down peering into his face, relieved to see he's still breathing. His number catches my eye, and I peer at it. I grow cold at what I see—it's fake. I touch it, and it feels similar enough. But when I press on it, the replica drops to the floor revealing a scar on his neck that appears to have healed long ago. He knew. He looked Mila over, knowing her number indicated she only had weeks left to live, and he never said anything. He could have saved her. He could have saved all of us.

"Come on," Ryder hisses, grabbing my hand and forcing me to move forward with our rescuers. My jaw is tight from clenching, the anger a slow burning fire in my chest. Betrayal is everywhere. The doctors. The nurses. The aides. Anyone who isn't a resident is our enemy.

We reach an elevator shaft, the whirring noise of the motor grating my nerves as we wait. I stuff my fears, clenching and releasing my fists as I cling to my fury instead. When the doors open, my indignation drives me forward. Everything is a lie. I no longer care if we live or die. Let the whole place burn and everyone in it.

"The kids!" I look at the woman for an answer. "Is someone getting them?" She shakes her head no, and I weaken, leaning on Ryder for support. "We have to go back," I insist, and move to hit the emergency stop button. One of the men pulls out a gun and places it to my temple.

"Hey! Don't!" I hear Ryder shout behind me as I raise my hands.

"Quiet," the man says, moving his gun from my head to point it at him. "Get back there with your friend," the man orders me, his eyes staying on Ryder. I move to the back, lowering my hands to take Ryder's in mine. We've escaped one prison and entered the next.

"Lower your gun," the woman says. "We're supposed to save them, not kill them."

"Just her," the man says, nodding in my direction. "There's no order to save him."

"Wait, what?" I look at each of our rescuers, but it's hard to gauge what's going on when all of their faces are covered by masks. I look to Ryder, and he gives a small nod. He knows what they're talking about. Everyone knows what's going on but me. I open my mouth to protest, but the woman speaks up.

"We save him, too." She turns to me. "We can't save the children," she says, but her voice borders on apology. "It's too risky."

"But they're just kids," I protest. "If we don't go back, they'll die."

"They might already be dead," the woman murmurs. I shake my head, even though she's voicing my worst fears.

"Devon and Mila are up there," Ryder says. "We might not be able to save everyone, but those are our kids. We have to go back for them."

The woman doesn't say anything, and it's apparent the conversation is over. I want to argue, to fight my way back to the third floor. But what can I do? We have no power here.

The elevator reaches the bottom floor, and the doors open with a gust of cool air. We step out onto the concrete to what seems to be some sort of underground tunnel. Directly in front of us is a waterway, which stretches toward narrower tunnels in both directions. Where we are is wide open, with pipes above us and fluorescent lights on the walls. If any of the lights burn out, we'll be in complete darkness.

We remove our masks, and I widen my eyes when I finally see who are rescuers are. The woman is Patrice, the girl that went missing. Two of the guys I only know by name—Shane and Keith. But the third guy, the one who pointed his gun at Ryder and me, I do know.

"What the hell, Thom?" Ryder demands. "You tried to kill us!"

"No, I saved your life."

"You were going to shoot us," I say.

"I needed you to see things my way. You were getting in the way of the mission. We have a plan, and if we don't stick to it, we'll lose more than just a roomful of kids."

"But they're *kids*!" I yell. Patrice steps in front of me, blocking me from Thom.

"Noelle, you need to understand. We're here to save *you*. Once the boat gets here, we're leaving and can't come back. Everyone we've stunned will wake up soon. If we're not out of here before that happens, this whole mission will have been for nothing. Even more, there will be no more chances. They'll be on to us."

"I'm not that special," I mutter.

"It's not about being special," Thom snarls. "It's because you're the pawn."

"Excuse me?"

"The pawn," he repeats. "They have your brother, and they're trying to extract information from him to get to the rest of us. So far he's kept quiet because we're still here. If they get you, all bets are off."

"Look, I get it. But trust me, I'm not that special," I repeat. "I know my brother, and there's no way he'd say anything, no matter what they did to me."

"I don't think he'll talk either, but with the right motivation, he could."

"What kind of motivation?" I look to Ryder. He briefed me on all this last night, and I thought I understood. But now I'm not so sure.

"Torture," Ryder says. "Rape. Cutting you up, piece by piece. Bringing you to the brink of death over and over. You name it, they'll do it to you, all in the name of getting Skye to speak. I don't think any man could stand there and watch his sister mutilated in front of him without doing the one thing that would bring her mercy. He'll speak so you can experience a quick death because that's what will happen if they get you—you'll die."

"You mean The Enforcers."

"You know about them," Thom says.

"Yeah, Ryder says they're the ones who took over the government and are running facilities like ours. But I still don't understand. What's the point? Why limit our lives like this?"

"It's a lottery system for most," Thom explains. "The world was getting too populated, thanks to modern medicine. People are living longer. Resources are dwindling. We were set to run out of clean water by 2025."

"That was twenty-five years ago," I say.

"Yes, and the population was set to reach eight billion that year with no population control, and reach almost ten billion this year. With those numbers, our world was also on course to run out of oil, natural gas, and even clean air. Food was becoming scarce. Even more, families with sustainable income were becoming a rare commodity. Most families needed government assistance. There were more people living in tents on the street than those who had homes. Something had to be done. So The Enforcers created the numbers system, assigning a different number to each person upon birth. They even had a spokesperson."

"Dr. Mark Shreveport," I say. We'd learned about this guy in school, a man of medicine who discovered the secret to learning the true lifespans of each individual human as it pertained to disease and natural causes. With a team of scientists and engineers, they developed a device that discovered each person's expiration date—at least, that's what we were led to believe. When the number devices became mandatory, a huge uprising followed. Our history books were filled with photos of protests and marches decrying the practice. It only took a few years for the numbers to become the norm. My generation, the Genesis Generation, was the first to be born into this practice, while our parents had memories of life before known expiration dates.

"The facilities became a way of monitoring those near the end," Thom continues. "Each number device has a needle inside, which injects the wearer with a highly concentrated dose of pentobarbital at the end of the countdown. Within seconds of injection, the wearer's brain functions slow down so much, they stop breathing. There's no chance of surviving. However, some people had become wise to what was going on, figuring out a way to remove the device as their number came close, and realizing they could live past their expiration. The government response was to secretly add a trigger to each device, forcing the needle to release early if tampered with."

"Then why do they still need to monitor us?" I ask.

"Because it's not foolproof," Thom says, pointing to the back of his neck as proof. He turns his head, and I can see that it's healed. "We got our hands on the magnetic key that safely removes these devices, and then copied it with a 3D printer. There's a group of us that have far exceeded our expiration dates. Some of us live off the grid in Armstrong Redwoods where your brother was captured, fighting the good fight to save others from an untimely death. The rest are in Cuba, the only country that refuses to go along with the numbers. They have asylum there, but Cuba is small, and the rest of the world has shunned the island, not allowing any kind of transmission to occur between the country and anywhere else. And because of its size, Cuba only allows a limited number of people in. You are one of those people, thanks to your brother."

"How could that be possible if he's been captured?" I ask.

"He secured your spot years ago, knowing the chances of him getting caught were high."

I wanted to ask why he'd risk any of this. Why wouldn't he just save himself by leaving the country for Cuba? But that would be ridiculous. Skye never played it safe. If there was a chance he could make a difference, he'd do it.

And I couldn't play it safe, either.

"Thom, we have to get the kids." I put my hands on my hips, matching his narrowed eyes.

"I told you, we're on a specific rescue mission. We can't risk losing you."

"But you can lose me, right?" Ryder cuts in. Thom tilts his head, appearing ready to listen. "Look, I agree that she can't get caught. But there's nothing stopping me from going on my own rescue mission."

"Unless it leads anyone to us."

"It won't. If I get caught, I get caught. All I'm asking is that you give me thirty minutes. If I'm not back before then, you leave without me. Deal?"

"We won't leave without you," I say. I look at Thom, and then Patrice. "Right?"

"Thirty minutes," Thom says, ignoring me. "When you get to the third floor, shoot out the cameras with this." He hands Ryder a gun with a silencer. "If it's your life or theirs, make sure it's theirs. Otherwise, the stunner will buy you the time you need without killing anyone. He places the silver stun device in his hand, then shows him how to use it. "That's all I can do to help you. Now hurry, or we're leaving without you."

Ryder turns to me, and his face appears blurry through my tears. I am so grateful he's risking everything to give the kids a fighting chance. I just don't know what I'll do if he doesn't come back. He could get caught. He could return too late. This could be the last time I'll ever see him.

"Please come back," I whisper.

"I promise," he says. I see it in his eyes, though—he's not sure. I throw myself in his arms and he wraps himself around me, pulling me in tight. "I'll be fine," he whispers into my hair. I lean back, looking into his eyes.

"I know you will," I whisper back, even though I'm unsure. I kiss him, not even caring that we have an audience, afraid I'll never feel his lips again, his arms around me, the smoothness of his skin, his heart beating against mine.

"All right, wrap it up. We have a boat to catch," Thom says. Ryder releases me, kissing my forehead before turning away. I watch him as he goes, but I'm distracted by the light heading our way from a fast-approaching boat. As it gets closer, I see Colby steering the motor. I also see Shane and Keith exchange a look as they adjust their bags.

No one is going to wait for Ryder. It's apparent. If I don't do something, we're leaving without him. I'll never see Ryder, Mila, or Devon again.

I break into a sprint as soon as the elevator doors open, reaching the inside of the car just in time. I hear Thom swearing as footsteps pound the concrete.

"Close it!" I scream. Ryder is already slamming his fist against the button. Shane races toward us, and I watch him until the doors completely close. I don't relax until we start moving. Ryder and I fall against each other, arms clutching, mouths searching, hearts racing.

"Why'd you do it?" he cries, tears streaming down his face. "It's a suicide mission. You know this, right? I can't guarantee I'll even make it to the kids. Anything can stop us. You were safe."

"They were going to leave without you." My own tears won't stop, and I wipe my eyes against his shoulder.

"You don't know that."

"I do," I insist. "I just do. But if I go with you, they won't leave. After all, I'm the mission, right?" He leans back and looks down at me. Then he shakes his head.

"You're something, all right," he says, then laughs. "I hate that you're here, and I'm glad you're here."

We reach the top floor. As soon as the door opens, I place a chair in the way to block the door so it can't return to the underground, and Ryder aims at the camera and shoots. I'm sure this only gives us a few minutes before someone notices. Are any of the nursing staff or security even awake? I have no idea. I suddenly realize just how in the dark we are. There's a plan in place and we know none of the details. Now, we're on a rescue mission that's sure to fail. Thom must have known it was going to fail. He didn't care because it was just Ryder. But now it's both of us, and I'm the vested interest. We're so screwed.

I try not to think of this as we quietly creep into the children's area. Twelve cots and the room is filled with the sounds of sleeping. The nursery door is ajar. Ryder follows close behind me as we creep to the door. Inside, Hannah is cradling Mila. I breathe a sigh of relief seeing the tiny body in her arms, drinking from a bottle. The aide looks up, her eyes widening when she sees me.

"What are you doing here? You're not supposed to be here."

I hold a hand behind my back, indicating to Ryder to wait where he is so she can't see him.

"I just wanted to see her," I say, stepping forward. She takes a step back, looking around. Judging by the nervous expression on her face, I figure she's the only staff member on this level. "Can't I just hold her?" I ask.

"I'm sorry, Noelle, but rules are rules. Now, please just go downstairs. I don't want to call this in, but I will if you don't leave."

I look down, making my face disappointed while I motion behind my back to Ryder. He rushes forward at the same time I do. He grips her shoulder just as she's about to scream. As she goes down, I take Mila from her arms. Hannah lies motionless on the ground, her eye wide open.

"No, *I'm* sorry, Hannah. You lied to me," I hiss. But I can't stay mad. Because of Hannah, I opened my heart to this precious baby. Once my heart opened, it wouldn't close. I let Ryder in and was finally able to look forward to every tomorrow I had left. I look down at Mila, her deep brown eyes shining in the low light of the nursery. This little girl gave me a reason to love, which gave me a reason to live.

"I'll get Devon, and then we can get out of here," Ryder says, stepping around me to move into the children's room. I follow him out, watching as he goes from bunk to bunk until he finally finds the boy. I watch as he rouses him, then whispers something in his ear. Devon reaches up, putting his arms around Ryder's neck. Ryder stands, holding Devon close to him in a bear hug, then joins me at the edge of the room. Both of us stop, surveying the cots.

"We can't leave them," I whisper. I look up at Ryder, who's already looking at me.

"I know," he says, a pained look on his face. Both of us are aware of the complications we're considering. Our rescuers only planned on the two of us, and we've just added a dozen. Sneaking out with this many kids could be dangerous. What if one of them cries? Fights us? Does anything that messes up the plan? Kids are unpredictable. We have less control over them. Their presence could mean all of our deaths.

But how will I feel tomorrow if we're safe, and they're not? There's no one to protect them if someone tampers with their expiration date. They could all be killed a number of ways, and no one would know any better. If I leave them, they're done for.

"You wake that side, and I'll start over here," I say. I move toward the first cot without waiting for him to respond.

14

Exodus

Noelle

∞

The elevator is packed as we take the long ride down to the underground. Everyone is crammed close together, foot to foot so we can all fit inside. We didn't go into detail with the kids about why we were leaving, and to their credit, they didn't ask. Most importantly, I lay out the rules to stick together and not say a word. The ride is silent as the number above our heads counts down to one and then continues to drop. We reach the underground, and my hands feel sweaty. I know we've exceeded our time limit, but I also know they'll wait. Being the pawn has its advantages—no one is leaving without me. But they also won't be happy when they see the extra baggage we've brought along.

Sure enough, Thom repeats some of the same words he used when I escaped into the elevator.

"Calm down," I say.

"No, you calm down," he shouts, which makes no sense because I am calm—at least on the outside. "What were you thinking? We have a boat that barely fits the nine of us, and you've brought…" He starts counting the kids. "Twelve kids and a baby? Seriously?" He shakes his head, his mouth set in a firm line. "No. We're not bringing them. They're staying here."

One of the girls clings to me, whimpering. I smooth her hair.

"No one is leaving you here," I say to her. Then I look at Thom.

"I'm not going if they can't go. You'll have to leave without us." I hold his stare, hoping he bends and doesn't actually leave us here. He can't. There's too much at stake if he leaves me.

Thom breaks eye contact first, and I know I have him. He breathes in deep, running his hands through his hair, glancing at Colby who's still sitting inside the boat. "I didn't want to do this," he says, and the next thing I know he's pointing a gun at me.

"Drop it," Ryder says from behind me, and I see his hand extended with the gun Thom gave him. "If you shoot her, I shoot you. But if you drop the gun, you'll live to see all of us get out of this cave alive. The choice is yours."

Thom's eyes never leave mine, and his gun remains trained on me. "She's too much of a liability if she doesn't come," he says, his eyes narrowing. I refuse to look away, trying to touch any humanity that exists inside him. As soon as I break eye contact, I know my life will be over.

"We can have it both ways," I say. "Take the kids, and you can have me, too."

"It's not that simple."

"But it is."

He won't let up. I prepare myself to die, but keep my eyes locked on his. We stay frozen, a few seconds feels like hours. He finally lowers his gun and I breathe a sigh of relief, releasing all my clenched muscles as he places the gun on the ground.

"Kick it over here," Ryder says, keeping his gun on Thom. He obeys, and I reach down to pick it up. I put the safety on, feeling strange as I maneuver a baby and a gun at the same time, then I stick it in the back of my pants. I hope I won't have to use it. If I do, I hope my childhood shooting range lessons will come back to me. For now, I just want to get out of this tunnel and on our way to safety. The longer we stay here, the more we open ourselves up to never getting out.

"We'll have to make two trips," Colby says, standing in the boat. "Noelle, Thom, bring half the kids with you, and then Ryder can follow with the rest of the kids, plus Patrice, Keith, and Shane."

"No. The kids will all go in the first ride."

"There's twelve of them," Colby argues.

"They can squeeze together. There's enough room."

"We're wasting time, just do it," Thom says. I begin ushering the kids on the boat, one by one. As they step on, Colby uses a part of the stunner to remove their numbers.

"Just go with them," I reassure the girl who's still clinging to me. "I'll be with you in a little while. I promise." She reluctantly lets go of me and joins the kids in the boat. Devon remains with Ryder, and I don't try to push him to join the others. I don't think Ryder would want that either. Mila stays secure to my chest, wrapped tight in a blanket.

I hear several booms in the distance, and my heart plummets. The rioting is getting closer. It probably means nothing for us right now, but our limited time is becoming more real.

"Go," I say to Colby, even though I'm not the one in charge. Not officially, that is. Ryder and I have turned the tables on their well-constructed plan.

"Stop right there!"

I whip around to see guards running from the other end of the tunnel. There's more of them than we have bullets. Ryder pulls his gun out, regardless, and I do the same. Out of the corner of my eye, I see Colby holding something in his hand. Everything goes in slow motion as I turn toward him and see what it is. *A grenade.*

"Run!" I scream, racing toward the narrow tunnel from where the boat came, holding Mila tight against my chest. I glance back to see if Ryder is behind me. He is, pulling

Devon with him. The blast pushes past us, and we fly forward. I land on my side, my body huddled around Mila. She's crying, letting me know she's still alive. I can't see anything in the pitch black.

"Ryder!" I pat the space around me, shrinking back when I touch someone.

"I'm right here," he says behind me. "Devon is, too. We're okay."

"Me too," a female voice says in the direction of the person I just touched.

"Patrice?" A light clicks on in her hands, and I see her face, covered in blood. "You're hurt! Are you okay?"

"I'm fine." She winces as she says it, then tries to put the headlamp on. After several attempts, she gives up and hands it to me. "Sorry, it's a little bit of a mess."

I wipe the bloody strap on my clothes and put the headlamp on. Then I shine it toward Ryder and Devon. They're both okay. An eerie crack sounds above and behind us, and I know the tunnel is getting ready to give way.

"Come on, come on!" I scramble to my feet, and start to run, Ryder and Patrice close behind. I cringe when I hear the crumbling. I don't know what this means for the facility, but if it goes down with the tunnel, we're done for. There's no way we can outrun that kind of destruction.

"It's three miles," Patrice gasps behind us. I know she's slowing, and I don't want to wait for her. I feel selfish, but I know we'll all die if she holds us up.

"Stay with us," I beg her.

"I am," she squeezes out.

We reach what I presume to be the halfway point before I slow to a walk. My adrenaline is at an all-time high, and I know I could run all the way to the end of the tunnel, even with Mila strapped to my chest. But we're far enough from the blast that even if the building did go, we'd be fine.

"Do you think the water is safe to drink?" Ryder asks.

"No," Patrice says, resting her head on her hand as she sits. "But I have a water bottle in my pack we can all share, plus purification tablets for later." She leans over while Ryder goes through her bag, producing both the bottle and tablets. We all take turns. I rifle through the diaper bag I packed for Mila, using some of the water to make her a bottle of formula. She takes greedy gulps, hiccupping in between as she recovers from crying.

"Poor girl," I say. Looking at her brings back everything that just happened, and the shock washes over me. *The kids.* "They're gone," I whisper. I look to Ryder, who's tending to Patrice. "It's my fault." I sink to the ground, cradling Mila as the panic speeds through my heart. "I killed them all."

"We don't know that," Ryder says, but his expression says otherwise. He touches my foot, but I pull away.

"It's true! If it weren't for me, they would all be warm in their beds and we would be a long way from here."

"They were going to start expedited expirations this week," Patrice breaks in. Even under the headlamp's dim light, her face is shockingly pale from running and loss of blood, and her hand trembles as she continues to hold her head.

"How do you know that?" I ask. She doesn't answer me, pulling a strange box from her vest pocket instead and bringing it to her mouth.

"Colby, do you copy?" It takes me a moment, but I realize she has a walkie-talkie, straight out of the 1990s, just like ones I'd seen in a magazine of classic toys. It seems so clunky and large, almost cartoonish.

"Colby, come in," she tries again. There's still no answer. I know it's pointless, that there's no way they survived that blast. As far as I can tell, Colby's grenade was a suicide bombing, meant to kill everyone so *their pawn* could get away. But still, the fact that Patrice is trying to reach him gives me hope.

"Colby, do you copy?" she repeats. Her voice echoes through the cave, and I hold my breath so I don't accidentally miss a sound. But nothing comes. Patrice looks at me. Her expression is even more tired. "I'm sorry," she says. My face crumples, the tears pouring from my eyes. That's when we hear it. Static. We all lean in closer.

"Patrice." It's faint, but I recognize Colby's voice. It takes everything I have not to cheer, but the grin on my face is in sharp contrast to my tear-stained cheeks.

"Colby, are you okay?" Patrice asks.

"Ask about the kids," I say, but she shushes me.

"We're fine. The explosion pushed…boat downstream. The passage…blocked, so we're…other direction." The static interrupts every other word.

"And the kids? Are they okay?"

There's more static. He's speaking, but this time we can't decipher it.

"10-9. Can you repeat that?"

"They're fine," he says through the static, and I pound the air with my fist. "I can't say the same for the soldiers, but we're all okay." He says something else underneath the static.

"Colby, you're breaking up," Patrice says.

He continues to talk, but we can't make out anything he's saying.

"Colby, come in." The static continues.

Patrice lowers her arm and rests her head against the wall, taking short breaths.

"We can stay here and rest for a while," Ryder says. She turns her head, taking a few more breaths before speaking.

"We can't," she says weakly. "I need to reach the team. They don't know about the change of plans, about the kids, or why all of us are running behind schedule."

"Can you radio it in?" Ryder asks. She shakes her head.

"No. This is a two-way. Wait…" She lifts her head, wincing with the movement.

"Just rest," Ryder says. "Tell me what you need."

"My bag," she says. "There's a radio in there that I took off a guard."

Ryder rummages through the bag, pulling out a radio with a clip on the back.

"Tune it to channel four," Patrice instructs. He does, then hands it to her. She speaks in what sounds like another language, but nothing I've ever heard before. She waits and then tries again.

"Code," she says to me in response to my questioning look. "If anyone knows about this ship, the whole mission is over." She kicks her foot on the ground. "Not that it matters. This tunnel is like a fortress. No radio waves can escape."

"But the walkie-talkie worked," Ryder points out.

"Because we're still in range," she says. "Our walkie transmits directly theirs when they're close enough. But to get the radio to work, it needs to be able to reach the tower, and that's outside the tunnel."

We rest for a little longer. Patrice is the one dictating the schedule, and in her defeat, she's making no more moves to stand. Her pale skin is shining with a layer of sweat. Every time I look at her, I can almost feel her discomfort. Her breathing eventually evens out, and she smiles at me when she catches me watching her. She's still bleeding, but since she's alert, I assume that's a good sign.

"Why was the facility going to kill the kids before their so-called expiration dates?" I ask. She turns to me, and I can't miss the pride in her expression.

"Rioters were targeting other facilities, finding their way in. They didn't know we were already on the inside. They'd planned on taking action before anyone could stop the process."

"But how do you know all this?"

"I became a shadow," she says, smirking. "I've been under the radar since I got here, which has allowed me to sneak into places I'm not supposed to be and hear conversations I'm not supposed to hear. They'd already started on the elderly, which I believe you noticed."

I recall the conversation I shared with Spring when I told her about the residents I'd noticed missing from our floor. "You were there."

"I was in the tree above you. No one saw me." She winces, closing her eyes in pain. She takes a few moments and then continues. "There's more. Nurse Sherry was offered a large sum of money to turn you over to The Enforcers. I heard her on the phone when she thought no one else was around. I heard every word. This was a few days ago, just after Skye's arrest. When the lockdown happened, we knew we couldn't wait any longer."

It was all too much. Everything was happening so fast.

"Just a few days ago, I thought I only had one hundred days left," I whisper.

"No one knows the day or hour when these things will happen," Patrice says. "No scientist, no engineer, no government or Enforcer. Only Infinity knows."

"You believe in Infinity?" I ask.

"With all my heart," she answers. "Don't you?"

"No," I say, but doubt washes over me. I've been wrong about so many things. "I don't know. It seems too...magical. Too convenient. Ryder, what about you?"

He looks over at me, appearing to mull over my words. Devon is leaning against him, his eyes closed, his chest rising up and down as he sleeps.

"I'd like to think there's more than just this," he says. "I don't really give it a lot of thought, though. I guess I just like the idea that we live forever."

"I'm not sure liking an idea and believing are the same thing," I say. His face breaks into a sheepish smile.

"Maybe you're right," he says. "But I can't believe we just stop existing when we die. There's something inside us, some kind of energy. When we die, I think that energy is free to return to the source, to join everyone else's energy, to finally be whole as we all join together. Maybe the only thing that keeps us separate is our bodies."

"It sounds like you've given this a lot of thought." I give him a pointed look, even though I like the things he's saying. Still, *liking and believing aren't the same things*. "We should probably keep moving. Is he getting too heavy? Should we trade?"

"Nah," Ryder says. "I got him. How about you, Patrice? Are you able to keep moving?"

"As long as we don't run anymore," she says. "Once we reach the other side of this tunnel, I can call for another boat that will take us to the sub."

"A sub? We're going down in a submarine?" I ask.

"It's the safest way," she says. "It's cloaked in a way that allows radars to believe they're passing through it when really they're going around it. The shield bends all transmissions, giving the illusion there's nothing there. We'll reach Cuba in just a few days, and no one will be the wiser."

My mind goes to Skye, locked up somewhere as they try to extract information from him. My stomach turns at the thought, a dull ache expanding in my chest as I realize the hell he's going through.

"What about my brother?"

Patrice grunts as she eases herself to her feet and pulls her backpack on. Her head has stopped bleeding, but a spidery red trail covers one side of her face. "We're working on that," she says, but she offers no other information.

We travel slower than before. I feel both dread and excitement over what lies on the other side of this tunnel. I'm not sure what to expect—it's either our road to freedom or we're running right into the enemy's hands. We travel in silence until the small red glow at the end of the tunnel grows larger. The rosy sunlight gives me hope, and I walk a little quicker to reach the end.

"Wait," Patrice says. We stop as she leans against the wall. "Things are different out there than they were before. People are angry and ready to fight. No one knows who the enemy is, and everyone looks like the bad guy. Are you still armed?"

"Yeah," Ryder says, flashing his gun. I pull mine from behind my back and then put it back.

"Be prepared to use them. I don't have one, but if you give me the stunner, I can use that. I'm probably just paranoid. There may not be anything to be worried about. But just in case, stand your guard."

We nod, and Ryder slips the stunner off his hand and gives it to Patrice. She pushes off the wall and staggers forward, and we follow close behind. The sunlight grows brighter as we get close, my nerves and excitement playing off each other. The headlamp is no longer necessary. I slip it off and hand it back to Patrice.

When we finally reach the end of the tunnel, it's disappointingly and thankfully underwhelming. The smoggy sky is an orangish-pink, the red orb of the sun flowing through the cloudy covering. The air is noticeably thicker, unlike the filtered air of the facility, but the soft breeze whispering through my hair and across my skin feels refreshing. A bird sings in a nearby tree, and it's absolutely breathtaking. I can't remember the last time I've seen a bird, having been cooped up in the dome for what feels like forever. I can't stop drinking in the world outside.

"Look, Devon," I say, holding Mila close to my chest so I can lean down and point at the bird. It tilts its red head toward us, seeming to survey us. Perhaps we look as strange to it as it looks beautiful to us.

A bullet whistles through the air out of nowhere.

"Patrice!" Ryder yells. I turn to see her on the ground, her neck gushing blood, her eyes wide open. I hug Devon, shielding his view of the gory scene. The radio is in pieces a few feet away. Another whistle, and cement flies off the entrance of the tunnel.

"We have to get out of here!" I grab Devon's hand and start running. Ryder doesn't follow. I turn and see him pulling the stunner from Patrice's grip. "What are you doing?" I scream.

"We might need it." He slips the backpack from her shoulders and then races toward me. We run together, trying to find someplace to hide. Bullets sail past us, ricocheting off the pavement. I get the sense they're trying to miss us. Their intent becomes clear when I see the armored truck stopped yards in front of us. They're shepherding us toward capture.

"This way!" I veer to the right and run through a courtyard. I clutch Mila's tiny body, cradling her head against my chest. All this running, and I pray I'm not jostling her too much. Ryder follows behind, Devon wrapped around his side. The bullets have stopped, probably because a building shields the sniper's path. But soldiers are now on our trail, their rustling gear giving them away as they run after us. I dive into a storm drain, landing hard on my knees. Ignoring the pain, I begin crawling with one arm, the other holding Mila against my chest. I pass rotting carcasses of rats, the smell turning my stomach. I don't let it stop me. Devon crawls behind me, in front of

Ryder. I have to hand it to the kid. This is more than he should ever have to go through, and he hasn't complained once. All it would take is for him to refuse to keep going, and we'd all suffer because of it. He's not giving up, though. He's crawling at the same pace as me, ready to do whatever it takes to get out of danger.

The drain widens enough that we can stand. Soon, we reach water and have to wade through it. I hoist Mila higher on my chest as the water gets deeper, trying not to think about what we're traveling through. Garbage and more rat carcasses line the edge of the water. If that's the worst of it, I can deal.

"Think we lost them?" Ryder asks. He's carrying Devon on his back, the boy's legs wrapped around his chest to keep from getting his feet wet.

"I hope so," I say. It seems they would have reached this part of the tunnel if we hadn't. "Do you know where we are?"

"No clue. But eventually, we have to reach some kind of water. I'm hoping it's a river and we can just travel downstream until we lose them completely."

I know it can't be far away because I can still see within the shadows. Sure enough, the light gets brighter and the end becomes visible. My heart sinks when it's apparent the end has been capped to keep the garbage from flowing through.

"We have to turn back." I want to cry. Every path seems to lead to a dead end.

"No, keep going," Ryder says.

"It's blocked off, though. We'll never get through."

"It's not permanently fixed," he says. "Trust me. I've been in one of these before. A bunch of friends and I found one when I was a kid. We used to jump off it into the water below, but we had to remove the cap first. I think one of the guys kept it as a souvenir. It makes for a great table."

We reach the end, and sure enough, the cap gives slightly when Ryder pushes against it. I take the other side and we both shove. The grate slips off the sides, disappearing from view as it falls. Both of us peer over and take in the rocky ravine.

"Now this...this is a problem," Ryder says. He looks at me, and then more pointedly at Mila. "Can you handle this with her? Want me to take her?"

I look down, unsure. "I think I'm okay," I say, but my voice wavers. Ryder clasps Devon's shoulder.

"What do you say, bud, ready to do some rock climbing?" Devon looks at the rocks and then grins up at Ryder.

"Are *you*?" He swings his legs over the edge of the drain before dropping to the rocks closest to us.

Ryder turns to me, rolling his eyes with a laugh. "That kid," he says. Then he motions at Mila. "Wrap the blanket around me. I'll carry her through this." I smile gratefully as he pulls Mila from the wrap. I pull it tight around him, triple knotting the ends. She's awake, and I know she'll be hungry soon. She also needs a diaper change. But we don't have time for that. I take Mila back from Ryder so he can drop below the drain. Once he's on the rocks, I hand her to him, ignoring her complaining cries. Once she's secure, I turn and climb out, my belly hitting the edge of the drain before I lower myself to the rocks. Devon waits until my feet hit the ground before he leads us down the ravine.

"Stay close," I warn him. "We're not out of danger yet."

We don't rest when we finally reach the water. I dig through the backpack at Ryder's back while we walk, pulling out a protein bar for each of us. I place a few tablets in the water bottle and then fill it with water. According to the package, we can't drink it for another thirty minutes, so I replace it in Ryder's backpack.

A helicopter's whirring blades overhead deflate my hope of escape. We run into the woods for cover, continuing our path along the water. The helicopter comes closer, the rhythmic pounding matching my rapid heartbeat. I finally see it circling above. It drops down toward the water, and we run deeper into the forest.

"How are they finding us?" I feel like the mouse in a cat's game of catch, and they're just playing with their food.

"I think I know," Ryder says. "Devon, come here." The boy comes close, and Ryder turns him around. His number stares back at me.

"They're tracking us," I breathe. Ryder takes a deep breath, holding the stunner close to Devon's neck. I'm suddenly grateful he thought to grab it. But I can sense his hesitation.

"Do you know how to use that?" I ask. He shakes his head.

"Not a clue. I wasn't paying enough attention."

"I think I was." He hands me the device, and I strap it to my palm. With shaky hands, I hold it over Devon's number. If I do this wrong, I run the risk of releasing the needle. I hold my breath and touch the stunner to Devon's number, and the magnet connects. When I pull away, the number comes with it. I exhale as Devon touches the back of his neck.

"It's itchy," he says.

"Try not to scratch it," Ryder instructs him, shooting me a grateful look over his head.

I do the same to Mila, my hands steadier now that I know how easy it is. We bury the numbers where we stand, then continue further into the forest. The sound of the helicopter fades as we go. I sense another danger, however, in the form of smoke.

"Do you smell that?" I ask Ryder. He sniffs the air, then nods.

"They're smoking us out," he says. "We need to move faster. Take Mila, and I'll take Devon." Once Mila is wrapped around me, we start jogging. The smell of smoke is faint enough, but we don't know how fast the fire is moving, or if we're heading right into their trap. It's hard to know where to go when we're not even sure where we are.

We see a house as soon as the first flames become visible. I race to the door, pounding on it to get the attention of whoever is inside. Several cars are in the driveway, and Ryder peers inside each one, looking for one that's unlocked while I continue knocking. I try the door, and it's locked. So I break the window with one of the potted plants and then reach around to unlock the door.

"Hello? Anyone here?" I yell. "You have to leave, the forest is on fire." I search the rooms, finding no one. Open suitcases and clothes are piled in the bedrooms, wine bottles and cheese plates in the kitchen, and an itinerary lies on the table. I glance at the clock on the wall, and then back at the itinerary. Everyone is at the lake for the day.

A key hook rests below the clock with several keys. I grab one and press the button, hearing a distinct double honk from one of the cars outside. I run out as Ryder is opening the door. The fire is kissing the trees closest to us. I toss Ryder the keys and climb into the passenger side. He throws the car in gear, and we speed down the gravel driveway. As I look behind us, the fire is just closing in on the house.

Journey

Ryder

∞

The view from my rearview mirror shows the black plume of smoke spreading across the sky like spilled ink, growing smaller as we drive further away. We're not out of the woods yet, so to speak. We stay silent as I drive. Noelle is likely thinking the same thing I am—without Patrice, we have no idea where we're going or what we're supposed to do. With no radio, the sub is no longer an option. Right now, we're just in survival mode. Once we reach safety, we can figure out the rest. Problem is, I'm not sure what safety is supposed to look like.

Devon is sleeping in the backseat, his head resting on his window. Noelle feeds Mila from the treated river water and formula. I keep my eyes on the road, hoping some sort of plan will manifest itself. I feel the weight of the situation on my shoulders. All of their safety depends on me.

My stomach drops when I see a line of cars stopped about a mile up the highway. I slow, my mind rolling through different scenarios as I realize it's a checkpoint. It's highly possible they aren't looking for us, that this is just a precautionary checkpoint tied to the protests and riots. However, none of us have numbers. If they look at the back of our necks, we'll be taken into custody immediately. Even if they don't initially think to check our numbers, they will when they notice Devon's dark skin and Mila's mocha complexion compared to Noelle's and my paler appearance.

I touch the map screen on the dash, keeping one eye on the road as I fumble with different route options.

"Here, let me help," Noelle says, expanding the map to show a different route. "Turn right here," she says.

"Where?" There's no road, not even on the map.

"Just turn," she says. I take a deep breath and crank the wheel, driving off the road and into the tall weeds that line the highway. A closer look at the map and I see where she's directing us. I keep driving, my speed at a crawl as I pray nothing is in my path. The weeds block our view in every direction except behind us, which is now mercilessly exposed after we mow it down. Every muscle in my body is tense as we keep moving forward, knowing we could still get caught by a sharp-eyed officer, or killed if this unplowed path leads us to a cliff. I don't fully exhale until my tires touch pavement once again.

"Left," Noelle instructs. I turn, and the roadway is clear, running parallel to the road we abandoned. I drive at a regular pace, keeping my head straight as we pass the checkpoint slightly above us. But my eyes follow the checkpoint until I can no longer keep watch. No one stops us. No one runs after us. We continue down the road as if we're a family of four on a Sunday drive—not one running for their lives.

"What now, navigator?"

Noelle grins beside me as she studies the map, making it smaller with her fingers so she can view more of it. She breathes in deep, and when I glance at her, her eyes widen.

"What?" I ask. She shakes her head.

"I might know where to go, but I'm not sure. For now, keep driving on this road until you reach the 'T.' Then turn left, then right so we're back on the highway."

She continues moving the map with her fingers. I can't help continuously watching to see what she's uncovered. After a while, she laughs, hitting the side of the door with her fist.

"What's wrong?" I ask.

"Not wrong. Right! Skye told me about this place, but I brushed him off. How much gas do we have?"

I check the gauge. It's about three-quarters full. "We probably have about four hours before we need to fill up if this car's mileage is anything like my old one."

Her brow furrows, her mouth puckered as she concentrates on the map.

"We might have to get creative on the way there," she says. I give her a sideways glance, and she slips me a smile.

"How creative?" I ask.

"Somewhere in between siphoned gas tank and brand new car. Have you ever—what do they call it—hot-wired a car?"

"Once," I admit. "It was a classic car from the '90s. These newer models make getting to the wiring almost impossible. But older models practically hand you the keys and pink slip. My friend's dad had this old 1998 Mercedes-Benz E-Class in his garage, and we stole it for a joyride. Jack and I figured it out together, going off a video on StreamTube. We were 14, and he made me drive. I'd never driven a car in my life. Still, we managed to put the car in neutral, drift it down the street, then hot-wire it till it sprang to life. We stayed out all night, though I drove at a snail's pace because I was too afraid of getting in an accident. I did pretty well until we got back to the house. I took off the whole side of the garage when I tried to pull it back in. I ran home, and my friend took the blame. He never even mentioned my name."

"You let your friend take the fall?" Noelle's eyes are wide, but she's practically laughing.

"Hey, I never claimed to be a nice guy," I say. "Besides, it was his idea and his dad's car. He didn't even get in that much trouble." I frown as the memory tugs at me.

"Why not?" she asks.

"He was gone a year later." It's like a knife to the gut every time I think of someone who's expired. So many people died needlessly because of The Enforcers. Jack could have grown up, had kids, and made something of himself.

"He had this thing for building." I try to hold back my emotions, but my voice cracks, giving me away. Noelle moves Mila so that she's sleeping in the crook of her right arm and then takes my hand in hers. "His house was filled with furniture he crafted on his own. Once, he even made a playhouse for his younger sister. If he'd been allowed to grow up, Jack would have probably built his own house."

She squeezes my hand, holding tight for a few seconds before letting her hand rest in mine. I brush my thumb over her fingers, soothing myself by the softness of her skin.

"We'll stop this," she says. "I don't know how, but we will. We'll be part of the movement. It's already started, thanks to Skye. It's not a secret anymore."

We reach Highway 5 a few hours later. Noelle is leading us to a forested area in Arizona. I didn't even know Arizona had forests. The state is a nightmare, and I'm not looking forward to it. My grandparents had once talked about Arizona as a tourist destination, telling me about the Grand Canyon, this natural phenomenon carved by the Colorado River. They'd gone camping in the first years of their marriage, spending their days hiking the cavernous landscape. I used to look at the photo album of their trip—this retro book with real photos under a plastic film—awed by the different shades and textures of the canyon and the vibrant colors of the sky. This was before the huge earthquake of 2025, when the canyon crumbled into the river, taking thousands of people with the destruction. The area had been overly developed with resorts and high-end hotels, and heavily trafficked by tourists. There had even been a gondola system arched across the canyon. The weakened landscape didn't stand a chance, and the canyon was reduced to rubble in a matter of minutes. The loss proved catastrophic for the state. Tourism stopped, and money ran out. Now, Arizona is a state rife with crime. If we can even make it across the California border with no money and limited gas, our survival in this sketchy state is slim.

I can't even focus on that yet. We've reached a stretch of highway that crosses open land. The next gas station is thirty miles away according to a sign I pass, and our gas tank is teetering on empty.

"Is there any food?" Devon asks from the backseat. I look at him through the rearview mirror, noting the bags under his eyes and the crease on his cheek from sleeping against the seatbelt.

"We can split the last protein bar," Noelle says. My own stomach has been rumbling for the last hour, and our limited food supply adds to my list of worries tumbling through my brain.

"You two split it," I say. "I'm getting kind of tired of protein bars."

"Sorry, we ran out of steak and eggs," Noelle teases. She halves the bar and hands a piece to Devon.

"Where are we going?" Devon asks, his mouth full.

"To a magical place called Arizona," Noelle says.

Devon nods as if he's heard of the place but then looks out the window because he obviously hasn't.

"We're going to have to stop soon," I say, nodding my head at the gas gauge. Noelle peers over my shoulder and winces.

"Is there a rest stop coming up?" she asks, even as she checks the map. "There's one about ten minutes away. Do you think we can make it?"

I shrug. "What then?" I ask.

"I don't know," she admits.

It's the longest ten minutes of my life. The car sputters as we reach the turnoff, and I coast the last dozen feet, stopping on the side of the road. We almost reach the parking lot. It doesn't matter; our use for this car is done.

I bring Devon to the bathroom while Noelle goes to the women's room. I'm so damn tired, I can't even think straight. The lack of sleep and hours of driving are catching up with me.

"When will we get to Risona?" Devon asks as he washes his hands. I smile at the way he says it. Another man comes out of one of the stalls, and I eye him carefully. I adjust Devon's collar as he holds his hands under the hot air blower, hoping the man doesn't notice our numbers are missing. A thought slowly crosses my mind.

"We still have a lot more driving," I say. "Hey, go wait with Noelle, okay?"

Devon skips out of the bathroom while I pretend to wash my hands.

"Cute kid," the man says. "Is he yours?"

"Yeah," I say. "I mean, he's my stepson. His mom passed away a few years ago, and he had no one to go to. I adopted him after her death."

"That's real noble of you," the man said.

"It's nothing. He's a great kid." I clap him on the shoulder as I pass him, and he crumples to the ground. "Sorry, man." I put the stunner back in my pocket, then drag the man into the handicap bathroom and lock the door. I go through his pockets, searching for his car remote, maybe some cash. Nowadays, no one carries cash. A few people do, but it's a rarity. Why carry cash when everything is on your ID bracelet? I eye the man's ID bracelet, tempted to take it. But what then? Once the man is reported missing, they'll ping his ID bracelet and we'll be found. I leave his bracelet alone and take his remote instead, hoping he has enough gas so I don't have to do this again.

Noelle is sitting on a bench with Devon when I come outside. Mila is crying, and Noelle jostles her lightly to try and soothe her. She looks up at me as I come close.

"I've changed her, fed her, everything," she says. "She's just so unhappy. Probably sick of this whole road trip."

"Join the club," I say. I hold up the car remote and Noelle's eyes widen. "We're changing cars. Wait here." I leave her and start searching the lot for the car that matches the remote, pressing the button and keeping an ear open to hear. There are only a few cars in the lot plus a semi-truck. I pray it's not the truck, and disappointment settles in the pit of my stomach when I hear the low beep as I get closer to it. Damn. He's a truck driver. There's no way I can blend in with the crowd in this huge monster, let alone drive it. I get up in the cab anyway, searching for something we can use. I find a cooler packed with food and a half-eaten candy bar on the seat. I eat the candy, relief radiating through me as the sugar hits my bloodstream. I leave the truck with the remote inside and head back for Noelle.

"What happened?" she asks. She's holding another bottle to Mila's mouth, who has quieted long enough to drink.

"He drives a semi. I'd rather wait for someone with a car that I know how to drive." I open the cooler and grab a sandwich off the top, then let Devon and Noelle at it. I can feel my tiredness leaving as the food hits my stomach.

"Here's someone." Noelle nods at a car pulling into the parking lot, taking a spot close by. I don't move, keeping my head low as I eat my sandwich, watching him leave the car and head for the bathroom. As soon as he's in the door, I set my sandwich down and follow him. He faces the urinal, his back to me, and I pretend to wash my hands again. My hands are probably cleaner than they've ever been inside a public restroom. He takes an abnormally long time to piss, and I can only wash my hands for so long before I look like a fanatic. I glance behind me, noticing his number. It's in the 900s. If he's on this stretch of highway, he's likely taking his own road trip, probably a bucket list kind of thing during his supposed final three years.

He finally finishes and stands beside me as I pretend to check my teeth in the mirror.

"I swear, road trip food is the worst," I say, glancing over at him. He nods, a friendly look of agreement on his face.

"I've had more junk food than I've had in my life," he says. He sticks out his hand. "Kevin."

My hands are still wet, and I dry them on my pants before taking his. "Jerrod," I say, giving him my father's name.

"Is that your family out there?" Kevin asks.

I nod, my nerves getting the best of me now that the plan's not spontaneous. I reach in my pocket just as a loud snore sounds from the handicap bathroom. I had almost forgotten the trucker was in there. Kevin turns to look as I reach in my pocket. Then I think better of it.

"Yeah, want to meet them?" I ask. Kevin looks back at me, a confused look on his face. "I mean, they've never met anyone from…where did you say you're from again?"

"I didn't," he says.

"Yeah, you did. Oregon, right?" I ask, recalling the state on his license plate.

"I guess I did," Kevin says, his face relaxing.

"Trust me, my wife will get a kick out of it. She's been bugging me to move there since the day we got married."

We walk out of the bathroom together. Noelle turns away quickly when she sees us walking together. I'm sure she's wondering what's going on.

"Amanda, sweetheart, this is Kevin. He lives in Oregon. You know how you're always saying you want to move to Oregon."

"Oh yeah," Noelle says without missing a beat. "They have so many more trees, and the housing prices are a bit lower there. I bet you live in a mansion, don't you, Kevin?"

He laughs and shakes his head. "Not exactly," he says. "But I do have some land. I have a picture of it on my phone." He searches his jacket pockets, then the back pockets of his pants. "Hm, I must have left it in the car. Wait here." He heads for his car, bending over the driver's side seat as he reaches for his phone. I'm right behind him. He drops inside the car, his knees hitting sidewalk when I clasp him on the shoulder.

"What the hell are you doing?" Noelle hisses as she rushes over. Devon follows behind, and I'm suddenly ashamed because he's witnessing this. I want him to always think of me as the good guy. I still have the gun Thom gave me, and I'd use it in a heartbeat if someone threatened us.

But this is different. Kevin is one of the good guys, I'm sure of it, and we're no better than low-life thieves right now.

"Hey bud, can you wait over there?" I ask. He looks confused at my request, and then his mouth sets as it becomes clear. He glares at me, and then heads for the bench, sitting and crossing his arms while he stares at his feet.

"How are we supposed to get him out of the car?" Noelle asks.

"We aren't." I head to the other side of the car and pull him into the passenger seat until he's in a sitting position. Then I strap his seatbelt on.

"This isn't funny." There's panic in her voice, and I know this must all look really strange to her. I close the door, and Kevin's head leans unnaturally against the window. I'll have to do something about that.

"I'm not trying to be funny," I say. "We need him." She opens her mouth to protest, but I place my hands on her shoulders. "Trust me, Noelle." She takes a deep breath, closing her eyes as I'm sure she thinks of a list of names to call me. When she opens her eyes, she appears a little calmer.

"Why do we need him?" she asks, each word enunciated slowly.

"Because we have twelve more hours of driving, and I can't do this again. We need money if we're going to make it to Arizona, and neither one of us has a cent to our name.

We're supposed to be dead in just a few months, everything we own has been given to family or charity. We don't exist. But this guy does, and he has an ID bracelet we can use to get gas and food."

"Then why can't we just take the...oh." She smiles sheepishly as the realization comes to her. "They'll track us once he wakes up," she says. I nod.

"I know taking a hostage is going to a new extreme, but we're on a life or death mission here. This guy could be our ticket out of here."

"And what happens when he wakes up?" she asks. I lift my shirt, revealing Thom's gun.

"He'll probably go along with the plan," I say. "I'm sorry he took the front seat, but I figure it will be easier for you to keep your gun on him from behind. You still have that gun, don't you?"

"It's in the backpack," she says, rummaging through it before pulling it out. She checks the bullets before snapping the safety back in place.

"Keep it handy, just in case." I look over at Devon, who's kicking the ground. I know he's refusing to look at me, even as he's well aware that I see him. "I'll be right back."

Devon doesn't speak when I sit next to him, just continues to scuff his shoes on the concrete. I keep quiet, sitting back on the bench next to him. I swing my feet in the same rhythm he is, hitting my feet on the ground just like him. It takes a few minutes for him to realize what I'm doing. He puts his hand over his mouth until his smile disappears, then turns away from me. I rub his back, expecting him to jerk away, relieved when he doesn't.

"I'm not perfect," I tell him. Devon doesn't move, but he stays still, listening to what I'm saying. "I used to think my dad was perfect, that he always knew the perfect things to do or say. I felt safe with him because he was in charge. I didn't have to think about where my food came from, how the bills were paid, or worry about my safety because my dad was there to worry about it, and he always had the answers. It wasn't until I got older that I realized he didn't always have the answers. There were some tough times when I was a kid, and I didn't know because my parents hid it from me. I always had food, but sometimes they didn't. When my dad was in between jobs, I didn't know that he'd borrowed money from my aunt so we wouldn't lose our home, or that other kids didn't get their clothes from the secondhand store. When he did get a job, I didn't know that he took on extra hours so that I could continue my swim lessons. I also didn't know that my dad hacked into my aunt's account and stole money from her, even after she helped him out." That had been a shock to learn, that my perfect dad was far from perfect and that his mistake was mine to repay when I was left in her care. "My dad wasn't perfect, Devon, and neither am I. That guy out there? I'm doing something wrong, and I hate that you have to see this. But I'm doing this because if I don't, all of us will be in much worse danger. I have to do one small, wrong thing to make things extremely right. Does that make sense?"

Devon turns to face forward, still not looking at me, but not looking away, either. He swings his legs again, but he doesn't look angry anymore.

"That's why I made you come over here," I continue. "It's not because I don't want to include you, or that I want you out of the way. But I don't want you to see me when I'm doing something bad."

He nods, keeping quiet for a moment. Then he looks up at me.

"Is he dead?" he asks. I shake my head.

"No, he's just sleeping. He's going to come with us, and we're going to do everything we can to make sure he stays safe."

"Promise?"

"I promise we'll try," I say. "But you need to know, this isn't the last time you might see me doing something that feels wrong. Remember all those soldiers who were chasing us?" He nods. "If we get chased again, I might have to kill people, but only to make sure we stay safe. You might see some scary things before this trip is done, but please understand that everything I do is to keep you safe." I wrap my arm around his shoulder and he leans into me. I kiss the top of his head.

"Thanks, Ryder," he says, putting his arms around my waist and squeezing. Then he hops up and heads for the car, getting in the back seat and shutting the door as if this has been our car all along.

Risona

Noelle
∞

Kevin likes country music, judging by the stations he has programmed into his satellite radio. He snores lightly while Ryder tries to find a different station. His head rests against the pillow I found in the trunk. I also found his suitcase, a tent, and a sleeping bag, plus a box of food that ensures we won't go hungry. Most of it is junk food, but I decide this really isn't the time to worry about nutrition. The paperwork on the floor of the passenger side shows that he has a reservation tomorrow for a campground in San Diego, which coincides with everything he packed. I'm not sure if the place will just brush it off when he doesn't show up, or alert his family—if he has any family. I don't want to find out. With any luck, we'll be in our safe place in Arizona, and Kevin won't be anywhere near us when they do discover his absence.

"Did you want me to take over driving?" I ask. I've noticed the dark circles under Ryder's eyes, and that he's jerked the car back on the road more than once. "I don't know how long this guy will sleep, but this might be your only chance to get some rest."

"I think we have at least three more hours," he says, putting his blinker on and drifting to the side of the road. "That would be amazing."

"Well, it won't be fully amazing," I say, shifting Mila in my arms. "You'll have to hold Mila while you sleep."

"Even better," he says, looking back at me with a grin. "She'll help me sleep like a baby."

"Let's just hope she stays asleep," I say. We trade spots and I get in, pushing a button so that the car seat and mirrors adjust automatically to fit my height and body size. Ryder has Mila secured in the blanket wrap so she won't fall if he completely loses consciousness, and maybe she'll even sleep more soundly. I look forward to the days when she's awake more than she's asleep, but for now, this is extremely convenient.

I merge back on the highway and then coast with traffic. We'll be on this road for at least as long as Kevin is asleep. There won't be another turn off for several hours, making the map unnecessary. As I turn it off, I realize we'll have to memorize it at some point. If our plan is to let Kevin out before we reach the place Skye told me about, the last thing we need is to lead him—and any authorities he alerts—directly to us.

"It would almost be easier to kill him," I whisper, then I glance in the rearview mirror at Devon, hoping he didn't hear me. It's silly to shield the eight-year-old from any of this. He ran from a bombing, almost saw his friends die, he's been shot at, and now he's sitting in a stolen car with an unconscious hostage. "How are you doing, Devon?" I ask him. He keeps his eyes on the road.

"Good," he says, his tone dull. He hasn't warmed to me as he has to Ryder. It's enough that he's talking to me at all.

"This has been kind of a crazy couple of days, hasn't it?" He nods while I'm still looking at him, apparently done talking.

I turn the radio up, landing on some classic rock station as a Coldplay song ends, followed by an oldie by Taylor Swift.

"What kind of music do you listen to?" I ask Devon. He tears himself away from the window and looks at me with a blank stare. "Do you listen to music?" He shrugs but doesn't offer anything. I feel ridiculous. I'm trying to forge this connection with him when we're not even facing each other. I should probably just let him stare out the window and keep to myself.

"I don't know what it's called," he says, breaking his silence. "My...my mom and dad always listened to her."

"Can you hum one of the songs, maybe?" I turn the radio off so I can hear him. He starts to hum, and I have no idea what he's singing. Then his humming turns into broken lyrics.

"At last…the skies…blue…" he sings, and I laugh.

"Wow, that's reaching back!" I touch the button on the radio. "Play Etta James," I say, and instantly, "At Last" fills the car. Devon grins in the back seat, but I don't miss that his eyes are shining. His little voice sings under the music, carrying the words he knows while he hums the rest. His cheeks are soon streaked by tears, but the smile remains on his face. I can't imagine what it's like to be him, to live without his parents for almost longer than he knew them. I'm sure he's thinking of them now, Etta James' voice pulling at memories of a time before death was familiar.

The song ends, and Devon wipes his eyes. He takes a deep, shuddery breath, appearing less stony than before.

"No more," he says as the next Etta James song starts. I switch it back to the station I was on before, and Beyoncé lightens the mood.

"Did your parents listen to that song a lot?" I ask. He nods.

"It was the last song I remember listening to with them," he says. "Before they…" He pauses, his voice cracking.

"Before they died?" I ask, and he nods. "Was it playing when you all…" I hesitate, unsure whether to continue. He nods again, and I feel hollow in the pit of my stomach, like a black hole is absorbing pieces of me. "I'm so sorry, Devon."

"It's okay," he says, looking out the window again. "Sometimes…" He takes a deep breath. "Sometimes I forget what they look like. But that song helped me remember."

We split a bag of chips from the trucker's stolen lunch, passing the bag back and forth until it's empty. Shortly after, Devon falls asleep against the window, leaving me alone with the road and my thoughts.

"If you ever find yourself in trouble, this is where you need to go," Skye said, pointing to a spot on the map splayed out between us. We were supposed to be helping my parents plan their Day 101 party, which felt morbid and awful all at the same time. But Skye had pulled me aside, insisting I pay attention to this archaic document. The fact that he had a paper map amused me, but his face showed no sign of humor. He told me he was afraid of being watched if he used the map on his phone, and I'd rolled my eyes as his weirdness shone through. It was common knowledge that anything we did on the internet could be seen through tracking, but I highly doubted anyone was paying more attention than just seeing how they could advertise to us.

"You're not that important, Skye," I said. "The government is not keeping tabs on any maps you look at."

"You'll see," he said. "I wish you were right, but you're not."

"You're just one in billions of people. You actually think what you do matters to the government?"

"More than you know."

The traffic slows to a crawl as we near Santa Clarita. I take the opportunity to turn the dashboard map back on so that it shows the rest of the route to our destination. We have roughly nine hours of driving left, according to the map. I magnify it, turning it on satellite mode. As far as I can tell, it's just a sparsely forested area of Arizona, no structures to be seen. The roads are so faint, I'm surprised there's even a route that follows them. Over the next hour, I take the time to memorize every turn, quizzing myself repeatedly until I can dictate the route from memory. Then I delete the coordinates from the map, plugging in a new location before turning it off completely. If we get caught, if Kevin snoops, if the government is paying attention, the only location this map will show is one that is thousands of miles away from where we plan to end up.

Ryder stirs as I pull into a gas station in Indio. I'm busy unfastening Kevin's ID from his wrist as Ryder stretches in the back seat.

"That was exactly what I needed," he says, moving carefully under Mila as he takes his seatbelt off.

"I can keep driving," I say, opening my door with the bracelet in hand. He shakes his head.

"I'm good now. Besides, we need to start thinking about how to secure Kevin before he wakes up. The last thing I need is for him to cause an accident."

He meets me at the pump, folding me under his free arm, cradling Mila in the other. I rest my forehead against him, ready for all of this to be over. When I look up, he presses his lips to mine.

"There's rope in the trunk," I say. "It's with his camping gear."

"You say the most romantic things."

I swat him while he ducks, then take Mila from him. I never fully appreciated how much juggling moms do when they have babies. Somehow I manage to fill the gas tank and keep Mila asleep at the same time while Ryder rummages through the trunk. He throws the rope in the back seat, then heads into the convenience market with the bracelet, returning ten minutes later with a bag of groceries.

"You know, there's a ton of food in the trunk," I point out. He wrinkles his nose.

"If you're into eating Twinkies and soda the rest of the trip, go ahead. If not, I got all of us a sandwich. I even got one for Kevin when he wakes up."

"You're the nicest kidnapper I've ever known," I say.

"Have you known many kidnappers?"

"You're the first."

"Then the standard's pretty low," he says.

Devon and I take a bathroom break, and then Ryder takes over driving while I feed Mila from the back seat. Devon sits next to me eating his sandwich, a weird combination of jelly and lab turkey. At some point, Ryder managed to figure out all of Devon's favorite foods, and they're nothing I ever would have guessed. Like M&Ms and soda. I like both, but never together. Devon is apparently into strange combinations.

We drive to a secluded street lined with warehouses. There's no foot traffic, so it's the perfect place to tie a person up without getting caught. Ryder uses this as a teaching moment to Devon, first telling him that this is not something he should ever do, and then demonstrating a few knots he learned in Boy Scouts. I stand by amused, the bottle at Mila's mouth as I watch alongside Devon. I wait for Ryder to sit back and let Devon try a few knots, but he doesn't. I suppose having an eight-year-old tie up our hostage would be crossing a few lines. By the time Ryder is done, Kevin is pretty much stuck there for life.

"How is he going to go to the bathroom?" I ask.

"We'll have to get creative, I guess," he answers, stealing my line. I don't even want to ask what that means.

Kevin doesn't stir until we reach the border. He groans, moving his head against his pillow. Then he vomits. Ryder swears, taking the next exit so he can pull over. I open my window, doing my best to take only small breaths. Regardless, the sour smell permeates the car, turning my stomach. As soon as the car stops, I unbuckle and get out, retching in the dirt as I hold Mila against my chest in the wrap. Devon leaves the car, too, but seems more interested in what's going on than grossed out.

"Where am I?" Kevin moans. "Why am I tied up?" When I look over at him, he's struggling against the rope. It appears most of the vomit hit the blanket we draped over him to hide his bindings. I try to reclaim control of my stomach, feeling guilty as Ryder handles Kevin on his own.

"You're in the desert," Ryder says from inside the car. I can see the sunlight glint off his gun, even though Kevin isn't going anywhere.

"You're that guy! From the rest stop!" Kevin yells, and I hear rattling as he tries even harder to break free. I push down my nausea and pull my gun from behind my pants. I keep the safety on as I train it on Kevin, moving to a place where he can see me. "And you're his wife!"

"Not exactly," I say, and then release the safety and aim at his head.

"Oh shit," Kevin moans, squeezing his eyes shut, preparing for the worst.

"We're not going to kill you," Ryder says. Kevin opens one eye, looking at me and then the gun in my hand.

"You're not?" he says.

"Not if we don't have to. But if you make things difficult, we'll have no choice."

Kevin seems to accept this, then looks down at the vomit-covered blanket on top of him. His face looks pale, and I'm afraid he's going to throw up again.

"Get that blanket off him," I say, and Ryder slips it off and throws it to the ground.

"Keep your aim." Ryder moves to the back of the car while I keep the gun pointed at our hostage. Devon stands near his door on the driver's side, watching everything with wide, interested eyes.

"Sweetie, come over here where I can see you," I say. Kevin turns his head to Devon, and then to the small lump Mila is making in the blanket wrap at my belly.

"You guys are terrible to bring your kids into this," he says, narrowing his eyes at me.

"Sir, we're doing this *because* of the kids," I say, refusing to let his words penetrate me.

Ryder covers Kevin with the sleeping bag, tucking it around him as if he's tucking him into bed.

"Are you hungry?" he asks Kevin. The man doesn't speak, staring off into the distance in defiance. But then he looks at Ryder.

"I have to go to the bathroom," he says. I groan.

"I knew it," I say. Ryder shoots me a look, then turns back to Kevin.

"Number one, or number two?" he asks. Kevin glares at him.

"I have to piss."

Ryder nods. He removes the covering and then looks around the back seat for something. I keep the gun on Kevin, but my eyes on Ryder, wondering what he's up to. Ryder re-emerges with an empty bottle.

"All right, you're going to have to trust me on this one, Kevin," he says, taking the lid off the bottle. I smother a smile, realizing what he's going to do. I'm glad I get to hold the gun and not the bottle.

"Wait, no. You're not coming anywhere near my… You can't." Kevin pulls again at the ropes, but Ryder's Boy Scout knots remain tight.

"It's either this or piss your pants," Ryder says. "Your choice."

Kevin looks down, and I realize he's concentrating. He's going for the latter; he's actually going to pee in his pants. I shake my head, dreading the rest of the ride in a stinky car. But then Kevin looks up.

"If you cut off my dick, you might as well kill me," he says. Ryder laughs, bending to unzip Kevin's pants.

"Dude, I'm not interested in dismembering you or even hurting you. As far as I'm concerned, you'll be free in a few hours and we'll be far away from you. Now hold still and try not to pee on me."

I keep pointing the gun at Kevin just in case he tries anything funny, but I focus my eyes somewhere just past him. It takes a few minutes, but I eventually hear the sound of liquid filling plastic. I'm impressed; this couldn't have been easy.

Once on the road, Ryder lets Kevin in on what's going on.

"So you're saying the numbers aren't real?" Kevin asks. Ryder turns and points to the wound at the back of his neck where his number once was. "Shit, man!" Kevin exclaims. "How did you do that? I thought it killed you if you tried to remove it."

"It does," Ryder says. "Unless you have a device to remove it." He fishes in his pocket and then pulls out the stunner. "This is what I used to put you to sleep," he says. Kevin jerks toward the window. "Relax, I'm not using it on you. But I can take your number off. I see you only have about three years left, is that right?"

Kevin looks out the window. I see the number on the back of his neck. 973.

"Two and a half," he says. He sighs, and I know exactly how he's feeling. The dread before the one hundred-day mark is actually worse than being locked up in the facility, on countdown to expiration. It's in those final hundreds when the unknown is scarier than the actual end, trying to figure out everything you want to experience before you can never experience it again.

"You can live longer than that," Ryder says, holding up the stunner. Kevin looks at him, then eyes the device.

"You'd do that for me?"

"Kevin, I'd do that for everyone. That's our goal. One way or another, we're ending this. It's time we stood up to The Enforcers and take back our country. This whole population control ruse has gone on long enough." He waves his hand. "Just say the word, and I'll do it."

"All right," Kevin says, turning his head again and leaning as best as he can while bound. Ryder keeps one hand on the steering wheel, and with the other, holds it against Kevin's number. The number hits the back of the seat before dropping to my feet, revealing a raw patch on Kevin's neck, just like the rest of us. I pick the number up cautiously, avoiding the needle folded inside, and toss it out the window.

"There. Now you can live forever," Ryder says.

I can see Kevin's grin reflected in the side view mirror.

The red Arizona hills eventually give way to cityscape, the traffic slowing down as we get closer to Avondale.

"Are we in Arizona?" Kevin asks. I hear the fear in his voice, matching the vibration in my nervous knees. My gaze lands on a man with a thick beard, a rifle slung over his back like a satchel. He's looking around him with crazy eyes, and I turn my head before he can see I'm watching him. "Don't make eye contact with anyone," Kevin warns.

"What do you know about Arizona?" Ryder asks.

"A lot. I grew up here. I escaped a few years ago, but it wasn't easy. We're actually just a few miles from my old house."

Devon is still looking out the window, and I touch his hand. "Don't look out the window until I tell you that you can."

"Why not?" Devon asks.

"There's a lot of bad people here," Kevin says from the front seat. "If someone sees you looking at them, they might not like it. They could shoot you, or rob you, or any number of other things. It's best not to draw attention to yourself."

We stay silent, facing forward like robots. It's so tempting to turn, especially as the activity on the sidewalks surrounding us increases the further into town we drive. A gunshot blasts to my right and I duck down, taking Devon down with my hand.

"It's nothing," Kevin says. I can hear the fear underneath his tone, barely noticeable, but enough to keep me on edge. "It's just some guy shooting out windows on the building."

We can't get out of this town fast enough. "Is all of Arizona like this?"

"It's bad," Kevin says. "But Avondale is probably the worst of it. At least, that's what it was like when I lived around here."

The stoplight is red in our direction, even though there's hardly any traffic. The only car I've seen moving on the street is ours and the one stopped in front of us. The rest are lining the side of the street, their tires missing, windows smashed, doors removed—it looks like someone took a baseball bat to each car down the line, taking out their aggression on glass and steel.

"Just move around them and go," I say, nodding at the car still idling at the stoplight. "It's not like there are any cops around here to stop you."

Ryder puts the car in reverse but then parks it again when he looks in the rearview mirror. I start to ask what's going on, but he puts his hands above his shoulders.

"We have trouble," he says.

I jump when I see a body move past my door, matching the shadow that crosses on the passenger side.

"Get out, all of you!" a man roars outside the car. He starts to open the door, but it's locked. He lifts the bat in his hand, and Ryder flings his body to the side to avoid the glass that showers him. His door opens and he's dragged outside.

"Ryder!" I scream, but I don't have enough time to say anything else before I'm showered in glass. I'm yanked out of the car, a large hand covering my mouth as I clutch Mila against my chest. The hand is replaced by a cloth, and I try to hold my breath. The smell overwhelms me anyway, and I'm falling

falling

falling....

Captured

Ryder

∞

I'm in the swimming pool. My pool. No, it belongs to someone else now. But it still feels like my pool. Except the pool water is thick. It keeps pulling me down. I'm trying to breathe, but I'm swallowing water instead. I try to grab hold of the side, but my arms won't move. I'm slipping under the water, and my head feels light, floating, peaceful. There's nothing to worry about. If I just stop fighting, everything will be all right. *Let go.*

"No!" I scream. I open my eyes as a bucket of water flies into my face. I sputter as laughter surrounds me. "Noelle!"

"Your girlfriend is fine," a deep voice says. "She's more than fine."

I realize I'm tied to a chair that's lying on its side. I move my head, looking into the face of the man speaking to me. He looks like he's lived in the sun his whole life. His skin is a reddish brown, almost black, his cheeks pockmarked, his eyes red around black irises. He wears a cowboy hat over a bandanna, just like the field workers did back home, but he doesn't look like he's been plowing any land. His hands are bruised, and he cracks his knuckles while meeting my stare. His lips are chapped and split in the middle, but that doesn't stop him from giving me a wide, leering smile, revealing a mouth of rotten teeth.

"You leave her alone," I say. He responds by kicking my forehead. My neck cracks involuntarily as my head snaps back, my ears ringing from the blow.

"We're in charge, hero," Cowboy says, then nods at someone behind me. I'm lifted to a sitting position, which makes my heavy head spin even more. Now I can see the cage that's behind him. Noelle is lying on the ground, still unconscious. Kevin is sitting against a wall, untied and rubbing a bleeding wound on his cheek. Devon is also sitting, his back straight, his eyes wide. Mila isn't in the cage, and an icy tremble grows inside me, afraid of what happened to her. I lock eyes with Devon, wishing I could tell him it will all be okay. I don't know if it will.

"Hey buddy," I say. His eyes glisten, and his lips tremble. "Hang in there. We're going to get out of here." I'm met with a slap across the face, which is better than being kicked but still hurts like hell. The pain goes all the way to the bone. The man peers at me, his face inches from mine.

"Don't make promises you can't keep," the man says, the decay of his mouth meeting my nose. I look beyond them, still searching for the baby. I finally see her in one of the men's arms. He's cradling her, but his face appears amused when he sees me watching them. He places his massive hand on Mila's head, his fingers curling around her skull.

"All I have to do is squeeze," the asshole says, tightening his hand. I feel helpless as Mila starts to cry.

"Not yet," the man in front of me bellows, and the Massive Hand releases his grip. "We might need her to help our friends talk."

His intention is clear. They can torture me all they want, kill me even. But I couldn't handle it if they killed Mila, Devon, or Noelle, especially in front of me. I keep my reaction in check, but inside, I'm cowering.

Noelle moans, curling into a tighter ball. One of the guys kicks the bars, and the sound echoes off the concrete walls. Noelle looks up, appearing drunk as she tries to keep her eyes open and head straight. My soul aches as I watch her gradual realization that Mila is missing. She looks down at her chest, then around the room. Suddenly alert, she wobbles to her feet, nearly falling as she clings to the bars.

"Where's my baby?" she forces out, her voice weak even with her resolve. She finally sees me in the chair, and her eyes widen. I nod at the man holding Mila, and she follows my gaze. "Give her back," she pleads.

"Not yet, princess. We have some questions, and your boyfriend's answers could decide whether you die quickly or slowly." Cowboy peers into my face, blocking my view of Noelle. "We'll start with an easy one. What are you doing in our town?"

"It's a free country," I mutter. The words are barely out of my mouth before he's on me, a knife at my neck. My heart is racing. I know he could kill me without thinking twice. But will answering him really help our situation? We're going to die no matter what. I'm afraid to answer even the simplest questions because I don't know if I'll be able to keep anything inside. *Please kill me quick.* It's the only thing I can think right now.

"All right, hero, here's another question. How come none of you have numbers?" Cowboy presses the knife to my skin. I stay silent, even as I feel the tip pierce me. The pain doesn't compare to my throbbing head. Cowboy mutters under his breath, releasing me. "Get the baby," he calls over his shoulder.

"No!" Noelle screams.

"Shut her up!" The man closest to the cell nods at Cowboy, then slams his gun against Noelle's fingers gripping the bars. She cries out, dropping to her knees.

I hear Kevin consoling her. I'm relieved he's there, despite the irony—a captive taking care of his former captor. I won't look up, though. I see the boots of the man holding Mila, and my stomach turns, afraid of what they're going to make me see.

"Last question." Cowboy kneels down so that I'm looking at him. I wonder what he'd do if I let loose the contents of my stomach. Already, I can feel the familiar pain, the dizziness in my head, the nausea building a tunnel in my throat. "Where are you headed?"

This is the one question I can't answer. If I say anything, I'll lead them right to the very people who can stop The Enforcers. I'm nobody. None of us are necessary when it comes down to it. But if these assholes find the safe house, the entire mission will go up in smoke. Billions of people could die if I open my mouth.

I shut my eyes, holding my breath as I wait for the inevitable. The baby is screaming, and I don't know what they're doing to her. I don't want to know. Cowboy is on me again, forcing my head up.

"Look at her," he hisses in my ear. "I want you to watch her die."

"We're going to Cedar Grove," Noelle cries out. My eyes fly open.

"No!" I can't see her around Massive Hand, though I'm relieved to find that Mila's unharmed. She's mad, probably hungry and uncomfortable. But so far, she hasn't been hurt. "Don't say anything else," I command Noelle. Cowboy releases me, stalking over to the cell.

"What do you know about Cedar Grove?" he demands. "Who told you about it?" Massive Hand has moved out of the way, and I note the defiance in Noelle's eyes. Her fear has been replaced with steely determination. I have a newfound respect for this woman's strength. I already knew she was tough. But faced with threats toward Mila, I don't think any of us would stand a chance against Noelle—bars or no bars.

"My brother," she says. "Skye Edison. Perhaps you saw him on the evening news the other night."

Cowboy glances over at the man with the gun guarding the cell. "Keys," he says. The guard tosses them to him, and Cowboy puts the key in the lock. He pauses before turning.

"Don't do anything funny," he commands. He unlocks the door and eases it open. "Just you. The other two stay in here." He tilts his head in my direction. "Moe," he says to Massive Hand. "When we're gone, untie her friend and lock him up with the others."

I internally panic. *Gone?* Where is he taking her? What will he do to her?

Cowboy closes the cell again, once Noelle is out, locking it and handing the keys back to the guard. He takes Mila from Moe's arms and hands her to Noelle, a move that confuses me. Noelle and I lock eyes. She's not afraid. She's going to tell him everything. There's nothing I can do.

Once in the cell, I sit next to Devon on the bench. My head is throbbing, my body aches, and I'm sure my face is a mess. Still, Devon leans into me without hesitation, throwing his arms around me and burying his head in my side.

"I'm sorry we dragged you into this, bud," I say, rubbing his head. I don't know what else to say. I'm conflicted about how to feel. If we'd left him, he would have died in two weeks, just like his number dictated. No. He would already be dead, thanks to the expedited expirations Patrice told us about. So, it's good that we saved him. But now, we're probably going to die in this concrete cell. I've made Devon's final hours a living hell.

"Think we'll survive this?" Kevin asks, almost as if he's read my mind. He scoots over to us. I shrug. We all know the truth, even Devon. But I can't bring myself to say it in front of him. I don't want to shred any hope he has left.

"We might," I finally say.

"What's Cedar Grove?" Kevin asks. I eye the men guarding our cell. Does it matter if I say anything now? I don't know what Noelle is saying, but I'm certain it's the truth.

"It's just some place." I eye Kevin, and he nods after a second, seeming to understand my hesitation to speak. It all feels trivial, but if there's any chance that Noelle is changing her story, I don't want to be the one to blow our cover. "Look, I'm sorry for kidnapping you," I say. He smirks.

"Obviously crime doesn't pay," he says, which makes me laugh.

"I guess not." We're both quiet for a moment. There's a clock ticking somewhere in the room, counting down the seconds of my life. *Click. Click. Click.* The guard taps his gun with the rhythm, occasionally whistling some song that's in his head. A faucet drips across the room, a hose— the same one they used on me—attached loosely and draped over the sink. We're surrounded by rows of shelving. I realize we're in some sort of warehouse.

"Can you at least tell me your name?" Kevin asks. "I know Noelle's now, and you know mine. But I don't know yours or the kid's."

"Ryder," I say. "And this is Devon. The baby's name is Mila."

"Ryder," Kevin repeats. He sticks out his hand. "Nice to meet you, Ryder and Devon, I'm Kevin." We shake hands. "I get the feeling you're not really a bad guy," he says. "At least not like these guys. Can you at least tell me why you took me hostage? I'd like to know something before I die."

I release Devon. His head continues to rest on my side as I lean back against the bars.

"We escaped from a facility," I say. "You know, one of those places people stay at in their last one hundred days. Noelle and I arrived on the same day. I knew something was off, though. I have for a while." I pause, looking around at the men surrounding our cell. Screw it. So what if they know? The guy with his back to us has only 243 days left; I'm sure the truth would be of some interest to him.

"We discovered the numbers were fake," I say. I can almost see our guard's ears perk up. He's stopped tapping his gun and whistling, but his back still faces us. "There was a group in there ready to break us out. They wanted Noelle, specifically. Her brother is part of—" I pause, realizing I'm treading on secret information these other guys shouldn't know. "At any rate, we were able to escape. Unfortunately, we don't have anything to our names. No money, no phones, no car, no home, nothing. As far as the world knows, we're as good as dead. We stole one car until we ran out of gas. With no money, we had to steal another car and, well, you. We needed your ID because it's a long drive and I didn't want to steal anything else."

"Were you going to kill me?" he asks.

"If we had to," I say honestly. "But I didn't want to. We were going to let you out after getting gas again."

He nods, looking at his feet. Then he looks back up to me. "I was going to kill myself," he says.

"What?"

"My wife left me last year. The closer I got to my date, the harder it was. She tried to support me, but I guess it was too much for her. I stopped working. I didn't leave the house. I couldn't enjoy anything, knowing I only had a short time left. Anytime something good happened, I couldn't shake off the feeling that it all had an expiration date. A limited number of holidays, time with friends, or even the small stuff like my morning coffee. Meghan took care of me the best she could. Then one day, she was gone.

I didn't even cry. It made it easier to deal with it now than when my final one hundred days came." He shakes his head. "It was worse knowing the day I'd die than not knowing at all. I'd rather die today, unexpectedly, than know the exact day that I'll die." He touches the back of his neck, rubbing the spot where his number used to be. "Now you're saying the numbers are fake, and that I'm not dying in two years. How do you know? What if I die anyway, even without that number on my neck?"

Before I can answer, Cowboy comes back in the room, Noelle following behind him, holding a bottle to Mila's hungry mouth.

"Let them out. We're escorting these guys to the mountain," Cowboy commands. The guard already has his keys in hand, and he fiddles with the lock.

"Hold up. You're what?" I look to Noelle for confirmation, and she nods.

"It's okay," she says. "They're on our side."

"They have a funny way of showing it," I say, touching the side of my head. She winces as she realizes the extent of my injuries. When we exit the cell, she touches my head lightly, peering at the wounds. Her finger brushes a lump and I grimace.

"Sorry about that," Cowboy says. "We have a shower if you want to clean up. There's some food, too."

"How about beds?" I ask, still unsure what we're doing and if we can actually trust these guys.

"We got those, too," he says. "Anything you guys want, it's yours."

"I still don't get it," I mutter, taking Devon's hands in mine as we all follow Cowboy from the room.

"I'm still processing this, too," Noelle says. "Seems my brother is a bit of a celebrity in these parts. He's part of the rebel elite. He'd been planning on springing me before he was arrested, and now it's just like you said—if The Enforcers capture me, they'll get Skye to talk and blow the whole operation." She shakes her head. "Like he'd talk, though. He wouldn't sacrifice the lives of all these people just because I'm his sister."

"I don't know," I say. "You're pretty special." She grins, then leans toward me. I meet her halfway, brushing my lips against hers. Just the simple touch is enough to send sparks through me. "If that makes your brother strong, then consider me weak."

"Really? You'd give up everything to keep me safe?" she says.

"I didn't want to," I admit. "I tried to be strong, but I knew where they were headed. I couldn't even handle it when they held Mila in front of me. But if you were the one in front of me, there's no question. Even if we were going to die—which I knew we were—I couldn't bear to watch you get tortured, knowing I could stop it." I shudder just thinking about it, what almost happened. "I still can't believe all that is over."

"Well, Duke isn't that bad," she says.

"Duke?"

"Yeah?" Cowboy turns around just as we reach the elevator. He laughs. "We haven't properly met, have we?"

"Oh, we've met," I say, turning my head to show him the mark he left. "But names? Nah, we never exchanged them."

"I'm Duke," he says. "And that's Moe. That guy there," he says, pointing to the guard. "That's Big Dan. Then there's Jareth, Paul, and Shem."

"Great, now we're all friends," I say, rolling my eyes.

"Look, man, I'm sorry. But we're the welcoming committee. We've had a few spies 'round these parts looking for Cedar Grove. If they reach us, they're practically knocking at the door. Luckily, no one has ever gotten past us." Cowboy Duke appears proud, and I can only guess how they've stopped anyone from getting closer.

"And how do you explain the missing bodies?"

"Nothing to explain," he says. "Let's just say we know how to clean up our messes."

Duke takes us down to the basement. The difference between upstairs and here is night and day; starting with soft lighting along the ceiling and walls, and continuing with fur throw rugs on ash wood floors. It's like something out of a magazine, and nothing like the rundown town we drove into—and definitely not like these thugs leading the way.

We're shown to our rooms. Kevin gets his own, and Noelle and I get a room with the kids that has two queen beds. Despite the change in Duke's demeanor, I don't fully relax until the door closes behind him. Even then, it's hard to loosen up. I let Devon take the first shower in the bathroom that's connected to our room. I stand next to the bed, glancing across a small table, at the jacks in the walls, the lights on the ceiling.

"Do you think they've bugged the room?"

Noelle rolls her eyes, but she gets up and looks around the room with me anyway.

"I believe they're on our side," she says, sitting down on the bed once she's satisfied there are no microphones or cameras anywhere in the room.

"I won't believe anything until we're at Cedar Grove," I say. "Even then, I don't know if I can trust a single person."

"I know what you mean." She strokes Mila's hair, then wipes her milk-stained lips. "But Duke knew everything Skye told me. He showed me photos of the two of them together. He says he'd take a bullet for Skye, and I believe him. When he realized I was Skye's sister, everything about him changed. He didn't force me to talk. In fact, he gave me more information than I knew."

"Like what?"

"Like..." She looks away, and for the first time I recognize the look of anguish on her face. I move closer to her, resting my hand on her knee. She closes her hand over mine, gripping me tight. "Like, where my parents are."

"Your parents? I thought they—"

"Died," she finishes. "I know. Me too. But apparently the rebels got them out, thanks to Skye. They're in Cuba right now, waiting for…" She doesn't finish, a sob escaping her throat. I wrap my arm around her pulling her into me.

"It's a lot to take in," I murmur into her hair. I try not to think of my own parents, but I can't help it. I've been angry with them ever since they left, unable to even mourn their deaths. Now, I don't know what to feel. There was no one on the other side of their facility walls to break them out. Do I even care? I don't want to. They didn't care enough about me to spend their last moments with me. They didn't even say goodbye. Good riddance. I bite my trembling lip and hide my anguish when Noelle looks up at me.

"I wonder if they know I'm coming," she says. I kiss her forehead, keeping my lips there, inhaling her scent. Her skin tastes salty from sweat and grime, yet I could breathe her in all day.

Devon curls up on the bed once he's showered, dressed in an oversized shirt and shorts that our captors-turned-protectors supplied for us. On such short notice, they didn't have anything child size, but Devon doesn't seem to care. I give Noelle next dibs on the shower, taking over baby duty. She's made a makeshift bassinet out of a dresser drawer, padded with a folded blanket and placed between our two beds. Milk drunk, Mila stays asleep in the small crib. I lie down next to Devon on the bed, and he turns to face me.

"Are we going to die?" he whispers. His eyes are clear, and he asks so seriously, so matter-of-fact, that my heart hurts for him.

"One day," I say. "But not today. And not tomorrow. And not anytime soon. We're safe now." I hope it's true. I mostly believe it's true. If it's not, then it won't matter because we'll be dead. "Are you okay?"

He nods. He closes his eyes, a small shudder escaping his lungs before his breathing slows. Once he's sleeping, I close my eyes, too. I drift in and out of sleep, slightly aware of Noelle's body folding around mine a short while later and the weight of her arm across my belly. It's the last thing I remember before I finally slip into blissful unconsciousness.

18

The Hero

Noelle

∞

Once Ryder falls asleep, he stays that way. I nap for a little while on the bed behind him but get up once I hear Mila stirring. Ryder doesn't even move when I crouch near the bed and lift the baby from her crib before she opens her mouth. There's a small kitchenette in our room, and I warm a pot of water on the stove before making her another bottle, but Mila has no interest in staying quiet. She cries until the bottle is in her mouth, then hiccups around the nipple, until finally settling into her meal. The boys remain asleep. It's almost eight at night, according to the clock on the stove, and the baby is wide awake, her eyes looking around the darkened room. I burp her when she's done, but the way she moves her body shows me that she's not going back to sleep.

"I guess we can go explore," I whisper, holding her in front of me. I take in her wide, espresso eyes, feeling my heart swell as she gazes back. I wonder if she loves me as much as I love her.

Opening the door quietly, I peek into the empty hall. I can hear voices in the distance, and I make my way toward them. The end of the hall opens to a large room. The men sit at a long table, playing cards while a fire roars nearby. I hesitate at the threshold. Two of the men from upstairs are there—Moe and Shem, I believe—but they're all I recognize. Everyone else looks just as brutal as the guys who brought us here, some even appearing to have fresh wounds on their knuckles as they grip their cards. I don't want to think about how they got them. Duke promised us safety, and I believed him at the time. But what if I was wrong? It wouldn't have been the first time.

"You can go in."

I turn around, and Duke is standing behind me. He smiles, transforming his gruff features into a friendlier expression, and I relax in spite of myself.

"Come on, Noelle. The answer is *tomorrow*."

I turn, smiling at the code. It's the answer to the riddle Skye made me say repeatedly the last time I saw him.

🌀 🌀 🌀

"Again," my brother had ordered outside my parents' house. Everyone else was inside, saying their final goodbyes to my parents at a farewell party I never wanted to attend. I also didn't want to leave the house and was irritated that Skye had dragged me outside.

"I never was, am always to be, no one has or will ever see me, and yet I am the confidence of all, to live and breathe on this terrestrial ball," I huffed. "And the answer is *tomorrow*. Now can we go back inside?" He ignored me, taking my shoulders so that I faced him. I tried to shrug him off, but he kept his grip.

"I'm serious, Noelle. Trust no one unless they tell you this."

"You're being weird." I twisted out of his grasp and stalked to the house. I didn't know why he had to be this way. I felt him on my heels, which made me even angrier. Skye seemed more intent on talking to me then saying goodbye to our parents. I whipped around, and he almost ran into me. Now it was my turn to get handsy. I pointed my finger at his chest, moving forward as he backed up against a wall.

"You don't even care that this is the last time we'll see our parents," I hissed. My anger threatened to seep out of my eyes in the form of tears, and I blinked rapidly to ensure my weakness didn't show.

"I'm not heartless. They're my parents, too. I love them, but I don't agree that they have to die."

"Not this again."

"I'm serious, Noelle. This whole numbers game is just that—a game. Nothing and no one can predict the exact date of their death, not even a computer."

Skye's long-ago words raced through me when Duke faced me earlier this afternoon, minutes after escorting me from the one cell room. "I never was, am always to be, no one has or will ever see me, and yet I am the confidence of all, to live and breathe on this terrestrial ball," he'd said.

"The answer is tomorrow," I replied. It was then that I knew he was on our side, even after I'd seen him beat and torture Ryder. It became more clear as he explained his current role as guardian of Cedar Grove, and a few of the rescue missions he'd taken part in, including one that still left me breathless. "We saved your parents, Noelle," he'd told me, a reality I still couldn't believe. He shared how he'd helped them escape, starting with removing their numbers and ending when they disappeared from the facility's records as if they never existed. It had all been within the first few days of their arrival, and no one ever noticed they were missing. It angered me when he told me this. For the past five years, I thought they were dead. Now I find out they're alive, and I haven't been able to see them.

"No one even let me know!" I yelled, no longer afraid of this man in front of me. "Someone could have gotten me, brought me to them, saved me from all this."

"We couldn't," Duke said. "At that point, we weren't sure if The Enforcers were on to us. We took a huge risk getting your parents, and luckily no one was paying attention. But we couldn't guarantee that with you. If we took you out of your normal life, it would have raised flags. We had to wait until you were in the facility."

"What took you so long?" I muttered. "I was in there for almost two weeks."

"By that time, they *were* watching you."

Now in the hallway, Duke pats my shoulder then brushes past me. The conversation doesn't break when I walk in, though Moe nods at me, acknowledging my presence. I sit gingerly on the hearth of the fireplace, letting the warmth take away the chill from the basement. Duke hands me a beer, and I swig it gratefully, watching as he makes me a plate of food from a nearby buffet.

"Do you guys eat this way every day?" I ask when I take the heaping plate from his hands.

"We own this town," Duke laughs. "Of course we eat this way every day."

"Can I take a plate back to Ryder and Devon?"

"If you want. Or they can just grab food from the fridge when they're up. Everything we have here is yours, sister of Skye." I roll my eyes at this reference, but I'm inwardly proud of my brother. He made all of this happen. Now we just need to make sure he gets out of this alive.

I stay up late with the guys, even after Mila falls asleep again. They invite me into their poker game, with Duke fronting me money. I lose it all. During the time, I hear stories about my brother I never knew: the family he saved before the authorities came to take their father; the orphanage he emptied—leaving behind aides passed out and tied up in one of the rooms; the safe houses he set up in Arizona located in places no one would suspect—the home of a pastor and his family, a frat house, a yoga studio, a synagogue. It was much like the Underground Railroad we'd learned about in school, but the hero was my brother. Duke even told me about the bombing at the White House, an act that killed dozens of Enforcers during a closed-door meeting.

"He almost got caught that time," Duke says with a laugh. "But your brother is slick."

"Except he eventually did get caught," I say, leaning back in my chair, tossing my cards on the table. The last of Duke's loaned money is swept up with the rest of the pot by the guy across from me.

"We got sloppy," Duke says. "But we'll rescue him."

"When?"

"We have a mission in place. But first, we need to get you all out of here. We'll escort you up the mountain first thing in the morning, and then you're on the next flight to Cuba."

"No."

Duke narrows his eyes. "What do you mean, *no*?"

"I mean, I'm not leaving until my brother is safe. I want in."

He shakes his head. "Noelle, we promised your brother we'd get you out of harm's way. This isn't a negotiation. We already have a team in place that is trained for circumstances like these. You do not have this kind of training, and you would just be in the way."

I look away. The old Noelle would have given in, agreed to whatever he said. But I'm not her anymore. I've had my whole life turned upside down. I've been faced with the lies of my life. I've changed. But I'm also the same. I was raised with courage and taught to be a fighter. I know who I am.

"What family do you think Skye came from?" I ask Duke. "He was raised by the same parents I was raised by. I learned the same lessons he did. We were both taught how to fire a gun, how to survive the elements in the wilderness, how to block a punch, and how to disarm a soldier. Everything that Skye knows, he learned it first in our family."

"It's different," Duke says. "Skye has been a part of an elite group of rebels and has learned more than the "Boy Scout" lessons from your childhood."

"If I weren't holding Mila…"

"I have no doubt, princess," Duke says, then gives a sideways grin to Moe. I burn inside, looking at them through narrowed eyes.

"Since you're so accustomed to holding babies, here," I say, handing Mila to Moe. Before Duke can react, I grab his arm, flip him over the chair, and hold the knife that had been sheathed at his waist to his neck. I straddle him, my legs wrapped around his in a strong lock. I haven't done this move in years, but it comes to me as if I've been practicing it every day. "That's the 'Boy Scout' move I was taught by my father, a man who served as a Navy Seal for twelve years. And there's more where that came from." I give Duke back his knife and stand while the guys behind me laugh. I don't want them to know how nervous I am to have just done that, or how it surprised me just as much as it surprised Duke.

"If you had that in you, why didn't you use that on my men when they nabbed you?" He refuses my hand that I hold out to him, and stands on his own.

"It's kind of hard to attack when you're unconscious," I say.

"And you don't think that can happen again?"

"It could happen to anyone," I argue. "Even your special team could be taken down unexpectedly. I should be there. I'm capable of handling my own, but even more, I'm his sister."

"Which is exactly why you *shouldn't* be there." I start to protest, but he cuts me off. "Noelle, if you're part of this rescue mission, you're playing right into their hands. They'll have you right where they want you. They'll torture you in front of Skye to get him to talk, and then they'll kill you."

I shake my head. "You and I both know he won't talk, even if they remove my fingernails one by one."

He knows I'm right; I can see it in his eyes. He stares me down. I don't look away, meeting his stare with defiant eyes. Finally, he sighs.

"Even if I agreed, I'm not the one you have to convince," he says.

"Then who *do* I speak with?" I ask, hands on hips.

"Her name is Birgitte, and she's leading the team out of Cedar Grove. If you convince her, you're in. But good luck with that. She has the whole operation planned out to the second. Adding another person will cause wrinkles to the entire execution."

"Don't worry about me," I say, gathering Mila from Moe's arms. "I'll find my way in." I leave the room before anyone can say another word, and before they can see the doubt in my eyes. I'm not a fighter. I might know a few fancy self-defense moves and how to shoot a gun, but I've never been in a situation dangerous enough to use them. I didn't even fire a gun once as we ran for our lives. What makes me think I can actually be a part of a rescue mission to save my brother? I must be out of my mind.

"I am, aren't I?" I whisper down to Mila, kissing her forehead. "I'm batshit crazy to even consider this insane death mission."

I sneak back into the room, turning the knob as I close the door so that the click doesn't wake the boys. The bathroom light leaves a soft glow in the room, and my heart expands when I see the way Devon is curled against Ryder, his little face pressed into his chest with Ryder's arm wrapped around him. It's so endearing, so natural.

I lay Mila in the dresser crib on the floor between our beds. She stirs a little but, thankfully, settles without waking. I start to unbutton my shirt, glancing over at Ryder as I do. His eyes are open, and my fingers pause on the third button. The light from the bathroom casts a soft glow on the room, shining in his eyes as he watches me. Without speaking, he leaves the bed, crossing the room and closing the space between us. His hands cover mine, pressed between my breasts, his face inches from mine.

"Hey," he whispers, lacing his fingers through mine.

"Hey," I return, my need growing from a grain of sand, to a boulder in my chest. I tighten my grip on his hands, looking from his eyes to his mouth, then back to his eyes. Still grasping my hand, he leads me to the bathroom. I glance over my shoulder, assured that the kids are still sleeping before I close the door behind us.

We don't speak; there's no need for words. He turns me around and leans me against the door, his hand behind my neck as my face tilts toward him. His eyes search mine, and my breath catches behind my pounding heart. I trace the bruises of his face, and he turns his head to kiss the tips of my fingers. I open like a spring when his thumb brushes my cheek, relief flooding through me when his mouth crushes on mine. I breathe him in, clinging to him as he presses me between the door and his hard body. His kiss deepens and I clutch his hair to pull him closer. So much closer. I can't get close enough.

We don't have to hide. We're not running. There's no one watching and our days aren't numbered. Time is ours, once again. The realization that we have our lives back flows through me, just as his hands pull at me, undress me, bring my skin to his. His lips and tongue tangle with mine. He fumbles with the shower, then draws me under the spray once it's warm. I melt under his hands as he gently shampoos my hair, pausing to kiss my face before massaging my scalp some more. He even conditions it, running his fingers through my long hair until it's free from tangles. When he's done, I do the same for him, moving my hands slowly as I memorize the landscape of his head, the feel of his hair between my fingers, and the slope of his neck. He closes his eyes while I press my fingers into his scalp, moaning lightly as I pull at his hair. I study the shape of his lips, the way his beard accentuates his jawline, his thick lashes as his eyes remain closed. Carefully, I tilt his head back and rinse, standing on my tiptoes so I can free his hair of soap. My body presses against his, and he wraps his arms around me, straightening to look at me.

"You're so beautiful," he says, a trail of shampoo heading dangerously down his forehead.

"I'm not done," I whisper. I wipe the suds from his face before they reach his eyes.

"I think you are."

His mouth claims mine, catching my breath and pulling the yearning from my chest. I taste the water and the saltiness of his skin as he kisses me, our bodies slipping against each other. I don't want to let him go, unable to get enough as I memorize the feel of his body, the taste of his mouth, and the fire that's spreading from my very center to his.

He guides me, his mouth still on mine, until my back is flush with the shower wall. With my foot resting on the bench in the corner, he presses into me, releasing the pressure that's been mounting for—I don't even know how long. I push back, meeting each thrust as we greedily take each other. His palms are pressed against the wall as he drives deeper, his back muscles rippling under my hands, his tongue twisting with mine. A melting coolness starts at the top of my head, running over my face, down my neck, enveloping my shoulders and chest until my whole body releases with his, his arousal exploding within me.

He stays inside me for a few moments longer as we catch our breath. Then he lifts his head, pressing his forehead against mine. This close, his eyes are a blurred ocean. Our lips meet, brushing against each other in their own silent affirmation of what just happened. The water is cooling, and I shiver. Ryder runs his finger over my goosebumps, lightly laughing, then reaches over to turn off the water.

"You need some sleep." He opens the door and grabs the towel off the rack, pulling it around my shoulders.

"I needed you, more." On my tiptoes, I kiss his mouth, then step out of the stall before handing him his towel.

He gives Devon the whole bed and joins me in mine, his shape formed to my body. I'm comforted by the weight of his hand on my hip and fall asleep with his arm as my pillow, his breath in my ear, and his heartbeat marking time against my back.

19

Life

Noelle

∞

M y dreams are a confusing mashup of everything that happened over the past day, from explosions in tunnels to being chased on tilted streets lined by the Arizona hills. Ryder is with me, but just out of my grasp as I reach for him. I keep trying, my fingers grazing the tips of his without ever grabbing hold. Then everything disappears, replaced by Skye's face.

"You thought I was crazy," he says, his pale blue eyes piercing mine. "Who's the crazy one now?"

My eyes fly open and I'm back in the warehouse, Ryder sitting on the edge of the bed rubbing my shoulder. He kisses the side of my neck as I leave sleep for awake, stretching in the bed as my dream slips from my memory, evaporating until all that's left is an unsettled feeling.

"What time is it?" I ask.

"It's just past nine," he says.

"Mila!" I panic when I don't see her in the dresser bed.

"Don't worry, Devon's feeding her," Ryder says as I look around. Devon sits in the shadows of the room's corner, his feet hanging off the chair as he holds the bottle to Mila's mouth. He's humming as he feeds her.

"Oh my goodness, he's so sweet," I whisper.

"He's pretty special," Ryder agrees. "She was starting to stir, and I didn't want her to wake you. You were snoring so loud, though, you didn't hear a thing."

"I don't snore!" I say, smacking his hand away from my shoulder.

"Okay, okay!" he says, laughing. "I guess it was more like purring."

"Or it was the strange whistle coming out of your own nose," I shoot back.

"This strange whistle?" He nuzzles my ear and makes a snarling noise as he nips at my skin. I laugh as the tingles race through my body and pull away before the temptation turns painful. The night before rushes back to me, and I can't help wishing we could have had more time alone. It makes my decision to join the rescue party that much more difficult. A remnant of my dream finds me again, and I remember Skye's face. Most of all, I remember the guilt. He tried to tell me about the numbers, and I shot him down repeatedly. Even still, he saved me from River's End. Now it's my turn to save him.

"Are you excited?" he asks. I pause, unsure what he's referring to.

"We're going to Cedar Grove," I say, and he nods, his smile wavering.

"You're not excited?"

"No, I am!" I grin, trying to prove it. I'm not ready to tell him about my decision yet. I know he'll just talk me out of it. "It's a lot to take in. These last few days have been a whirlwind, and we've spent the last day and a half fighting for our lives. It's hard to believe we can actually relax."

"I'm looking forward to relaxing with you," he murmurs, leaning in and brushing his mouth against mine. I ache inside. How can I tell him? He'll never understand.

"I am, too," I whisper. I open my mouth and invite him in. The kiss is brief, but it suggests the need that still lies underneath. He pulls away and leaves the bed.

"I need a cold shower to wake up," he says, backing away from me. The look in his eyes tells a different story. I don't think showers will ever be the same.

"You sure that's all you need a cold shower for?" I glance down at his obvious arousal, then duck as he tosses his shirt at me. My eyes linger on his naked upper body as he disappears behind the bathroom door.

I turn my attention to Devon. He's set the bottle down on the table next to him and is softly talking to Mila. Her eyes are focused solely on his. The whole thing is so endearing, I hate to interrupt, but I know she probably has a gas bubble trapped in her tiny chest. "Did you want to try burping her?" I ask. He gives me a shy smile, then a nod. I help maneuver her so that her head is on his shoulder and his hand is behind her neck, then show him how to pat her back softly. He does, and she lets out a belch, along with a stream of spit up.

"Ugh!" He loses his fondness for her with a look of disgust, which makes me laugh. I dab at his shoulder before picking her up.

"Babies are pretty gross, huh?" I say. He nods, wrinkling his nose, but he doesn't appear scarred from the experience. He helps me change her, putting her socks on after I swap out her wet diaper for a clean one. By the time he's dressed himself, Ryder is out of the shower, towel drying his hair with another towel slung low on his hips.

"You should probably get dressed," I say, trying to keep my eyes no lower than his face. I fail when his hand rests at the top of the towel. I bite back my grin without success. "Seriously, Ryder. Go get some clothes on." The look in his eyes is wicked as he grabs a clean pair of clothes off the dresser and returns to the bathroom.

Kevin is already up when we reach the back room, sitting at the same table as last night's card game. In front of him is a huge plate of eggs and pancakes, and behind him is a buffet of steaming food.

"Dig in," he says. "Duke's leaving in a half hour." We follow suit, piling food onto our plates as if we haven't eaten in weeks. Even my dinner from the night before is forgotten as my stomach rumbles. Devon's plateful is larger than his stomach, but he appears determined to finish it all when he starts to eat.

"What about your wife?" Ryder asks Kevin. I look up at this.

"Wife? You're married?"

Kevin nods reluctantly, giving a side glance to Ryder. "Kind of," he says. "She left me a few weeks ago, made it clear she didn't want to see me again."

"Oh." I suddenly feel terrible. This guy we kidnapped has a whole backstory I don't even know. I don't know if I *want* to know. On one hand, we're kind of saving his life. On the other, we've interrupted the life he had. We didn't give him a chance. I glance at Ryder and he gives a quick shake of his head.

"No, it's okay," Kevin says. He puts his fork down. "I've spent the last few years in a dark state of depression. I couldn't handle the fact that my life was ending so soon. I had so many things I'd wanted to do, and hadn't accomplished any of them. With my expiration getting closer, I realized I was this huge nobody. I don't have kids, I haven't done anything remarkable, and I haven't changed anyone's life. I realized that when I died, that was it— Kevin Lark would cease to exist, and life would go on without me. I'd be forgotten. I wasn't even convinced my wife would miss me. She tried to help me out of my funk, insisting that I was throwing away my life by regretting the time I didn't have. It was easy for her to say. She was going to die an old woman according to her number, which made me feel worse because she was wasting her life on someone like me. Well, she finally had enough of me and left. When you found me, I'd sold everything I owned and was on my way to San Diego."

"For a camping trip," I say. He nods.

"Yes, something I'd wanted to do before I died."

"A bucket list item?" I ask. Kevin gives Ryder a sideways glance, and reality sinks in. "This was a suicide trip," I say, and he nods. "I'm so sorry."

Kevin smiles, then he takes my hand. "Don't be sorry," he says. "You two saved me. If you hadn't kidnapped me, I'd be dead. I had it all planned out—a campsite with a view of the ocean, a bottle of pills, and a note for my wife once they found me." He shakes his head, releasing my hand. "But ever since you two gave me my life back, I've had some time to reflect. I realized a few things. Most importantly, I want to live."

"I take it there's something else," Ryder says.

"My wife," Kevin answers. "I should just leave her behind and start fresh. After all, she broke our vows at the first sign of trouble. But I can't. I love her. She messed up, but I had my part, too. It couldn't have been easy for her. I need to at least see if what we had is worth salvaging."

"I don't know, man," Ryder says. "It's not safe. We removed your number. If anyone figures that out, you're as good as dead."

"We have a fake one for him." Duke is in the doorway, holding a number device. "And he has a direct line to us if anything goes down."

"So you agree with this?" I ask. "You really think this is a good idea?"

"Hell no," Duke says. "I think it's a stupid one. The guy has a straight shot to freedom, and he's stepping back into the fire. But I understand love, and that sometimes it makes more sense than common sense."

Kevin finishes his last bite of eggs and then kicks back in his seat. "Don't worry about me." He grins, tilting his head. "If I can survive being kidnapped, I can survive this."

Cedar Grove

Ryder

∞

We stay at the warehouse long enough to see Kevin off before climbing into Duke's SUV. The windows of the car are heavily tinted, hiding us from the view of anyone on the outside. We're piled in the back, Devon in the middle with Noelle and me on each side. Noelle's face is turned away as she watches the scenery, stroking Mila's hair absentmindedly, as the baby sleeps against her chest. She feels a million miles away. I reach across Devon and touch her shoulder. When she turns, her smile doesn't reach her eyes.

"Are you nervous?" I ask. She shakes her head, then tilts it.

"Maybe a little," she admits. "Which is crazy because this is the easy part. Everything is supposed to get better, isn't it?"

"Yeah, but it's still something new. We don't know what to expect." We reach a gate, the third one we've gone through. I've noticed machine guns and cameras stationed in trees at each one, even as the gate swings open easily. But this one's different. Armed guards come out of nowhere, surrounding our car. My heart pounds as one of the guards orders us from the vehicle. Just like yesterday's run-in with Duke and the gang, the SUV doors fly open and strong hands force us out.

"It's fine," Duke says to us, raising his hands as they pull him out. They pat us all down. Duke and his men had confiscated our weapons yesterday, so the guards don't find anything except Duke's knife.

"You can get this on your way out," the guard says, slipping it into his pocket.

"Whatever," Duke mutters. "If there's even a scratch on it, you'll pay. That knife belonged to my grandfather."

Duke takes us the rest of the way in. The trees give way to a mountain, a cave carved into the side. We drive in, the light of day replaced with artificial lights lining a tunnel. It goes straight for about ten minutes before Duke takes us through a series of turns—"the maze," he tells us. He explains that it's the last safeguard before our destination. Anyone who gets lost in these tunnels will be crushed by the security system.

"One wrong turn and the tunnels constrict on whatever enters. You're lucky I'm the one driving."

Luck is an understatement. Duke is taking each turn as if he's made this drive a thousand times. I doubt Kevin's car had a navigation system that could direct us with this much precision.

He finally slows the car. The light—at what appears to be the end of the tunnel—is blinding as we get closer. I shield my eyes as we enter the light, emerging on the other side. When I look again, I'm greeted by Utopia. Seriously, the place is Infinity on Earth. Blue sky with bright sunshine, not a cloud of smog to be seen. Green grass surrounds leafy green plants. Children play tag while parents mingle nearby. Dozens of houses in all different colors, each with a porch and a garden out front. Large giraffes, a zebra, and small dogs chase each other. Devon flies out of the car as soon as we stop. He finds the nearest dog and starts a game of fetch.

"Well, I guess he lost his fear," I say with a laugh. Even Noelle appears relaxed, grinning as she opens her door.

"Where are we?" she asks.

"Cedar Grove," Duke says. "You're inside the mountain." We both turn to him.

"Wait, what? How is that even possible? The sun is right there," I say, pointing skyward.

"Pretty incredible, isn't it?" Duke says. "CGI isn't just for movies. Humans are pretty much gods now. We can create anything, even a place that looks, smells, and feels like the most perfect place you've ever seen."

"So, the dogs aren't real?" I ask, watching as Devon tumbles to the ground with a half dozen puppies.

"Oh, they're real all right. Most of this is real. But the sky isn't, neither is the weather, the smells, the temperature, or even the air. All of that is manufactured. But the plants, the animals, and the people—they're all real."

Noelle's hair moves with a breeze, and she brushes it away from her face, then smiles with realization—there's wind here, but it's artificial. "That's impressive," she says.

"Isn't it? You wouldn't have even know, which is why some people choose to stay here to welcome the next visitors before they head to Cuba."

Noelle stiffens. It's brief, and she pretends to be interested in her surroundings. I know she's pretending because she's chewing the inside of her cheek, even as she looks around with wide eyes. Some kids shout in the distance, and we both turn in the direction we hear them. Even from far away I recognize a few of the kids from the facility. They made it.

"Colby and Thom, do you know them?" I ask Duke. He nods.

"Yeah, they've been a part of the rebels for a while now. Don't head into Arizona too much, but I generally keep tabs on where they're at since they're always part of the action."

"Do you know where they're at now? Are they here?"

"Nah," Duke says. "They're headed for Cuba to train with the resistance. They'll be back, though, and when they are, you can be sure it's because things are going down."

I watch the kids across the courtyard for a little longer. Devon brushes up against me, sliding his hand in mine. When I look down at him, I see his attention is on the other kids, and he's hiding behind my legs. I free my hand from his and place it on his head, smoothing it over his hair as a way to convey that he doesn't have to do anything he doesn't want to do. We can see the kids are here; we don't have to do anything else.

Duke takes us to the welcome center, introducing us to Gretchen, a woman who can only be described as long. She's tall with blonde hair to her waist, and limbs that stretch like branches, which she uses for emphasis as she speaks.

"This is where I leave you," Duke says. Noelle gives him a hard hug goodbye, but I just shake his hand. He may have delivered us to the "promised land," but he also messed up my face pretty good.

Gretchen takes all of us on a train tour of the city, which submerges us below the grassy Utopia we arrived at. It's apparent Cedar Grove is larger than we realized.

"Think of it as a small San Francisco, but without the pollution, the stress, or the crowds," she says as the city unfolds. Below the earth is an entire community, with large skyscrapers—"earthscrapers," she corrects me—a maze of streets, storefronts, cafés… It's just as she says, seemingly modeled after San Francisco, but with a lot more parks. There are no cars, and most of the people we see are walking in the streets or riding bikes. Tour trams act as buses, dropping people at various places around the city.

"How is this possible?" I ask, watching the entire underworld pass by.

"Cuba mostly," she says. "They've supplied us with the engineers and some of the materials, and helped us tap into Earth's core power to keep the city running."

"That doesn't make sense," Noelle says. "They're a small island. How can they have enough of anything to help us?"

"Appearances are deceiving." Gretchen gestures toward the windows. "When you saw the mountain, did you see any of this?" We both shake our heads. "Cuba isn't just their surface. They've created an entire country beneath what the world sees. This right here is a much smaller version of what already exists there. It's how they've had room to take in refugees. And this sanctuary is just the beginning. We've started building a larger one in Africa, and have plans for Germany and Sweden."

"We need more than sanctuaries," Noelle says. "We need to stop The Enforcers from killing healthy people. Holing people up in caves won't work forever."

"You're right." Gretchen moves next to me and waves her wrist next to the window. The view outside disappears, replaced with what looks like a panel of holographic buttons. She quickly touches several of them, and the window shows a view of Cuba from far above the Earth. It zooms closer, reaching what appears to be a training camp, filled with soldiers. "The first phase is saving who we can. Part of this is to preserve humanity. But the second part is to increase our numbers. We're preparing for an uprising, but we're not there yet. This is so much bigger than just our country. It's happening all over the world."

"You can't keep this up forever. Eventually, The Enforcers will catch on," Noelle says. Gretchen nods, her smile appearing tired.

"They have your brother," she says. "We are well aware how fragile this whole thing is. This is the closest they've come to uncovering the truth about the sanctuaries. We've prevented them from discovering us in every way except human error. Right now, The Enforcers are likely torturing Skye and probing him for information, and they won't find anything because he knows how to close his mind. But no one knows how to turn off human emotion, save for erasing his memory or killing him. If they capture you, he'll talk. We know it, and so does he. That's why we saved your parents and you."

"So, he'll stay quiet," Noelle says, looking down at her shoes.

"Yes," Gretchen says. "That's our reason. But even more, because Skye insisted that if anything happened to him, we carry through with saving you."

The train slows to a stop, and the view of Cuba disappears, letting the artificial sunlight back in. We're in front of a tan two-story home with a large yard and a wide porch, and a swing in the corner swaying gently in the artificial breeze. Leafy plants serve as bookends to the porch stairs, resting at the top as if they've been waiting for us.

"Welcome home," Gretchen says as the train doors open. She turns to me. "I understand you like to swim. You'll find a large lap pool in the backyard. And there's a surprise waiting for you inside, Noelle."

Devon races in front of us, opening the red front door that leads to a large entryway. We follow him inside, and I hear Noelle gasp. She rushes around me and peers inside a large fish tank built into the side wall of the living room.

"You saved Fish!" Her finger traces the glass where a small goldfish swims among other colorful fish.

"You made it too easy," Gretchen says with a laugh. "We'd planned to grab him on your last night, and you left him just outside your neighbor's door."

Noelle is smiling, even as tears stream down her face. She gives me an embarrassed smile. "I know it's silly to cry over a fish. But he was the only friend I had." It's silly, but also endearing.

"I get it," I say.

The house has everything we need—a bedroom for each of us, lots of windows to let in the light, and a backyard with the promised pool and a play structure for Devon, who wastes no time to start swinging. There's a golf cart in the garage for transportation, along with bicycles and scooters, and a giant map on the wall so we can study how to get around. There's even a fully stocked fridge—at least, it appears that way.

"Keep an open mind," Gretchen says as I turn over a package of frozen burgers.

"Termites?" The food has handmade labels on it, which don't even try to hide what's in them. I pick up package after package, my appetite waning as I find insects where there should be lab meat.

"Things are different down here," she says. "Part of the overpopulation issue we're facing above ground is the demand for food. Instead of insisting on sustainable agriculture, the government caved to the demand and began manufacturing meat in labs. It was a quick fix, but not a solution. Also, it's expensive and unsafe."

"So you're forcing us to starve on bugs down here to help with the population."

"Actually, you'll find that insects have more protein than you think, and they're calorie efficient. 100 grams of termites provide around 75% more calories than 100 grams of steak. That termite burger is not only delicious, but it will definitely fill you up."

I pick up the burger again, peering at the "meat." It looks almost like a regular burger, no termite in sight. I put it down and pick up another package. I don't even need to read the label to know what's inside—ants. There's probably 1,000 of them in there. My skin feels itchy just looking at them. I peer into the drawer of the freezer, seeing both prepared foods and bags of frozen bugs, along with vegetables and even a gallon of coconut milk ice cream. Wait, with crickets.

"I guess we're going to have to develop different tastes," Noelle says. When I meet her gaze, she wrinkles her nose.

"It will be easier than you think," Gretchen promises. The kitchen leads right into the living room. Along with the fish tank, this room has a vision port, which serves as both a television and phone.

"Can I..." Noelle hesitates, and Gretchen reaches across to touch her arm.

"You can call your parents," she says, and I see Noelle fighting back more tears as Gretchen hands her a card with her parents' number on it.

"Not yet," she says, and Gretchen nods.

"I'll leave so you can start getting used to your new life. Stay here as long as you'd like, there's no time limit. But when you're ready, we'll take you to Cuba where a house identical to this one is waiting for you. We'll even take Fish."

Noelle hands Mila to me, who's ready for her next bottle, and follows Gretchen outside. In the kitchen, I find a wall panel that has options to make any kind of beverage, including formula. It seems humorous to me that I can make myself a beer and Mila a bottle from the same machine, but there you have it. I do just that, taking turns holding Mila's bottle to her mouth and then swapping so I can take a swig of my beer. We might be forced to eat bugs, but at least there's beer—and the amber liquid has never tasted so good slipping down my throat. I take a mouthful every time it's my turn to drink. Mila isn't too happy with this arrangement, crying every time I take her bottle away.

"Fine, have it your way," I say under her cries. I find a spot to sit in the living room where I have a clear shot of Devon playing in the backyard. I prop my feet up on an ottoman and rest Mila between my knees. With one hand I feed Mila, leaving my other one free for my beer. This is home. I feel pretty clever, and turn to see when Noelle is going to come back inside. She's still talking with Gretchen, and I almost turn around again until I realize Noelle is crying. She appears to be pleading with the woman, who is shaking her head. Eventually, Gretchen appears to give in to whatever Noelle is asking, writing something down on a piece of paper and handing it to Noelle. I flip back around when Noelle turns back toward the house. By the time she enters, her face is blotchy but dry, and she's concealing her grief with a smile.

"How's my girl?" she coos as she takes Mila from my lap. She nods at my glass. "Any more of those?"

"In the kitchen. Check the wall panel. You basically have a whole bar at your disposal, plus drinks that won't get you hammered. Hey, is everything okay?"

"Yeah, fine," she says as she retreats from the room. I hear the machine whirring in the kitchen. When she returns, Mila's head rests contently on her shoulder. Noelle sits in the chair patting Mila's back, then takes a sip of her beer. "Man, that's delicious."

"Something's going on," I say, unwilling to let this go. "You've been acting strange all day. What's up?"

She takes another drink of beer, mulling it around in her mouth for a while, allowing the silence to fester for a little while, before she finally speaks.

"There's just a lot to process."

"Like what?"

She closes her eyes, taking another sip. Then she sets the glass down and looks at me, her blue eyes darkening, her mouth set in a firm line.

"Like, they have my brother and are doing God knows what to him. Like, my parents are alive and have been for the past five years, and I'm only just learning about this now. Like, we're living in this beautiful place, our safety pretty much guaranteed, and millions of people are still dying before they're supposed to. Like, I've realized so much of my life was a lie, not because no one told me, but because I chose to live in my safe, little bubble. Skye tried to tell me. He was the only one telling me the truth, and I kept brushing him off. Now I'm safe, and he's not, and I'll never live with myself if he doesn't survive this. And…"

She takes a deep breath, still patting Mila even though the baby has already burped and fallen asleep. Her leg vibrates, capturing all the energy in the room as she bounces it up and down.

"And I'm joining the rescue team to get him out of there."

"What?" I peer into her face, trying to see if she's joking. Tears fill her eyes and she looks away.

"I know what you're thinking," she says.

"That you're insane? Yeah, that's what I'm thinking. We're finally safe, and you're ready to join a mission you know nothing about? We don't have to run anymore, Noelle."

"That's easy for you to say!" she says. "It's not your family. You don't have anyone left to care about. I do!"

I feel the heat burning a hole in my chest at the words, and I stand up, grabbing my beer from the table.

"Ryder, I'm sorry. I didn't mean it like that."

I ignore her, drinking the rest of my beer in one gulp. Then I chuck the bottle across the room. My anger turns to horror as it flies at the fish tank, shattering the glass. The water spills out on the floor, the fish carried out on the waterfall.

"Fish!" Noelle screams. I rush to the scene of the crime, sifting through the broken glass for flopping, gasping fish bodies. Noelle joins me, even as she holds Mila.

"What happened?" Devon stands in the doorway, his eyes wide as he sees us on our hands and knees among glass, water, and fish.

"Get me a bowl, quick!" He runs into the kitchen and is back in a few seconds with a large plastic bowl. I dump the fish I've saved into the bowl, and then carefully stand

and make my way to the tank, letting some of the spilling water flow into the bowl. Noelle places a few more in the bowl, and we both look in, taking a quick inventory. They're all there, even Fish. It doesn't look like any of them suffered much, either, though this bowl is too small for them to live in forever.

"Maybe we could put them in the bathtub until this gets fixed?" I feel terrible. "I'm sorry," I whisper.

She doesn't say anything. Instead, she leaves the room.

"Come on, buddy," I say to Devon. "Want to help me get these guys into their new home?"

"Yeah. How did the tank break?" he asks.

"Just me being stupid," I say.

We fill the bathtub completely, checking the temperature by hand to make sure it's close to the tank water. Then we slip the bowl into the water, letting both mingle as the fish float from their small container to a much larger one.

"You watch them, and I'll call the…management, I guess. I'll call them, and then clean up the mess. Deal?"

"Deal. Can I pet them?"

"I don't know much about fish. It probably wouldn't hurt, but let's wait and ask Noelle, okay?"

She's already in the living room when I return, picking up shards of glass and putting them in a paper bag. I hear her swear under her breath as a bead of red appears on her finger. Unsure where the First Aid kit is in this house, I grab a paper towel in the kitchen and wrap it around her finger, pressing hard on the wound to help stop the bleeding. I hold her hand a little longer than necessary, running my thumb over the soft skin of her fingers in apology.

"Thanks," she says quietly, taking her hand back. She goes back to cleaning up, and I join her. When there are no more large pieces to pick up, I search for the vacuum. I find a small robotic one that's just like the ones at River's End. I turn it on, then sic it on the water-stained carpet. It happily sucks up the glass shards we missed. Noelle sits on the floor nearby, watching the sloth-bot.

"Is Mila asleep?" I ask. She nods without looking at me.

"I put her in her crib."

The tension is crushing me. She's obviously bent on being mad.

"I'll call the repair guys," I say. "There has to be a number somewhere."

"Here," she says. She reaches into her pocket and pulls out a business card. I take it and see Gretchen's name on it. I turn it over and see a handwritten number with the name Birgitte.

"Which one do I call?"

"Gretchen," she says. "The other number is for me."

My jaw tightens, but I say nothing. Nodding, I leave to make the call.

"Wait," she says. I do, turning as she gets to her feet. She comes to me and wraps her hands around mine as I clutch the card. "I shouldn't have said that," she says. "It wasn't right. Just because your parents aren't here doesn't mean you don't know how to love."

"I know how to love you," I say. Then I realize what I just said. "I mean, I know I care about you." But the words are said. She loosens her hands from mine, and I know I've blown it.

"You…you *love* me?"

"There's no backing out of this, is there?" I ask. She shakes her head, a smile creeping onto her face. "Yeah, I love you. That's why I—" Her mouth is on mine before I can finish my reasoning, her arms around my neck, her breath mingling with mine. The card flutters to the ground as I pull her in, my kiss deepening as I'm filled with relief for having said it and fear in knowing I'm going to let her go.

"Ew!"

I break from Noelle and look over my shoulder at Devon in the hallway, covering his eyes.

"Hey, who's watching the fish if you aren't," I tease.

"They're just swimming in circles," Devon says. "It's not like they can get out. Besides, I'm hungry. What is there to eat here?"

"Bugs." I bend to pick up the card from the ground. "You look for something edible while I make this phone call. Then I'll make lunch for all of us."

Second Life

Noelle

∞

A ll I have to do is touch the last number. I stare at the remote in my hand and twelve numbers stare back at me, waiting for that thirteenth one before it rings through. Why was I hesitating? They were my parents, for God's sake. I'd longed to hear their voices for five years. I'd have given anything for this opportunity to speak with them again and yet, now that I had it, I was scared out of my mind.

"You have Skye," my mom had said at her party in our last hours together. It wasn't the same, and we both knew it. I'd talked to my mom almost every day of my life until I couldn't. She'd been my sounding board, my only friend. In this world with expiration dates, she was my forever. The morning of their Day Zero, I'd woken early and traveled to the coast. It was a rare day when the sky was clear, and I watched as it turned from deep purple to pink to blue over an endless sea. While I now know they never died, I thought it was my first day in a world without them and the emptiness was overwhelming. Alone on a cliff above crashing waves, I'd screamed into the wind, tears leaving frigid trails down my cheeks, I'd hurled every rock within my reach into the water below. It wasn't fair that they were gone. I'd felt more alone than I ever had in all my life.

It's been four days since Duke told me they were alive. Four days, and I feel paralyzed by the truth. I'm happy. Of course, I'm happy. But, I'm also nervous. I could have contacted them when we arrived at Cedar Grove but kept putting it off. My excuse was that I wanted to wait until we were settled. But that's all it was—an excuse. The truth is, I accepted their death a long time ago. It took months of tears, anger, and bargaining to finally reach the place where I could accept that the two people I loved most in this world were gone. I'm almost afraid to believe they're alive. So much of me doesn't quite believe it yet. The other part doesn't want to, because if anyone is lying, if this is some cruel joke, I'll plummet right back into that dark hole I had to dig myself out of when I said goodbye the first time.

Ryder has been incredible through all this. He hasn't questioned me once about why I haven't called before now, but he left the house with Devon as soon as I mentioned it was time. I think he knew I needed to be alone when I made the call, though I'm not sure he knows how conflicted I feel.

I hit the last number, my body one big heartbeat. I can barely breathe. I want to hang up as soon as it starts ringing. My eyes water at the realization that I'm about to see their faces and hear their voices for the first time in five years.

"Hello?" My mother's face fills the screen in front of me. Her hair is grayer and cut shorter, but her face is almost the same. Maybe a little plumper, but the same. Her eyes widen with realization.

"Peter, come quick!" she calls. "Oh, darling, my darling girl."

I dissolve into a puddle of tears right on the spot—sniffling, runny nose, ugly face and all. I can't even come up with words as I look at my beautiful mom, and cry harder when my dad comes into view.

"You grew a beard," I finally manage to get out, taking in my dad's full face of gray whiskers. He strokes his chin, his lip quivering as he grins, his eyes moist.

"Does it make me look old?" he asks, and I shake my head. My parents have never looked healthier, more alive. Their skin is bronze under linen clothing. My dad is in a light colored button-up shirt, and my mom is wearing a dress.

"Stand up," I say, laughing through my tears. "Turn around. Let me look at you!" They do, and I can't get enough of them. "You both are so beautiful!"

"Oh honey, you are too!" my mom says. "Your hair is getting so long. And you're so skinny! Are you getting enough to eat?"

"I was on some vegetarian diet at the facility," I say. "And the past couple days have been kind of crazy. But we're settled in our new home now, and the fridge is packed. I'll gain back all the weight I lost, and then some. That is, if I can get used to the, um, menu."

"Try sautéing the grasshoppers," my mom says. I check to see if she's joking and realize she isn't. I bypass the food topic and instead catch them up on the most recent details, telling them about Ryder, and about Mila and Devon, our stay at River's End and our escape, the drive to Arizona and our capture by Duke and his men—everything that led me to this very moment.

"Did you hear about Skye?" I ask, and regret it when I see my mom's face crumple.

"Emily, it's going to be okay. They're going to get him out," my dad says.

"They might not," she whispers, then peeks at me. "I'm sorry. I should be more optimistic. You've been through so much, and don't need to hear me being negative. Of course they'll get him out."

"I'm going to help," I say. My mom studies me.

"You're joking, right? Say you're joking."

"I'm not." I chew the inside of my cheek as her mouth sets in a firm line. Our years apart feel like nothing as she shoots me the same look of exhaustion she used to when

I was being stubborn. And just like old times, she is bent on protecting me from myself instead of just trusting me. I'd forgotten what it was like to have an over-caring mother. "I have to do this, Mom."

"Noelle, don't. I can't lose you, too. Just come to Cuba. We're safe here. No one has to pretend anything. No one can even get you here."

"I know, Mom, but how could I live free knowing that Skye is stuck here, his life in danger?"

"Do you think it would be any different if he was free?"

I know it won't. If he wasn't in prison, he'd be continuing the mission toward liberation, putting his life in jeopardy so others could live. If he survives this, it probably won't be the last time he's captured.

"That's why I need to stay," I say. "And it's why I need to help find him and bring him back. He'd do the same for me. He made sure all of us survived."

"You remember your training?" Dad asks. Mom looks at him, her eyes narrowing.

"Peter." Her voice is a warning, but Dad and I talk around her.

"It's been a few years, but yes. I surprised myself before we got to Cedar Grove when I used the moves on one of the guys. I had him on the ground, a knife to his neck before he knew what was happening."

"Good girl."

"No, *not* good girl," Mom says. "This isn't the time for heroics."

"And when is the time, Mom? I already have Ryder on my case about this, and everyone else is acting like a roadblock. But Skye's my brother! I don't care what anyone says, I'm going after him and helping to bring him home."

"She can do it," Dad says, wrapping his arm around my mom. "I taught Skye and Noelle everything I knew when they were growing up. She's a natural, and she'll annihilate anyone who crosses her path." He laughs, turning toward me. "Do you remember that one time I had to get you from the principal's office?"

I smirk, shaking my head with humor. I was fourteen, walking home from school when Brent Whitley wrapped his arms around me and tried to yank me behind a building. He hadn't seen it coming when I grabbed his arm, pulling as I whipped around, and then caught him with an upward thrust to the chin with the palm of my hand. He'd bit straight through his lip, and I would have felt sorry for him, but I also knew his reputation. As he lay bleeding and crying at my feet, I told him that if I got in trouble, I'd bring in numerous female witnesses who would have plenty to say about his aggressive persuasions. His friends narced on me anyway, which was why my dad had to get me. Somehow, Brent convinced the principal it had all been a misunderstanding. Still, a few weeks later, he was forced to leave school when many of his previous victims came forward, reporting attacks by him that started out just like mine. Once word got out that I'd roughed him up, other girls found their courage to speak out.

"Noelle gave that boy a lesson he never forgot," Dad says with a laugh.

"I thought the story had a few missing parts." Mom sighs. "I don't love this idea, Noelle, but I can see there's nothing I can say that will change your mind."

"Or mine," Ryder says behind me. I turn to see him holding Mila, Devon at his side.

"Oh, you must be Ryder," my mom says. "And Mila and Devon! Noelle, get out of the way so we can see these precious children."

My mom gushes over them, and then she and Ryder talk about me as if I'm not even there. It's so my mom, so familiar, and so much like home that I find myself tearing up again.

"Sweetie, we're just joking," my mom says as I wipe my eyes. She'd just finished telling Ryder about the time I'd discovered my first armpit hair as a teen, and how Skye had teased me mercilessly when he found out.

"I know, Mom," I say. I peek at my armpits now. "It's been a few weeks since I've seen a razor, so I think I can get French braids out of them by now."

Before we get off the phone, my mom surprises us with one last question I'm not ready to answer.

"So, will the two of you and my grandkids be here before Christmas this year, or what?"

I balk at the question, breathless by the weight of timing and the insinuation of our family roles. I've only known Ryder for a short time; we're still navigating our place with each other. I know I'll keep Mila no matter what, and I assume Ryder will keep Devon. I know I want to be with Ryder, and I'd be lying if the thought of forever hadn't crossed my mind. But when my mom says grandkids….Ryder told me he loves me, but we haven't discussed what comes next. It seems too soon. I look at Ryder for support, unsure what to say. He slips his hand in mine, squeezing it.

"You raise an interesting question, Emily," he says. "We're still figuring that out ourselves. But we'll let you know soon, okay?" She seems happy with this, and I make a mental note to talk with her in private later, halting any family talk from her until we've had our own conversations.

🌀 🌀 🌀

"Sorry about my mom," I say when we're finally off the phone. Devon is back outside, taking advantage of the "daylight" hours before he has to come inside. I pull vegetables from a bin in the fridge and, with an inhale of courage, a package of grasshoppers for dinner.

"What are you sorry about?" Ryder asks. He eyes the grasshoppers, swallowing hard as he does. "How do we cook those things?"

"My mom said to sauté them, but let's try breading them and then frying them," I say.

"Good call." He grabs the carton of liquid eggs from the second shelf and the flour and spices from the pantry.

I scoot the crickets in his direction, then start washing the vegetables. I peel the potatoes, moving out of his way when he washes his hands. He kisses the back of my neck, and then busies himself at the stove, dropping the grasshoppers into the scrambled egg, retrieving them with a slotted spoon, and then dipping them in the flour mixture, moving them around with the spoon until they no longer look like bugs. With a sizzle, he lets them rest in the hot oil for a few minutes before setting them on the plate I've prepared with a paper towel. It's like a dance, one that's so familiar despite having never learned the steps. I've always cooked alone, and yet sharing the duties couldn't feel more natural, despite the bugs we're about to eat. We both move around each other as if we've done this many times before.

"What I mean is my mom's insinuation that we're a family," I say, returning to the conversation.

"Aren't we, though?"

My heart beats faster at this. "You know what I mean," I say. His back is to me as he continues cooking the grasshoppers, and I don't know if he's teasing or serious. "She's just being ridiculous, I guess. Same old mom."

"She's not that ridiculous." He turns to face me, popping a fried grasshopper in his mouth. "It's a conversation that hasn't been possible before now, but it's one we should have." His mouth is full as he speaks, and then he chews thoughtfully. "These aren't half bad. Here, try this."

I take the grasshopper he's extending. I'm not sure what to say because there's so much riding on this conversation and what it means for us. I have so many questions, but I can't seem to find the words. The grasshopper offers me a way to stall, as grossed out as I am. I put it in my mouth, trying to clear my mind as I chew. It's soon clear that bravery isn't required. I mostly taste the fried batter, though I'm aware of the crunch on the inside.

"So what do you say?" Ryder asks.

"It's not bad."

"No, about wanting to be a family? Do you want to?"

I give the slightest of nods, afraid to do anything more. What if he doesn't? I believe he does. I mean, he loves me. But that's different than something as permanent as a family. I could be reading him wrong. We've kind of been lumped together in all of this. What if this whole thing is just a matter of convenience, and it all blows up now that life is simmering down?

His face relaxes into a warm smile, and he gestures for me to come to him.

"I have to get the potatoes in the water," I say, nodding toward the boiling water.

"Then do it, and come here."

I do carefully, slowly, fearfully, unsure about all of this, and completely afraid he won't want the same things I do. When the last potatoes hit the water, he takes my hand and pulls me close, giving me no choice but to fall into him. He lifts my chin so that I'm looking at him, and he searches my face. His mouth turns up at the corner, and he lowers to mine, taking me with his kiss. I release my grip on the counter and cautiously place my hands at his waist before wrapping my arms around him. Every thought, every doubt, every fear falls at our feet as I lose myself in him, tasting him as his tongue dances with mine. He nips at my lower lip, ending with a soft kiss. He then holds me against his chest, his mouth against my ear.

"Marry me." His whisper catches me off guard, and I move to leave his embrace, but he continues holding me. "Don't fight it, Noelle. It's no accident we found each other."

"But it's too soon to even think about marriage," I protest.

"And our lives were supposed to end in just a few weeks. But we're still alive, and now we have this chance to start over. Let's get married. We're already a family, let's make it legal."

I tilt my head up so that I'm looking at him. His face is so hopeful, and I see in him everything I've been looking for. We met as two lost souls with no one left to belong to. He has his issues and I have mine, but somehow they all seem less terrible when we're together. He's my someone, my person, the one I want to do life with. I can't imagine living this second life without him. Nothing makes less sense. I feel my doubts and fears evaporate as I look into his eyes and see my future in the kaleidoscope of his irises. We belong together, I've never been more sure of anything. All the things I thought I'd never have—love, children, a long happy life—it's all possible with him.

"Yes," I breathe, and his face breaks into a grin.

"Say it."

"Yes, I'll marry you. Yes, I'll raise a family with you. Yes to all of it, as long as you're with me."

His mouth finds mine again, and we kiss until the fire alarms sound.

"Our dinner!" This batch of grasshoppers is completely black. But who cares? If he burned every grasshopper, I'd eat them anyway, and they'd taste divine, accompanied by this sweet life we both have with each other.

That night we make love slowly. There's no hurry, no hiding. He leaves the lights on low, taking in my body with his eyes before claiming me with his flesh. When he enters me, I feel complete, as if we have no beginning or end and are made of Infinity. He whispers in my ear, telling me every way he loves me. His words penetrate my skin, sink into my bones, become my soul.

I clutch his muscled back as he kisses my shoulders, running his lips against my collar bone. He makes me feel beautiful, taking his time to savor my body and taste every inch. Then he slips away from me and continues his exploration. My breath catches when he reaches my core, my fingers running through his hair until he makes me lose my senses. I cry out into the pillow beside me, ecstasy running through me in waves until they finally subside and he returns to me.

He holds my hands over my head and claims my mouth, taking me completely as he moves purposely, methodically, deeply. His body tightens and he expands within me before he lets out a low moan, wrapping me in his arms as he releases his energy. I feel the relief immediately, as if I've been holding my breath up until this very moment. The air is sweeter, easier. He collapses on my chest and I stroke his hair, damp with sweat, and kiss his salty forehead. He keeps his arms around me, and I feel like I'm one huge heartbeat combined with his.

I awake alone in bed, the dim morning light shining through the window. I peek at the clock, groaning when I see how early it is. It's not even six yet. The door nudges open, and Ryder enters with a tray. I can hear Mila whimpering in the background. He groans, wrinkling his nose, but there's a smile on his face. He places the tray on the bed, which holds two cups of coffee and a plate with bagels smothered in cream cheese.

"I was hoping we could wake up a little more, maybe have a repeat of last night before she woke up," he says.

"Welcome to family life," I tease, pulling back the covers so I can get her.

"Stay here. Drink some coffee. I'll get her." He leaves before I can protest. I sip the coffee. This is a first, and I like it. No one has ever served me coffee in bed. I could get used to this.

He returns, insisting on feeding her so I can eat, even as his coffee grows cold.

"I can always make another cup, it's no big deal," he says when I protest. I think he enjoys this whole family man thing.

Once she's happy and he's finally able to eat, I waste no time bringing up the hard stuff.

"I haven't forgotten the mission," I say. He chews, regarding me for a moment before swallowing.

"I know," he says. "I don't like it, but I know." He looks down at Mila, who's resting on the bed between our legs. "I want to go with you."

"No," I say. "I mean, I want you there. I don't want to spend a moment without you. But it's too dangerous."

"And it's not dangerous for you?"

"It's dangerous for anyone. But I'm not going into this blindly." I told him about my dad's years as a Navy Seal, and how he trained Skye and me when we were little.

"I might not have grown up as a would-be assassin, but I'm not some lame duck, either."

"I'm not saying you are." I stroke Mila's leg, and she kicks at my touch. "Besides, who will watch the kids?"

"I'm sure there's someone who can stay with them," he says. I shake my head.

"They're not you or me, though. It should be one of us. It should be you. If something happens to me, you should be here with them. They can't lose both of us."

"And I can't lose you."

I don't respond. I sip the last of my lukewarm coffee and then grab the dishes, leaving Ryder with Mila. I hear him rustling on the bed behind me, and Mila's soft noises as he picks her up to follow me.

"Noelle, you have to understand this isn't easy for me."

"I know." And I do. I'm as freaked out as I am determined by this decision. I haven't even found my way into the mission, and I'm terrified. But I have to. I'll regret it forever if I don't.

"I'm only going to ask you one last time. Stay. Please stay. Let the rebels do whatever they have planned to get your brother, and stay here with me where you're safe. We'll have a nice wedding, any kind you want. We can stay here or go to Cuba, I don't care. But stay with me. I couldn't handle it if I lost you."

I put the dish down in the sink and dry my hands. I walk over to him and he wraps his free arm around me, kissing the top of my head. I look up and see tears in his eyes, and I have to look away or I'll start crying, too.

"I have to try," I say, and I feel him deflate next to me. "I'll ask to join the mission. If they refuse, I won't fight it and I'll come home. But if they accept me, I'm going with them. I know I'm safer here with you. I know I'm risking my life. But Skye would have done it for me. I have to be a part of this."

"He wouldn't want you to die," Ryder says. He keeps his arm around me, but it hangs loosely against my shoulder. I grasp his hand, squeezing it.

"Will you support me?" I look up at him, and in spite of his opposition, his face softens into a smile.

"You know I don't want to."

"But I know you will."

He wrinkles his nose, then kisses the tip of mine.

"Forever. But you better come back to me. We have a wedding to plan."

"And a big move to Cuba."

To this, he grins. "I better brush up on my Spanish."

Mission

Noelle

∞

"**A**gain."

I grimace, but pick myself up and take a ready stance, bracing as my broad attacker barrels at me. My body complains as I crouch at the last moment, but I fight through the pain as I meet Derek's solid middle and throw him over my shoulder as if this three hundred pound man was a third of his weight. I don't try to hide my grin as I hear him grunt while hitting the ground behind me.

"Better," Birgitte says. "Again."

We've been at this for days, going through different modes of attacks. She'd surprised me when she first agreed I could join the mission, but I'd realized early on that it was a test, and they were going to beat me into quitting. This was apparent by the numerous drills they put me through. It seems they were aware of my training as a child. Of course they were—they knew my brother. However, they underestimated what I was capable of. Hell, I underestimated my capabilities. As they ran me through the gauntlet, I kept a cool demeanor, doing everything they asked without hesitation. But inside, I was shaken. I was sure I'd fail. By the end of the day, I was bruised and run ragged. In the evenings, I'd soak in an ice bath, trying to undo the damage to my muscles. In the first hour of the morning, I couldn't even dress myself as my arms wouldn't lift above my head.

"Is it worth it?" Ryder had asked this morning as he helped me get my shirt on. I noticed his grimace as he took in the huge bruise covering my right side.

"My brother is worth it," I said.

By the end of today's session, I finally see acceptance in Birgitte's deep green eyes, which appear even more exotic lined in kohl. The woman embraces femininity with a don't-fuck-with-me air about her. She has long, sleek black hair, which reaches her waist, even tied back in a thick braid. Her slender body is like liquid in her black catsuit. Her arms are covered in Japanese cherry blossom tattoos, which snake up her shoulders and end halfway up her neck. Her voice is silky, even when she's barking commands at me. I'm both intrigued and intimidated by her. She's dark and mysterious, making me feel plain and inferior in her presence. So when I see that she's pleased, I can believe I've done well.

"We're finished," she says. I glance at the clock on the wall, noting how much earlier we're ending the drills. "I need you in your best shape, soldier," she says. "Take the rest of the day off. Go to bed early, then be here at 0300 hours. We head out tomorrow."

I turn and head for the showers before she can see my surprise or any lingering fear. I'd asked for this, but I doubt I'll ever feel ready. Birgitte had warned me what to expect. We're heading into a battlefield, into a war where anything is possible. We have moles on the inside and know exactly where Skye is being held. We know of some of the traps we'll face. But we don't know everything, Birgitte had admitted to me.

"Failure is not an option," Birgitte promised at one point as I rested during my drills. I didn't miss her faltering look. "We die trying," she said. Just like that, her usual determination returns to her tight jawline.

"We die trying," I whisper as the hot water washes over me. I make it as hot as I can stand, feeling my skin burn before it numbs to the temperature. I stay in there for twenty minutes, just standing under the water as the spray pelts my back. *I could die.* Ryder's face flashes in front of me, followed by Mila, then by Devon. My family. In a rare moment, I second-guess my decision to go. I know I can opt out any moment. Birgitte might even be happy about it. But I can't. I owe this to Skye.

◉ ◉ ◉

Ryder holds me all night long. When my alarm buzzes, his arms are still wrapped around me. I shut off the alarm and remain against him for a few more minutes. He stirs, nestling his nose against my neck.

"Stay," he whispers. I smile, scooting closer as he tightens his embrace. I breathe in, memorizing his warm scent, the feel of his body, how good it feels to be this close to him.

"I'll be back before you know it," I say. He sighs but doesn't argue. Reluctantly, I leave the safety of his arms, dressing in the dark, ignoring my screaming muscles as I do. It feels strange to strap on my bulletproof vest and sling my gun over my back when everything in this house is safe. Mila and Devon are sleeping soundly in their rooms. Our routine has normalized after only a few weeks. This space is our own, and we can breathe easy knowing no one can interrupt our safety. And here I am, wrapping ammunition around me and strapping guns to each of my legs. I lean over and kiss Ryder's cheek.

"Take care of my babies," I say. "And take care of you."

"Only if you promise to come back to me."

I inhale his scent one more time. I'll never get enough of it. "I promise."

A car is waiting for me outside, its headlights carving a sharp angle through the darkness. I slip into the backseat, resting my gun beside me. As soon as the door shuts, the car glides forward, the driver never saying a word. We ride in silence the whole way there. I stare out the window, my vision blurring through tears I keep biting back. I feel stupid crying. I made this choice, so why the sudden tears? I'm sure Skye never cried. But then again, Skye was always tougher than me.

We arrive at the facility and I get out. "Thank you," I murmur, and the driver nods in acknowledgment. He's gone as soon as I close the door. I face the dark building that looms in front of me before starting up the dimly lit path. Our plan moves through my mind on repeat with each step. Jet. War zone. Tunnels. Basement. Diversion. Skye. Escape. These are the pillars of our mission, which seem simple enough. It's the spaces between these words where my worry lies.

Birgitte wastes no time once I'm inside. We step into formation and she leads us to the hanger. A small, black jet rests in the center, and we each climb the stairs and find our seat inside. There are just enough seats for the six of us. The cabin feels even smaller when the pilot closes the door. I glance at the other rebels on this mission. Derek is arguably the largest of the group, his seatbelt straining against his bulging chest, and the muscles of his arms clearly defined under his tight, long sleeves. Jet is the exact opposite—short and lean. But I've seen his moves. Just like his name, he's fast. Boaz is slightly older than the rest of us but has a mind like a computer and a way with a machine gun. And Justin? I try not to stare too long at him. The dude loves anything war, from what I can tell. Every drill, he's the one going full force, giving it his all, as if the rest of us are on the wrong side. Birgitte only pitted me against him once, and it was enough. He's a former Seal, but nothing like my dad. From what Boaz told me early on, Justin snapped after the Canadian war and still suffers from PTSD. But he's also the one with connections on the inside, and so Birgitte overlooks his instability for what he can bring to the mission. As for Birgitte, she's quick in our drills, ruthless in battle, and an expert with any weapon she can find—and everything within her reach becomes a weapon. I once saw her strip Derek's belt from his waist and had it fastened around his neck, like a noose, before he could react.

Then there's me. I've managed to hold my own in every drill, but I don't pretend to be better than anyone here. They've been training for years. I'm banking on my childhood lessons, before I even knew we had enemies. I know they're aware of my lacking skills; I just hope I can keep up. There's no other choice.

My heart races as the aircraft moves forward, leaving the hangar to coast down the runway. My belly churns with fear, and I have to force down the energy bar Birgitte's given each of us.

"We don't know when we'll eat again," she warns when she sees my hesitation. It tastes like charcoal with a chewy consistency, but I choke it down anyway. As we eat, Birgitte repeats the plan she's told us every day since I joined the mission, the same plan I've breathed night and day.

"Skye is in Sacramento, California's state capital," she says. "They've disguised the building as an end-of-life facility, but it's really a prison for rebels, guarded by lifers who have bargained their way out of expiration and some of the nation's toughest soldiers, loyal to The Enforcers. We're landing about fifty miles away at an abandoned farm in Suisun City. A Humvee is there to truck us in—"

"Wait, a Humvee?" I interrupt. "I thought we were taking a bus in to keep a low profile."

"A Humvee," Birgitte says, her eyes narrowing on me. "Riots have increased across the nation, but particularly around government buildings. They've stopped all visitors from coming into the city, and that includes buses filled with tourists. Trust me, it's better than what they were doing before."

I glance at the guys, my gaze landing on Jet as he makes eye contact with me. He raises his hands like he's holding a machine gun, then makes whooshing noises while pretending to gun us all down.

"We've snagged a Humvee from the National Guard, and will look just like the soldiers when we roll in." Birgitte moves her gaze, glancing at all of us. "That said, be ready to move once we get there, guns at the ready. Shoot at anyone that shoots at you. And whatever you do, don't stop. You stop, you die. End of story."

She continues with the rest of the plan, and I try to tune in, but all I can think of is how I'm going to shoot at a civilian who's shooting back at me. Training with my dad is one thing. Tossing men who are bigger than me is one thing. Killing one of my enemies before they kill me is one thing. But killing a person who I'm ultimately trying to save? That's something else. *If you want to see your family again, you'll do what it takes to survive*, I scold myself. I hope I don't have to.

"One last thing, don't do anything stupid." She smirks. "Which, of course, means do anything to survive. If you're in the enemy's hands, you fight your way out. Never surrender. They're out to kill, so you better have the same mission."

***

We reach California in record time. It feels like I've barely had a moment to breathe. The jet makes its descent, landing next to a cornfield. Just like Birgitte says, a Humvee greets us as we climb down the stairs. We don't speak as we move from one vehicle to the next. The freeway is crowded at first, but traffic lightens the closer we get to Sacramento. By the time we hit Davis, it's like a ghost town. Cars are abandoned on the side of the road, riddled with bullet holes. Ripped remains of protest banners hang from the trees, their haunting messages dripping within the folds of the ones we can read. "The numbers are a lie. We're not dying, we're alive." The sun is just rising, and as far as I can see in the dim morning light, there are no signs of civilian life. Windows are shot out of buildings. Streetlights are dark. Blockades at every exit bar us—and anyone else dumb enough to brave this road—from slipping off the highway and finding refuge in the town. Every few miles, I see a Humvee like ours stationed on the side of the road, soldiers leaning on the truck with guns next to them. Each one waves us through as my heart pounds. I get the importance of this vehicle now. Any other mode of transportation and those soldiers would pump us full of metal.

The sign ahead says "Sacramento," with "sucks" spray-painted below. I mirror the faces of my fellow rebels, who look determined and prepared for the mission we're about to face. My hands are sweaty, but my skin is cold even under all these layers. This time, the exit is wide open, and we coast down the empty street. We don't even reach the end when protesters come out of nowhere, holding bottles in their hand. I realize they're Molotov cocktails, and I flip the safety as I raise my gun. Justin jumps from the Humvee before I can even take aim, running at the protesters while screaming unclear words. They scatter without throwing a single bottle bomb.

"Tell your friends," he shouts as he climbs back into the Humvee.

"Justin." Birgitte shakes her head at him but then rolls her eyes.

For the most part, any civilians we come across slip out of sight as we roll through the town. We go slow, joining a train of Humvees heading toward the capital.

"Gas masks," Birgitte orders quietly, slipping hers on. I do the same, following her gaze to the bodies lining the side of the road. Shouting voices meet my ears, and I watch in horror as I see soldiers hitting the numbers at the backs of people's necks, instantly killing them as they're injected with the needle's poison. The soldiers seem to be making a sport of it. One runs down a family, catching a mother as she falls.

"Run!" she screams before she's silenced. The soldier doesn't chase after the children from what I can tell through blurry eyes.

We're in hell. Smoke rises from former houses, now reduced to rubble. Soldiers laugh while kicking aside human remains. The living that dare to show their faces are dirty with tear-stained cheeks. Ash rains down on us from smoky skies. It's hard to believe the world looks like this. It's only been a few weeks since I prepared for my final one hundred days. Back then, the world was safe—at least as far as I could tell.

"How long has this been going on?" I ask Boaz, sitting next to me.

"Not long," he says. "Since Skye's arrest, when everyone else became aware that the numbers were a lie."

I look around with wide eyes. The place looks like it's been under attack for years, not weeks.

We break off from the line of Humvees, heading down a side street. I look over my shoulder to see if anyone notices, but the soldiers in front of us are all looking forward. It's likely that anyone paying attention will think we're patrolling neighborhoods, not embarking on the next step of our way into the capital.

We stop at the dead-end of an alley, and the engine cuts. Quickly, four people appear out of nowhere and block the end of the alley closest to the street. I hold my breath, my hand on my trigger as I prepare for the worst, but loosen my grip when I see that they're hiding us from view with large cans overflowing with trash. Justin gets out first, meeting them halfway as they near our Humvee, clapping one of them on the back.

"Is that our guy?" I ask Boaz.

"Which one?" he answers. "We have a lot of help on the inside. Unfortunately, the enemy has more."

We leave the Humvee and step through a hidden doorway to the right of the dead end, entering a dark passageway. Each of us has a headlamp, but only Birgitte's lights the way, keeping things dim until we reach our first destination. We make two rights, and then a left before we're ushered into the back of what appears to be a Chinese market. Spices line the walls, their ingredients listed in characters rather than words. Through a curtain, I can see fruit and vegetables rotting on abandoned tables.

"This way," one of the men whispers, leading us through a doorway. We push our way into a crowded room. Dozens of eyes watch us. Despite the number of people in here, including children, the room is silent. We squeeze through the crowd wordlessly, reaching the other side and another door. A woman sits at a desk in a large room, big enough to hold a few of these families, but empty except for her and her desk.

"Ms. Evans," the woman says in a thick Asian accent, bowing slightly to Birgitte. "We've been waiting for you." She gets up from her seat and leads us across the room to yet another doorway. Here, we find a dormitory with bunk beds and a refrigerator. She leaves us without instruction, shutting the door behind her. I frown, setting my gun down and loosening my vest.

"Don't get too comfortable, soldier," Birgitte says. "We're here only to fuel up before heading in."

"What about those people out there?" I ask.

"What about them?"

"They're in that cramped building with hardly any space to move, when there's a large office on the other side of the wall, and food and beds in here. Why do they have them locked in like cattle?"

"That's not part of our mission."

"It's inhumane," I mutter. Birgitte hits the side of the bed with such force, it shifts.

"Those people are not our concern," she hisses. "Neither are the bodies on the side of the road, the families being mowed down, the homes being burnt, the…"

I look up as her voice catches, alarmed at the sudden pause of words. She grimaces, glaring at the wall behind me. But I see the shine in her eyes as she fights back tears.

"We're here for Skye, okay? What you've seen is horrible. What's happening is horrible. Those people crammed into that little space? *Horrible*. But we're here for your brother. Once he's safe, then we can focus on the rest of the world. But not until Skye is safe."

I hear something in her tone, a familiarity when she says his name.

"You've known him for a while, haven't you?" I ask. She doesn't answer. Instead, she brushes past me and opens the fridge. I feel awful that I'm disappointed by the choices—a bowl of white rice, a container of strange looking vegetables, a bottle of soy sauce, and a pitcher of murky water. There's death and destruction happening all around us, and I don't like the food. Birgitte grabs the water and drinks without hesitation, then hands it to each of us, one by one. When she gets to me, I hide my discomfort and drink, disgusted by the metal taste.

"He saved my life," she says. Then she moves on.

Following our final bathroom break, Birgitte pushes the bed away from the wall, moving the boxes underneath to the side. She lifts a tiny latch, and the checkered floor reveals a two feet by two feet trap door. Justin goes down first, jumping through the hole and landing with a thud on what sounds like concrete, judging by the echo. I peer down, seeing the nothingness revealed by his headlamp.

Each of us follows behind, with Derek taking the rear, closing the trap door behind him. I can hear scraping above us as we're sealed into our tomb by boxes and a bed. We're encased in black, save for Justin's lamp. We keep ours off as he leads this portion of the mission, taking us through a series of twists and turns. The tunnel is a maze, but he moves forward with surety as if he's done this many times. He hasn't, of course. For weeks, he memorized a map of the city's water pipes until he had the exact course toward the capital ingrained in his memory.

It's almost an hour of silent travel before he stops. He lifts his finger to his lips, then points to a ladder. He holds his hand up, signaling for us to wait while he pulls a device from a clip on his vest and punches in a code. A few seconds later, the device gives a low buzz. My heart jumps as a scraping grate above us cuts through the silence. A face peers down at us, then extends his hand, motioning for us to make the climb. Justin nods at me to go first. With a deep breath, I grasp the cold, damp metal of the ladder, using Justin's knee as a boost to reach the first rung. When I reach the top, strong hands grasp me under the arms, pulling me the rest of the way into the capital building.

The Enforcers

Noelle

∞

"Put this on." The man speaks underneath a thick white mustache, handing me a soldier's uniform. The coarse material is pure black except for gold striping on the upper arms, forming a V. Zippers fasten in front, hidden by a strip of overlying material. I dress quickly, tucking my hair under a matching helmet and lifting the face mask so that only my eyes are visible. Everything is a little loose, and I work at the drawstrings to tighten the pants.

"Here, allow me," the old man says, stepping forward. He's wearing a custodian uniform, which seems strangely believable. He touches a button at my waist, and the pants cinch to my skin. He does the same for the jacket, and it molds to the shape of my bulletproof vest.

"A little looser up top," Birgitte says, nodding at my chest. I look down. Even with the vest, it's apparent I'm a woman. The man touches another button lightly, and my chest blends in with the rest of my body.

"There's more." Birgitte crosses the room and touches a button at the edge of my sleeve. Sharp spikes protrude from my sleeves, curving in a knife-like hook. "Hopefully you won't be close enough to anyone to use these," she says. "But if you are, these will do some serious damage."

Once everyone is dressed, we line up as we've practiced in our drills. This time, Derek leads the way, followed by Jet. Birgitte falls in behind me, with Justin taking up the rear. We march through the corridors, passing other soldiers in identical formations going in the opposite direction. Derek never fails to salute the lead of each line, just as they do to him. Not only have we spent weeks going over the rescue mission, but we've memorized the culture within the capital. The smallest mistake could expose who we are and what we're doing. The Enforcers likely know there's a rescue plan in place; it would be dumb to believe otherwise. This makes it even more important that everything is perfect—not even revealing one stray hair on my head.

We climb two flights up to the main level of the capital, taking each step in sync like the ticking of a clock. I keep my face forward as soldiers are trained to do, but my eyes take in everything around me; the women wearing calf-length pencil skirts and jackets, carrying clipboards and rushing from room to room; the cameras that are spaced ten yards apart, pointing down at us from all directions; a bird that found its way indoors and is desperately trying to find its way out; the tapestries on the wall, which seem medieval in nature, adorned with a lion crest . I've seen the lion before, but I can't place where. Here, the emblem is everywhere—embroidered in a stole around each statue's neck, repeated in the wallpaper of one of the rooms, and sewn into the lapel of every capital worker we pass. Without looking down, I realize it's also on my uniform. My question to its meaning is soon answered when we enter the main hall of the capital and stop before the huge banner taking up the top of one wall. A huge face of a lion eyes us from the banner, appearing mid-growl next to the words, "The strong shall inherit the earth." Underneath, in large letters, "The Enforcers."

The meaning is clear, and a chill runs through me. Extermination. Population control. Ridding the world of the less fortunate, those who are weak, and anyone who gets in their way.

We're waiting for admittance through closed double doors. Just knowing that each step is one closer to Skye has me on edge. That, and the fact that this could all go wrong without warning. Each second tightens around my throat. All I can see in front of me is the back of Jet's head, and I strain my ears to hear what the guarding officer is saying to Derek. We're finally let through, and I pass the officer without glancing in his direction. I feel his eyes on me, though. I can barely breathe. Even though my face is covered by my balaclava, I'm sure he's recognized me.

We continue in formation as the doors close behind us. In front of Jet, Boaz twists slightly. My breath catches as I see him look up, realizing that we've reached the next phase. Sure enough, he steps out of line and faces us.

"The cameras are now on a loop," he says with a grin. I relax, leaning against the wall in the empty corridor, same as the guys. Only Birgitte stands tall.

"We don't have much time," she says. "Ward is blocking the entrance for the next fifteen minutes."

"Ward?" I ask.

"The officer that waved us through," she says, a hint of satisfaction reaching her eyes. So he *did* recognize me, but for entirely different reasons. "This hallway leads to the stairwell. At the bottom is The Well, the Capitol's basement where they're holding Skye. From this point on, we don't need to march, but we do need to stick tightly together. If anyone questions us, attack. Don't hesitate, no mercy. We have no friends from this point on."

We jog forward, our bodies practically touching as we remain one solid group. At the doorway to the stairwell, we drop back into line. This time, Justin leads the way. I realize the importance of this when he stuns a surprised soldier with his device before the man can even react. Once the soldier falls, Justin peers at the number at the back of his neck.

"High quintuples," he mutters. "75,647."

"Looks like he'll live past 200," Boaz says. He winces when Justin smashes the number.

"Not likely," Justin says.

At the bottom level, Derek lifts his finger in the air to stop us, then eases the door open. Jet throws a smoking bottle into the darkness as we all remain silent. We hear footsteps running, and then large thuds, like objects hitting the ground.

"Now," Derek says quietly. I pull my gas mask from my pack, lowering my cloth headgear before slipping it on. I then turn on my headlamp, just like the others. We proceed with caution, and I move my head so the lamp's light catches anything in my path. From my count, there are six soldiers collapsed on the ground. I step around each body, and wince as I hear distinct thwacks behind me—Justin has ensured none of them will follow behind us, or see their expiration date.

We reach the door at the other side of the room, turning off our headlamps as Boaz types something into his tablet. The glow from the gap under the door shuts off, and we can hear shouting on the other side. I barely hear the door scraping open, but I distinctly hear the clinking roll of another gas bottle. When it's quiet, we light up again and leave the room.

"Two rights and a left," Derek directs as we advance down the hall. I trip over a soldier lying in the middle of the path, pitching forward. I'm pulled back just in time.

"Careful, Edison," Birgitte says, letting me go. I murmur my thanks, burning with embarrassment. We make the first right, and I hear a whistling sound zip past me.

"Get down!" Derek yells.

"Damn," Birgitte swears, pulling me down and covering me with her body. At the same time, she removes her mask and then fumbles with her vest. I hear multiple shots hit the wall above us. "Mayday! Mayday! We're under attack in the fourth leg."

"We have your position, soldier," dispatch returns. "Are there any fatalities?"

"Boaz, get the lights!" Derek says. Boaz doesn't answer. I raise my head, my light shining on the person next to me. My vision is blocked by my damn gas mask, and I remove it so I can see. Boaz lies still, his head in an awkward position.

"Get down, soldier," Birgitte growls at me, but I shake her off.

"I'm in this, too," I say, understanding what she's doing—keeping me safe above all others. If she wanted me out of danger, though, she never should have agreed to let me on the mission. She releases me, and I lean over Boaz's body, searching for any signs of life. His neck was hit, blood flowing from his throat. He isn't breathing, and his wrist reveals no pulse. His skin is still warm. "Thank you for your service," I whisper. "To your country, my brother, and to me." I take the tablet from Boaz's loose grasp.

"One man down," Birgitte says, her voice shaking into the radio. "Officer Boaz DeTurk was hit by enemy fire." She lowers the radio, then takes the tablet from my outstretched hand.

"I hope you know how to use this," I say, feeling awkward. Boaz is dead, and the mission continues. If I submit to the overwhelming urge to mourn, it will be difficult to recover.

"No, but Justin does." Birgitte passes it to him, and he starts typing. My gun is out, and I hold it in front of me, ready to shoot. The lights turn back on, and I prepare to shoot at anything that moves. Even though the shots continue to fire above our head, we're alone—not including one soldier whose unconscious body lies a dozen feet away. I note the location of each bullet hole in the wall, then determine where they're coming from. A patterned wall camouflages the mechanical guns, but once I see them, they're hard to miss.

"Here, hold this," Justin says. He gives Birgitte the tablet, then creeps forward on his forearms and thighs. In the short amount of time I've been around him, I'm not surprised when he reaches the guard's body, looks up to determine the location of each shot, and then stands, holding the guard in front of him as a shield. It happens so fast, the bullets flying into the soldier as Justin shoots out each gun with impressive precision. The guns finally stop. Justin drops the body and steps over it.

"Coast is clear," he says, a wicked grin on his face, taking the tablet back from Birgitte.

"Cancel emergency," she radios in. "We have the situation under control."

"Roger that," dispatch returns. "Check back in when you can so we know your team is safe."

"Couldn't he have done that without the human shield?" I asked Birgitte once Justin is out of earshot.

"You know Justin," she replies. "We're lucky he's on *our* side." She adjusts her pack and stands, taking a quick look around. "Come on, we're wasting time." She's already down the hall after Justin before I'm on my feet. This most recent attack makes it clear that an ambush can happen at any moment, and my skin crawls in anticipation of what the next surprise might be. I do my best to stay alert and appear confident as I catch up to the group, but inside, I'm shaken.

Justin directs us just behind Derek, navigating the maze of hallways from the tablet. We go slow, especially when we reach each corner, unmoving until Derek gives the signal. I hold my breath when Justin touches Derek's shoulder, stopping when Derek holds his hand up. The two of them huddle over the tablet.

"Stay here," Derek finally says. "Don't move until I give the signal."

He and Justin disappear around the corner. My heartbeat echoes in my ears as we breathe the silence. I glance at Birgitte, but her expression is stone. My nerves are so wound up, my teeth are chattering. But I mimic her expression, hoping no one notices. It feels like forever when I finally hear the faint sound of something falling to the floor, followed by the thwack against flesh. A moment later, Derek is back, motioning us forward. We reach Justin, who's applying wired boxes to the corners of a solid metal door. A soldier lies motionless a few feet away, curled on his side.

We've reached Skye's cell.

"Get in position," Birgitte says, her voice barely a hum. I crouch down, bent on one knee, my gun at the ready just like the others. Justin presses a button on the remote. Immediately, the door begins to creak. The area around each device turns red before the door collapses into a puddle of liquid metal. Justin goes in first, slowly, methodically. I hold my breath while I wait. He's more relaxed when he returns, a grin on his face.

"All clear," he says. "Skye is unconscious but alive. We're free to move."

The mention of my brother's name shoots straight through me. I swallow hard. The threshold is the last barrier to Skye. I look to Birgitte at the same time she looks at me.

"Go ahead," she says softly. I note the tears in her eyes and recognize something in her expression.

"No," I say. "We go together." I take her hand as if she isn't my commander, but my friend. She squeezes before letting go. Raising her gun toward the door, she nods me forward. I also raise my gun, moving cautiously as I cross the doorway and enter the dark room. My brother is chained to the wall, his hair, the same silver color as mine, hanging in his face with his head drooped. I've never seen him so skinny. Despite the cool air within the cell he's wearing next to nothing, and I ache to cover him.

"Skye," I whisper.

"Drop your weapon."

I hear the click and feel cold metal against my temple. I close my eyes, breathing evenly and keeping a tight grip on my gun. I will *not* drop my gun. We've gotten too close to give in.

"Birgitte," I say, opening my eyes.

"Your friend is fine," the voice says. "At least, she's still alive. But if you don't drop your weapon, I'll kill her." I feel a firm grip on my shoulder. In one move, I could turn the tables on whoever is standing in the way of this rescue. But I don't. I let him turn me around until I can see my commander, crumpled on the floor a few feet away, a soldier standing over her. The slight movement of her chest shows she's still alive.

"Derek!" I call out. "Justin!" The man at my back cackles in my ear.

"They can't hear you. Now drop your weapon, Noelle."

"Not until I know the others are safe." The man hits me in the head with his gun and I stumble forward. He grabs me by the jacket, pulling me upright, turning me and taking my gun at the same time. The move is quicker than I can react, but that's not what shocks me.

"Dr. Patrick?"

The last time I saw him, at least conscious, was when he was holding Mila, telling me how lucky that little girl was to have me. His warm smile had made me momentarily forget how cold and sterile River's End could be. Now, his sneer takes over his whole face. I glance down at his collar.

"I should have known," I mutter, seeing the lion insignia, the same one I've seen everywhere. "You're one of The Enforcers."

"No one can accuse you of being dumb," he says, lowering his gun and nodding just behind me. The other soldier twists my arms behind me and forces me to kneel. "But if you were smarter, you would have known long before."

"I figured out which side you were on," I say, feeling my arms tied behind me. "I know your number is fake." I glare at him. "You pretended to care for all those people, masquerading as a doctor. It's all a lie, just like all of our numbers."

"Ah, but I *am* a doctor, Noelle," he says. "Just the kind of doctor you only see once."

I narrow my eyes, realizing what he's saying.

"You're the—"

"Doctor of Death," he says with a nod. "Most people die with a simple injection in the back of their neck on Day Zero, thanks to that brilliant device. But mistakes happen.

Sometimes the needle isn't released, or the injection isn't strong enough. I'm there to make sure the job is finished. I also take care of early expirations, like when infants are surrendered. However, there's one baby I let live."

I turn my head, tears stinging my eyes as I realize the implication. The soldier standing behind me forces my face back toward Dr. Patrick. My anger at this man mixes with shame as the tears spill over.

"That's right, Noelle. If it weren't for my intervention, Mila would've just been another one of those abandoned babies, put to sleep and then burned in a mass cremation. Instead, she's a healthy little girl, isn't she?"

"Don't pretend like you did me any favors," I spit out. "Your only reason for saving her was to ensure I'd talk. If it came down to it, you would've had no trouble threatening her life. But the joke's on you. Mila is safe, and you'll never lay a hand on her. There's nothing you can do to get me to talk."

"Really, Noelle? Nothing?" Dr. Patrick steps aside, giving me a full view of my brother. Skye moves his head slightly. "Did I tell you about my other specialty?" Dr. Patrick asks. He doesn't answer, walking to a briefcase next to the wall instead. He picks it up and brings it a few feet in front of me. He unlatches it and the lid springs open. Inside are several vials and syringes. He chooses a needle, holding it up as if inspecting it. Then he picks up a vial.

"It's interesting how something so small can bring so much pleasure," he says. He inserts the needle, pulling back the plunger. A clear substance fills the barrel. "Oh, not for the recipient, mind you. But if a prisoner isn't cooperating, this liquid will change their mind really quick. Would you like a demonstration?"

He doesn't wait for me to answer. I watch in horror as he walks slowly, purposefully toward my brother's battered body. For the first time since I've seen him, Skye lifts his head, looking right at me. It's slight, but I don't miss the shake of his head.

Say nothing.

Dr. Patrick grabs Skye's arms and doesn't even hesitate before plunging the needle into his flesh, pushing the poison into him as he screams.

"Stop! No! Leave him alone!" I fight against the ropes holding me down. The soldier behind me wraps his hands around my neck and I gasp for breath. My head grows light, and I lose control of my muscles as my vision dims. When he releases me, I fall to the ground, watching helplessly as my brother writhes in pain. I sob as I watch his head twitch violently and hear his anguished cries at whatever is coursing through him. It only lasts a few minutes, and then his body goes limp. I press my face against the concrete, unable to do anything but sob with shuddering breaths. I'm yanked back to a kneeling position, and Dr. Patrick leaves my brother, making his way to me. I'm sure Skye is dead until I hear him moan, moving with each intake of air.

"Thing is, Noelle, I've used this method many times on your brother in an attempt to get him to talk, and he doesn't seem willing to open up. It seems he has an impressive pain threshold. Question is, just how much do you have in common with your brother?" He picks up another vial, inserting the tip of the needle in the top and drawing the liquid into its chamber. He flicks the barrel, and a few drops spurt out. I clench my jaw. Fear washes over me as he comes closer, holding the needle right in front of my face. "Here's the deal. One of you will tell me where your camp is, along with any other place you're hiding refugees and rebels, or you'll feel what your brother just went through. And Noelle, I'm a patient man. If you don't talk the first time, maybe you'll talk the second, third, or even tenth time I inject you."

"Don't..." my brother moans. Dr. Patrick leans away from me, glancing over his shoulder.

"Well, that was quick. Do you have something to say?"

Skye lifts his head again. I can tell it's taking all his strength. He looks at Dr. Patrick for a moment, then he turns his gaze to me.

"Don't," he repeats, then takes a few deep breaths. "Don't do...anything...stupid," he wheezes out, then collapses. Birgitte spoke the same words just a few hours ago. I'm renewed with a sense of energy coursing through me, my confidence returning as I remember this uniform has a secret Dr. Patrick doesn't know about. My fingertips find the button at the hem of the sleeve. Before the doctor can react, I slice my way through the ropes and slash the neck of the soldier holding me captive. Dr. Patrick lunges at me with the needle, but I sidestep him, tripping him with my leg and bringing my elbow down in the middle of his back. The needle skitters across the concrete, and I lunge for my gun lying a few yards away. I roll over, pointing the gun at him with my back against the ground at the same time he trains his gun on me. I don't hesitate, squeezing the trigger as I aim between his eyes. It's a clean shot, except for the explosion of blood, skull fragments, and brain matter. I wipe my face in disgust, then check the gun in his hand. He hadn't even had a chance to remove the safety.

I leave the body where it lies, stumbling to my brother. He turns his head as I aim my gun at the chains on the wall, falling forward as he's released. I gather his bony frame in my arms, holding him as I openly sob into his soiled skin.

"I'm so sorry." There's so much I'm apologizing for, I can't even put it into words. Seeing him like this, how he's suffered to keep so many people safe, is more than I can bear.

"Quit it," he wheezes out, but he gives me a weak smile. He turns his head toward the center of the cell. Birgitte is still lying on the ground, her hair covering her face. "Take me to her."

I wrap his arm around the back of my neck and stand, bearing most of his weight as I bring him up with me. One of his legs is obviously weaker than the other, and he drags it as we move slowly toward Birgitte. When we reach her, he sinks down, resting on his hip before lying in front of her. A few strands of her hair have escaped her braid, and he smooths them away from her face. He caresses her cheek with a shaky, dirt-stained hand. My suspicion about their connection is confirmed when he leans in and presses his lips against hers. She gives a low moan, and he moves back. Both of us watch as her eyes flutter open. She stares at him for a few seconds before it registers, then both of her arms are wrapped around him. I watch as the heroic, bold, badass woman—who kicked my ass into fighting shape—transforms into a soft creature in the arms of the man she loves. Birgitte holds Skye's face in hers, kissing his cheeks, his eyes, his lips, murmuring her love to him as they both cry. I give them their moment, heading for the door of the cell. I'm nervous about what I'll find on the other side, unsure if the guys are okay. My shoulders fall forward when they're nowhere to be found. I'm about to turn around when I hear shouting down the hallway. I steady myself, aiming at the direction of the voices, but then lower my gun when I see Derek, Jet, and Justin, followed by an army of soldiers in blue uniforms.

"Cuba has arrived," Justin says, his grin mirroring the one I can feel on my face.

Epilogue

Noelle

∞

"Good morning." Ryder kisses me on the forehead, as the smell of coffee fills my nose. I stretch under the blankets, not ready to open my eyes, though the aroma is coaxing me from sleep.

"Good morning," I say, finally peeking through heavy lashes at my sweet husband. *Husband.* The word still gives me butterflies, the same that come when I spin the simple band on my finger. We'd married a few weeks after the rescue mission in a quickly thrown together ceremony attended by a dozen children, a few giraffes, and my parents, who were shuttled back to the States for an emotional reunion. Our honeymoon was a submarine journey to our new home in Cuba, where we were greeted by my fish named Fish, and a new puppy named, well, Puppy. It's only been three months since we made this place our home, and I'm caught somewhere in between the newness of it all and a comforting sense of place, as if Cuba has been calling to us all our lives.

Our home is in the underground, the same artificial world we'd been introduced to back in the States. But it's different here. We're not in hiding, this is just how everyone lives to make up for space. Above ground is where many of us work, where our food is grown, and where we can smell fresh air instead of the filtered air underground. It's easy here. The land is valued just as much as the people who tend it, and we all do our part to ensure the land continues to thrive. Here, the sky is always blue and the air is always sweet.

"I slathered some extra grub butter on your toast," Ryder says, and I notice the tray next to me. Mila is already trying to grab at it, even as Ryder keeps a tight hold on her. We recently started her on rice cereal and some mashed fruits, and now she's realized she wants all of our food, too.

"Coffee and breakfast in bed, how did I marry so well?" I ask, taking the wriggling girl from his arms. She forgets the food and snuggles into my neck, babbling against her fingers. I smell the top of her head, a mixture of her lavender baby shampoo and the natural scent of her downy skin. I'd bottle it if I could.

"Well, if you don't eat it, I will. I've already had two slices downstairs."

"Not bad for someone who thought he'd starve before eating insects."

He gives me a sly grin, reaching for my toast. Even with a baby in my arms, I'm too quick for him. I bite into the toast, savoring the nutty taste of the grubs as he leaves to finish getting ready for work. Mila doesn't last long curled up in my arms. I only get a few sips of coffee in before she's ready to move.

Downstairs, Devon is hunched over a bowl of cereal next to his Uncle Skye. I stand in the doorway for a moment, taking the two of them in. Devon is as dark as Skye is light, two opposites sitting side-by-side. And yet, the two of them have formed an immediate bond. It's much different than the relationship between Devon and me. Now and then, I see his walls come down, especially when he needs some extra comfort and comes to me for a squeeze before he's off and running again. But Devon is a guy's guy. In the same way he latched on to Ryder, he's become Skye's sidekick.

My brother agreed to live with us for a while, even though I know it's only temporary. He's here to heal and get stronger. Eventually he'll join Birgitte back in the States, working alongside her, Derek, Jet, and Justin to rehabilitate the citizens who survived the war as they set reconstruction in place. The numbers no longer apply, the US government has been overthrown, and our country is now liberated under a new leadership who holds sustainability at the forefront. In a year or so, Ryder and I have the option to move back if we want, but I think we'll stay. Cuba feels like home.

I often think back to that day when we rescued Skye. Derek told me the story of everything that had happened while I faced Dr. Patrick. The three of them had been captured during the surprise attack, overtaken and dragged from the capital building. If it had happened any earlier, our positions in Skye's cell would have been revealed at large, and all of us would have been killed. But Cuban soldiers had already reached the capital. We couldn't hear it from underground, but the war had begun. A group of soldiers freed the three men, who then led them to where we were.

"We came to rescue you, but you had to go and rescue yourself, you crazy girl," Derek had said, ruffling my hair like I was his kid sister. Then he pulled me into a side hug. "You did good soldier," he said.

"I'm pretty sure you wouldn't hug the guys this way," I said, but I returned the hug, wrapping my arms around his waist. I was just so glad to be alive.

"Are you kidding? Jet, Justin, get over here." Suddenly I was in the middle of three large men, gasping for breath as they squeezed in for one huge bear hug.

"You going to stand there all day?" Skye asks, bringing me back to the present. I grin, coming forward to wrap an arm around my brother's shoulder.

"What am I going to do when you leave?"

"I'm not leaving now, sis."

"I know," I say. "But how can I make up for all these years in such a short time?"

"By not future tripping," he answers. "It's not like your days are numbered. We have all the time in the world."

"At least until Infinity."

"Ah, don't tell me you believe in an afterlife. You actually think there's an Infinity?"

"Skye." I shift my eyes at Devon, who's abandoned his cereal to play with the dog on the floor. *Sorry*, Skye mouths.

To answer, I don't know. Before, it was easier to not believe. I didn't want a life after this one because this one had once been such a disappointment. But now? I want this life to last forever. And if it can't, I want it to continue beyond my body. I want to always feel this much in love and this much happiness for all of eternity. Even if Infinity is a childhood story, I want to believe in it more than I don't. I know wanting isn't the same as believing, but it sure does feel the same.

"Hey dude, we've got to go," Ryder says to Skye. "You don't want to show up late on your first day of work." My brother takes the last bite of cereal, then gets up from the stool. His titanium leg peeks out from under his hitched up pants, and he straightens it so it's hidden again. He trots over to the sink to wash his bowl, and I marvel at how easy this new leg is for him. His injuries in The Enforcer's prison had included a shattered femur, left for so long there was no choice but to amputate. He's had his new leg for only a few weeks, and he barely has a limp. A few more weeks, and he'll probably outrun me.

"It's not like I'll be doing anything interesting," Skye says. "You know, the first day is just about filling paperwork. I probably won't even pick up a gun." They both work for the Cuban government. Ryder is on the receiving end, helping new arrivals get acquainted with the lifestyle and exotic diet of grubs, grasshoppers, and termites. Skye, on the other hand, is training soldiers heading back for the States. The war is over, but humanity has a long way to go before everyone is on the same page. I know it kills Skye that he still can't join the soldiers back home, but this is the next best thing.

"Sweets for my sweets?" Ryder asks, wrapping his arms around me and Mila. I lift my face, meeting his lips with mine. He lingers there, and I take the moment to wordlessly remind him of last night, and every other night since our wedding night. He exhales when we part. "Girl, you keep doing that and I'm never going to make it into work."

"Then hurry and leave so you can hurry back home," I whisper.

"Gross, you guys. It's not like you're in public or anything."

I turn my head and stick my tongue out at Skye. "Please, it's not like you and Birgitte weren't making out every second in your hospital bed. If she were here, you'd probably never come out of your room."

He grins, not denying it. Ryder kisses the side of my head and I turn back to him.

"Seriously, hurry home," I say.

I watch the two of them leave from the window. A shuttle is waiting outside, hovering just above the asphalt. Once they're in, it elevates and flies into the air, joining the sky highway, heading toward the outside world. This kind of technology hasn't hit the states yet, but it's an exciting advancement. Ryder loves how fast they travel. I love that they're hydro-powered.

I look back to Devon, watching as he patiently tries to teach Puppy how to sit on command. Mila squirms, and I place her in the highchair before grabbing a container of mashed bananas—her favorite. I still have another hour before Devon and I have to be at school. I yawn, hoping I have enough energy to make it through. Yesterday was my first co-ed, self-defense and combat class, and I gave it my all. My aim is to provide skills to everyone from housewives to future soldiers. I have no desire to go back into combat, but this class will put my skills to use and help pay it forward.

However, it doesn't compare to what's fast become my passion. It started out with volunteering at Devon's school, breaking up my day while Mila napped in a playpen in the corner. Soon enough, I realized I loved being in the classroom, surrounded by brilliant, young minds, seeing their potential and helping them achieve their goals. In a few weeks, I'll join classes that will help me achieve my new dream of becoming a teacher. All the energy I put into my regret of not having kids, I'm channeling it into caring for other people's children. It's not the same, but it fills that void in my heart.

Of course, it's nothing like being Devon and Mila's mom. I realize now this was who I was always supposed to be. It would have been wonderful to add more children to our family, to give Devon and Mila a baby brother or sister. I would have loved to have known what a child with equal parts Ryder and me would have looked like. But it's unnecessary. Maybe one day we'll adopt more children. Infinity knows there's plenty who've been orphaned because of The Enforcers, and Ryder and I have plenty of love to give. But for now, we're good with everything we have. We're a family of four with a fish and a dog.

Our number is perfect.

Author's Note & Acknowledgments

I don't know how to adequately express just how special this story is to me, but I'll try. The deepest and most profound thing about this book is that it came to me in a dream. On June 16, 2018, I woke up to the image of a man's face. That was all. But in an instant, I knew his story. He was dying of cancer, and he knew he only had a short time left to live. It didn't stop there, though. The story of Numbered began racing through me so fast, I jumped out of bed and ran downstairs where I spent two hours mapping out the story before it left me for good. I've discovered from experience that if you procrastinate with gifts from the muse, the muse will take them back.

So now I had this story, which brings me to the second profound thing about this book. I hadn't written in six months, and I was at a bleak place in my life where I figured I'd never write again. I'd already announced to my readership that I was taking a break from writing, but in my heart, I was done. The previous year had been filled with a few hardships and disappointments, and in the midst of all that, I felt like my well had run dry. To suddenly feel passionate about a story was more than a relief. It felt like I'd been holding my breath this whole time, and was now finally able to breathe.

And so I wrote. Most books take me a month or two to write, but I didn't want to rush this one. I broke all those rules about getting certain word counts in each day and writing to market. I didn't even write every day! Instead, I wrote from the heart as I was led. Because of that, I never resented the story or dreaded writing, and my fear of failure was pushed aside by my renewed passion.

However, I'm also human. Once I finished this book, I was plagued by some serious doubts about whether this book was everything I planned it to be.

Here's where my acknowledgments start.

One of my very favorite authors is Tarryn Fisher. Aside from being an incredible writer, she has the gift of gathering a community and inspiring people to help others as they can. One of the ways she does this is through a post she calls "Small Needs." In it, people share their needs, and those who can do so fill those needs. The morning she posted her Small Needs post, I was blinded by self-doubt. In my weakness, and in total humility, I offered up my own small need, admitting my doubts and asking for encouragement. I not only received reassurance, but I also met several wonderful women who offered their time and energy to read Numbered and offer feedback.

My very first thank you goes to Caitlin Foland, Natalin Altamirano, Tonya Loftice, and Yvonne Coneliano. The four of you offered such detailed insight on ways I could strengthen the story. Your help was invaluable, and thank you is too small of a word.

Through this Small Needs post, I also met my wonderful editor, Sarah Villanueva. Sarah is the kind of editor every writer dreams of having. She was thorough and quick, gentle and consistent in her critiques, and she also boosted my fragile ego with praise. Sarah, I value our partnership on this novel, and could not have done this without you. I can't wait to work with you again.

And, of course, thank you thank you thank you to Tarryn Fisher for being so accessible, so inspiring, and just so damn cool. When I look to authors who give back for all they've received from this writing life, you top my list. Thank you for creating the community that helped my modest novel grow. PLN for life.

My deepest and most mushy thank you to my sexy, handsome, brilliant husband Shawn Langwell, who is always my very first reader, is never afraid to be kindly honest, and believes in me way more than I believe in myself. Darling, I love you more today than yesterday, and tomorrow I'll love you even more. I'm the lucky one.

A huge thank you to MoorBooks Design who worked with me through a very tight timeframe to create a gorgeous cover. This is the second novel they have created for me, and I cannot rave about them enough.

I have a large community of people that have supported me throughout my novel writing endeavors. My New Life family, especially those I grew close to on the mentoring team: Jim and Barb Thornton, Curt and Cindy Newsom, Dan and Aileen McNamee, Ann Jones, and Elise Paulino.

My Press Democrat family. My Century 21 Bundesen family. My dear friend Wendy Dunnagan. My parents Gary and Nancy McLerran. My incredible grandmother Elsie Chretien. My sisters Melissa Spurgeon and Heather McLerran. My amazing kids Summer, Lucas, and Andrew.

And to my Creator...every morning I wake up with Thank You on my lips. I am constantly amazed by this beautiful life you have given me, and I am ever so grateful for this writing passion you've placed in me. Thank you.

Other Books by Crissi Langwell

The Hope Series

The Road to Hope

Hope at the Crossroads

Hope for the Broken Girl

Dessert for Dinner Series

Come Here, Cupcake

Forever After Series

A Symphony of Cicadas

Forever Thirteen

Other Titles

Loving the Wind: The Story of Tiger Lily & Peter Pan

Reclaim Your Creative Soul

Everything I Am Not Saying

Golf Balls, Eight Year Olds & Dual Paned Windows

**See all of Crissi Langwell's books at
crissilangwell.com**

About the Author

Crissi Langwell is the author of eleven books across several genres. Her passion is the story of the underdog, and her novels include stories of homeless teens, determined heroines, family issues, free spirits and more. She writes romance, magical realism, women's fiction, and whatever other genre fits her fancy. Beyond writing, Crissi is an avid bookworm and a weight training wannabe. She pulls her inspiration from the ocean, and breathes freely among redwoods. She lives in Northern California with her husband and their blended family.

crissilangwell.com